Catherine of Deepdale

Catherine of Deepdale

Millie Vigor

ROBERT HALE · LONDON

© Millie Vigor 2012
First published in Great Britain 2012

ISBN 978-0-7090-9639-9

Robert Hale Limited
Clerkenwell House
Clerkenwell Green
London EC1R 0HT

www.halebooks.com

Typeset in 10/13pt Palatino
Printed in Great Britain by the MPG Books Group,
Bodmin and King's Lynn

Acknowledgments

My grateful thanks to all those people I could not have done without. Jennifer Sutherland, Jim Budge, Robbie Burgess, Elma Johnson and others who during conversation inadvertently gave me ideas and snippets of information. Special thanks to the members of the Rebel Writers of Sandwick for comments, criticism, companionship and encouragement.

Special thanks also to the staff at Robert Hale Ltd, who have kindly and expertly led me along the road to publication.

Catherine looked down into the valley and at the little houses crouching there. Four days ago she had walked up the aisle of St Bart's church in Southampton to where Robbie Jameson waited to make her his bride. Excited and eager she had set out with him on a journey that had lasted three days, the last night spent in a bunk on a ferry boat. It had been a bad night and she had slept very little. They had left their luggage with a carrier and walked the three miles from Lerwick to Deepdale. She was tired, very tired, and thought she didn't deserve to have her expectations shattered this way.

'Catherine,' said Robbie, 'shall we go on?'

What other option did she have? 'Yes, I suppose so,' she said.

She was wearing the shoes she had chosen to complete her going away outfit and that had cost many precious clothing coupons. They were not the sort to wear for terrain like this. 'You should have told me we would have to walk; I'd have put my old shoes on if you had.'

Robbie looked down at them. 'I didn't even think about it,' he said.

'I wanted to look nice to meet your parents, but … I've been rained on, my hair is wet, my shoes scuffed and I'm tired and … oh, I must look a mess.'

Robbie slid the bags he was carrying from his shoulder and took Catherine in his arms. 'I'm sorry,' he said, 'I should have given it more thought, but you've nothing to worry about; I love you and that's all that matters. I don't care what anybody else thinks.' Raising a hand he touched her hair. 'Your curls look even better wet and nobody's going to look at your shoes. You've left the city; you're my country lass. Come on.' He picked up the bags and they walked on.

A country lass, was appearance not important then? As they got closer to the Jameson house Catherine's heart sank. Its walls were only fractionally above the height of the door. Its roof of thatch was not neat like those she had seen in the south of England. A net had been thrown over it, held down by rocks. To the left of the house was a stone barn and beside the house a stack of something black.

Robbie opened the door, dropping the bags as he went in. Immediately there was the clatter of a dropped pan and the screech of a woman's voice.

'Is that you, Robbie?'

'It is, Mam.'

Catherine stepped over the threshold and watched as the woman threw her arms round him and weeping and laughing hugged him to her.

Disentangling himself from his mother Robbie turned to Catherine.

'Say hello to Catherine, Mam,' he said and when his mother looked at her and back at him, a questioning look on her face, added, 'my wife.'

The expression on his mother's face changed rapidly. 'Your wife!'

Faced with this glowering woman Catherine gritted her teeth, forced a smile to her lips then listened as Robbie and his mother exchanged heated words.

'Yes, my wife.'

'You said nothin' about this.'

The smile on Catherine's face faded and died.

'I did, in the letter.'

'There's been no letter here.'

'But I sent ...' Robbie shook his head then said, 'she's a hard worker, Mam, she'll be a help to you.'

'Why would I be wantin' help?' spat his mother as she glared at Catherine.

What have I done to deserve this? Where is the smiling face, the arms to hold me too? If this was the way the woman was going to be it meant trouble. Catherine thought of her own mother who said the best policy was to meet trouble head on, so she took a deep breath, smiled, stepped forward and held out her hand. 'I'm very pleased to meet you, Mrs Jameson,' she said, 'I promise to do my best not to get in your way.'

Again the smile faltered and was in danger of disappearing before Jannie Jameson took the proffered hand. With bad grace Jannie said, 'Well, you're here, we shall have to make the best of it.'

So that's the way she wants it is it? Catherine tightened her grip on the hand in hers and stared, unflinching, into her mother-in-law's eyes.

Robbie watched anxiously as the two women confronted each other. 'Now, Mam,' he said, his voice a trifle too loud, 'how about some tea?'

Catherine maintained her grip and kept eye contact till Jannie looked away. Then she smiled and let go. Round one to me, she thought.

Jannie Jameson cut and buttered what Catherine thought rather flat scones. 'They're bannocks,' said Robbie when he saw Catherine looking at them.

Jannie poured tea into china cups, set a cup in front of Catherine then, with a casual sweep of her hand, indicated that she should help herself to food. Turning to her son, she began a barrage of questions. She spoke rapidly and in dialect and Catherine was at a loss to understand. With an occasional apologetic glance toward his wife, Robbie did his best to satisfy his mother's questioning.

'Daa'll be glad to have you back,' said Jannie, 'now that he's troubled with rheumatism. You'll be a help.'

Daylight had turned from dusk to dark. Jannie set an oil lamp on the table, took off the glass chimney, lit and adjusted the flame till it burned bright and clear. Catherine looked round the room. It was austerely furnished. A stove on short legs squatted in the fireplace, its hob hardly higher than a bucket of fuel standing by it. An old and sagging arm chair stood close by the fire. Other furnishings were in plain wood. Behind Robbie and in a corner was a piece of furniture that puzzled her. To her it was a large box on legs and too big to be a store cupboard, she wondered why it had a curtain in place of a door. She wrinkled her nose and sniffed. A combination of smells, cooking odours, cabbage, some sort of smoked fish, the musky smell of wet dog and something else that she couldn't put a name to hung over all.

The first flush of questions and exchange of news over, Jannie got up to tend the fire and set the kettle to boil again. The door opened and the man who came in ordered the collie dog with him to go to its bed, then he looked at Robbie. 'Boy, you're home,' he said.

'Ay, Daa, I am.' Robbie stood up, took Catherine by the hand, 'This is Catherine, my wife.'

'Your wife! You didn't tell us.'

So this was Robbie's father. Catherine held out her hand as she looked into John Jameson's pleasant face and kind brown eyes. 'I'm pleased to meet you, Mr Jameson,' she said.

The palm and fingers of the hand that enveloped hers were smooth and hard as leather. John Jameson looked down at her; briefly the corners of his mouth twitched into a smile and the hand that held hers gave it a quick squeeze.

'Welcome to Deepdale, lass,' he said. His voice was soft and mellow.

'Thank you,' said Catherine.

'You've chosen a hard road.' He squeezed her hand again, then let it go and went to sit in the chair by the fire.

What had made him say that? The little seed of doubt that had been sown earlier in Catherine's mind began to take root. Had she been foolish in not questioning Robbie more closely about his home?

'Where's the bathroom, Robbie,' she said, 'I need to spend a penny.'

'I'll get a lantern.'

She frowned. Why would she need a lantern?

'Here you are, I'd better come with you. Put your coat on.'

My coat! Oh my God, it's outside. Catherine shrugged herself into her coat and followed Robbie out and along to the end of the house. He stopped and held the lantern up so the light fell on them. 'I'm sorry,' he said, 'but we don't have a bathroom and the toilet, such as it is, is here.' He indicated a small building on the end of the house.

'Here … this is the toilet?' There was no mistaking the disgust in Catherine's voice. When there was no reply from Robbie she looked at him; searched his face for some sign of remorse, found none, then, as he opened the door and handed the lantern to her, wordless, she walked in and shut the door.

He was not there when she came out again.

Setting the lantern on the ground she felt in her pockets for cigarettes. She put one in her mouth, lit and drew hard on it, exhaled long and slow.

Night had come earlier than she had expected. Rain and wind had fled away leaving nothing more than a fitful breeze. The moon sailed across a rain-washed sky; its light illuminating the valley. In front of her a stretch of cultivated land sloped gently away to end in a patch of rough grass, then came rocks, a beach and the glittering waters of a bay. The hills behind her and to right and left of her had spread their arms around the valley and headlands guarded the entrance to the cove. The valley was enclosed and self contained.

Her cigarette finished, Catherine threw the stub down and ground it out under her shoe. She wrapped her coat tightly round her and folded her arms. She didn't want to go back indoors into that bleak unwelcoming domain. Why hadn't Robbie described the house he had grown up in, told her what it was like? Why?

The creak of a hinge and a door being shut meant that someone was coming. It had better be Robbie. It was. 'Why didn't you come back in?' he asked.

'Good question,' said Catherine, 'I have a few for you.'

'Oh.'

'You haven't been honest with me, have you? You knew your home was totally different from mine, so why didn't you tell me? And your mother treats me like dirt. Not the sort of welcome I expected.' Catherine clenched her fists and glared at Robbie. 'My parents made you welcome,' she went on, 'treated you like one of the family, but apart from your father all I've had is the brush off. You met all my family, nothing was kept from you, everything was open and above board, but *you*,' she jabbed at him with her finger and her voice rose as she went on, '*you* let me think your parents lived in a bungalow, on one floor you said, and had a sheep farm, "they keep lots of sheep" you said. Why have you deceived me? For that's what you've done. '

'I didn't tell you they had a bungalow or a farm,' said Robbie. But Catherine wasn't listening. She was feeling for cigarettes again.

'There's no electricity, is there?' she went on, 'What about water? Where do you get your water? No, don't tell me. There's no bathroom so how do you have a bath?' She gasped. 'Oh my God … you don't.' She gave a mirthless chuckle. 'It's no wonder your father said I'd chosen a hard road. Why didn't you tell me the toilet was a bucket in an outhouse?' She put a cigarette in her mouth, lit it then flicked the match away in an arc. Turning away from Robbie she drew hard and sucked smoke into her lungs. 'What else don't they have?' she asked. 'Is there a kitchen and does it have a sink? I suppose there's no possible hope of a washing machine.'

Robbie looked at her but said nothing.

'Well say something,' Catherine snapped, 'or are you just going to stand there and hope it will all go away?'

'I love you, Catherine,' he said at last.

'You could have fooled me. Did you think if you didn't marry me first I'd turn tail and run? Have I got a surprise for you, much more of this and you'd better not think I won't.' Robbie reached out to her, but she struck his hand away. 'If there're any more nasty surprises, things you haven't told me, mark my words, I'll be on the next boat out of here.' With a groan of despair she turned away from him. 'You should have told me.'

The keening cry of a lone gull made Catherine look up. You and me both, brother, she thought.

'You should have told me,' she said again, 'you should have been honest. You lied to me. How am I ever going to believe you again? How could we ever get on together without trust?' She blew a steady stream of smoke. 'Your mother knows nothing about me so why does she hate me?'

'You never did listen to me, Catherine, I didn't lie to you, it was just that I didn't tell you and you jumped to your own conclusions.'

'That's not fair, you should have told me.'

'Well, you could have asked.'

'I wouldn't have thought I needed to.' Cigarette finished, Catherine threw it away. From the bay came the soft swish of restless water and now and again the plop of a breaking wave. From somewhere on the hill behind them the bleat of a sheep was answered by another. And there was that smell again. She wrinkled her nose and sniffed.

'What is that smell?' she said, 'I smelt it in Lerwick, in your mother's kitchen and now here.'

'It's peat reek, smoke to you.'

'Hmm. So you burn peat. There's no electric, no piped water, telephone or car. It's a wonder you aren't still dressed in animal skins and living in caves.'

Robbie ignored this remark and for a while there was silence between them. 'Please don't leave me, Catherine,' he said at last, 'I couldn't bear it if you did. I can't think of life without you. I thought if I told you – well – you're right, I thought you wouldn't marry me.' He paused. 'I had to hope … I didn't want to lose you; it would have broken my heart.' He reached for her, took hold of her arm and turned her to face him. 'Please be patient. I'll do anything for you, anything at all, only please … please give me a second chance.'

'And if I do?'

'I'll make sure you never regret it. Things are going to change; it won't always be like it is now.'

'Hah, that's easy for you to say.'

'Believe me, I'll *make* them change.'

'And your mother? If I stay, living with her will be hell.'

'No it won't, you'll just have to learn how to deal with her. Surely if you love me at all you can do that for me, can't you? It won't be forever. There is somewhere for us, I promise.'

'I've got to think about it,' said Catherine and began to walk away.

Utterly dejected Robbie said, 'What are you going to do?'

Catherine gave a sardonic little chuckle. 'I can hardly get on a bus and go home, can I? I'll have to grin and bear it, I suppose … ,' she turned on him, 'but only until I've made up my mind.'

'Please don't leave me, give me a chance,' pleaded Robbie. 'Can't you see I had to get you here and hope you'd forgive me for not telling you everything? I had to believe you'd accept my way of life, after all, I lost count of the times you said you loved me enough to go anywhere in the world with me.'

'All the same, I wish you'd told me instead of letting me find out like this. If this is the worst … it is, isn't it? It has to get better.' She paused and waited for him to speak; when he didn't and while she waited the little seed of doubt that had taken root began to grow. 'You're saying nothing so there's bound to be more,' she said. 'You'd better tell me what's coming next. First of all tell me where we're going to sleep. I take it you do have beds.'

'Ah …'

'Oh no.' Seizing Robbie by the arms she shook him. 'What is it now? Tell me.'

'I think it's better if I show you.

TWO

'WHAT'S THE MATTER wi' you?' said John Jameson.
  'Nothin' wrong wi' me,' snapped Jannie as she opened the
stove, pushed a couple of slabs of peat in and clanged the door shut.
'Nothin' wrong wi' me.'

'There's got to be, you're fussin' about like an old hen.'

Jannie stood arms akimbo, 'Well,' she huffed, 'here's the boy home
from the war, brought a wife with him and never told us.' She shook her
head. 'He said he wrote, but there's been no letter here.'

'It's maybe gone astray.'

'No, no, he never was good at writin'. How many did we get from
him while he was away?' Jannie picked up the cat that was sitting on
her chair. 'Now, Puss,' she cooed as she put it on the floor, 'I need to sit
there.' She sat down, picked up her knitting and began to knit.

John took a pipe and a tin of tobacco from the mantelpiece. 'The lad
was at sea, he likely never had much time to write. There's no reason for
you to take on so, it's been a bit of a shock, that's all. You'll maybe get
to like the lass in time.'

'I would not have been upset if he'd married a Shetland lass, one
who knows what croftin's about.' Jannie's mood transferred itself to her
fingers, they flew furiously back and forth and the steel needles in her
hands flashed in the lamplight. 'No, he's got a soft one from south;
she'll be no use.'

John struck a match, put it to the pipe and drew on it till the tobacco
glowed red. As he puffed a small cloud of aromatic smoke rose to hover
above his head. 'He's made his choice,' he said. 'It's up to him.'

Jannie grunted. 'And what's she doin' out there now? Likely she's
makin' a fuss, cryin' because she's left her mam and wantin' Robbie to
hold her hand. She's not the sort of wife he needs. I can't think why he
married her.'

John puffed at his pipe. 'Poor lass,' he said. 'She must be very tired;

maybe you would be weepin' if you'd travelled as far as she has. You should be kind to her.'

'I can't do wi' a weepin' wife and it's not you that'll have to put up wi' her, you'll be away to your work; it's me that'll have her round me skirts.

'Well, you'll just have to get along wi' it.'

'Get along wi' it you say; she'll not want to dirty her hands ...'

Taking his pipe from his mouth John Jameson said, 'That'll do now. Leave it be.' He had not raised his voice but it was enough to leave Jannie in no doubt that she was to take note of what he said. He had silenced her just in time for the door opened and Robbie and Catherine came in.

'I take it we're sleeping in the end room,' said Robbie.

'Ay,' grunted his mother her eyes still on her work.

Robbie's duffel bag and Catherine's overnight bag were still where they had been put down. Picking up her bag Catherine followed Robbie through a door, along a short passageway and into another room. To her surprise there was no sign of a bed. Furniture consisted of an armchair on either side of a fireplace, a marble-topped chest with a large china bowl on it, a solitary wooden chair and another piece of furniture like the one Catherine had puzzled over.

'Where's the bed then, or are we sleeping on the floor?' she asked.

'It's here.' Robbie pulled back a curtain on the odd-looking cupboard.

Catherine looked from it to Robbie. 'You're joking,' she said.

Robbie shook his head. 'No, it's not a joke.'

'It's *got* to be.' Catherine, swallowing the lump that had risen in her throat, went to look and saw pillows and a quilt inside. Was there to be no end to the surprises Robbie was going to throw at her? 'What have I done to deserve this?' she said then, slowly and deliberately, emphasizing every word, 'You really cannot expect me to sleep in a box.'

'Why not? Lots of people do.'

'It's archaic for a start.' A nerve at the side of Catherine's mouth began to twitch. She put up a hand to try to stop it. 'What do I do if I need to spend a penny?' Then she gasped. 'Oh ...' A crooked smile twisted her lips. She giggled. 'I've got to sleep in a box and pee in a pot.' The giggle turned into a laugh, the laugh became uncontrollable.

'Hush,' said Robbie as he tried to take her in his arms.

'Get away,' she cried, beating at him with her hands, 'why have you done this to me?'

Trapping her flailing fists he crushed her to him, 'Hush now,' he soothed.

'Leave me alone,' cried Catherine as she struggled to escape, but he held her tight and abruptly she dissolved into a flood of tears. All energy spent, she gave in, clung to him and wept for the hurt, deceit and disappointment she had suffered, wept for her inability to walk away.

When at last her sobs lessened Robbie loosed his hold on her but still held her. 'I'm so sorry, Catherine,' he said, 'I'm a stupid idiot and I've done it all wrong. I should have brought you here before we got married and given you the chance to change your mind.' Tenderly he wiped the tears from her face. 'But I love you so much and I was afraid I'd lose you. Please forgive me; my life would be as barren as the hills if you left me.'

'I don't care, I don't care,' hiccuped Catherine. 'I am so tired.' Closing her eyes she laid her head on his chest. 'I am *so* very tired.'

'Oh, darling, I'll get some water so you can have a wash, you'll feel better.'

While he was gone Catherine looked again at her surroundings. The chairs that stood either side of the fireplace were upholstered; there was a rug on the floor in front of it while on the wall above hung a framed bible text. Floral curtains hung at the window. This must be the sitting room. Was it ever used as such? She looked again at the bed. Stared at it and hated it, thought of her own bed at home, of her family and her mother. Oh Mum, she sobbed, what have I done? There was no getting away from it though, like it or not she was going to have to sleep in the box. Her body ached with exhaustion her head throbbed and her eyes felt gritty and sore. Against her will her eyelids drooped then closed and her body began to drift, soften and relax. I've got to go to bed, she thought. Starting up she shook herself. Her body felt like lead. She ought to move … but there was no hurry, she would just sit a while … once again she let her eyes close.

The sea was rough, the boat pitched and tossed and her body, following its motion, moved incessantly in her bunk. All the time through the mattress and pillows the ever present hum and throb of the engines droned on in her head. If only she could sleep. But then she was slipping, sliding, falling. She reached out a hand to save herself. With a cry she started up and opened her eyes …

And there in front of her was … the box and Robbie coming back with a jug of water and a towel. 'You'll feel better when you've had a wash,' he said as he poured water in the bowl. 'I know it's only an old box bed, but it'll be warm and I'll be beside you.' He kissed her gently.

'Don't let the water get cold.'

Catherine got up, peeled off her clothes and threw them on the chair. The water in the bowl had cooled slightly, but she rinsed her tears away along with the dust and grime of travelling. She took her nightdress from her bag, put it on and crawled into bed.

THREE

KAY BURNETT WAS tidying her sitting room, wiping virtually non-existent dust from ornaments and photo-frames. At the windowsill, resting place for more ornaments, she did the same. Then, as was her habit, she looked out of the window at sea and sky to judge the state of the weather. Beyond the bay and above the headlands clouds rolled and chased one another, the sky was in a hurry. Beneath it the water of the North Sea tossed and turned, but in driving through the headlands it lost much of its power and only small waves rolled in to lap the shore.

Expecting to see neither man nor beast Kay gasped, put her hands on the sill and leaned forward. 'Now who can that be?' she murmured.

The hunched figure of a young woman, hair blowing in the wind, was sitting on the rocks by the beach. As Kay watched, the figure got up and head bent began to walk slowly back and forth. Not a happy person, thought Kay, and, wondering who it could be she could do nothing but stand and stare. If there had been visitors in the valley she would have known for comings and goings were common knowledge. Enthralled though she was she turned away and took her cleaning things through to her living room to put away. She put a slab of peat on the fire then picked up the empty bucket to refill it. When she stepped out of her door the person from the beach was walking toward her.

'Hello,' she said, 'did I see you on the beach, are you on holiday?'

'No.' The voice was flat and uninterested. 'I've come to live here.'

'*Live* here! Where?'

'We're at Robbie's mother's house for now. I'm Robbie's wife.'

'Is he home then?'

'We came yesterday.'

For a new bride, and she must be, thought Kay, her eyes should sparkle, not look dull. It didn't take long to guess the reason for it was Jannie.

'Have you come far?'

'From Southampton.'

'Oh, two if not three days travelling.' Kay took peat from the stack to fill her bucket. 'Poor girl, you must be exhausted.' Bucket of peat in hand and about to open her door Kay stood with her hand on the latch. She turned to look at the girl. 'Are you expected somewhere or do you have time to kill?'

'I am at a bit of a loose end.'

'I was about to make a cup of tea. Would you like one?'

A brief smile lit the girl's face. 'That would be nice.'

'I'm Kay Burnett,' said Kay as she put cups and saucers on the table. 'And your name is?'

'I'm Catherine.'

'So you've come from the south. I'm an incomer, like you,' said Kay. 'I came from Derby.'

'Did you know much about Shetland before you came?'

'Not a lot.'

'Then what made you stay?'

Kay laughed. 'I married a Shetland man.'

'Well, so have I, but that doesn't mean ...' Catherine stopped and turned her head away. Suddenly, her voice sharp, she said, 'Robbie wrote to tell her we were getting married, but she said there was no letter.'

'Oh, dear.' So Jannie didn't know.

Catherine shook her head. 'There was one, I posted it, but if she didn't get it she couldn't have known.'

'It must have been a shock for her then.'

'But that was no reason ...' there was a long pause before Catherine spoke again, 'I'm sorry; I shouldn't offload my troubles on you.'

'I gather Jannie didn't exactly welcome you with open arms,' said Kay. 'Is that what's making you unhappy?'

'Well I did expect ...' Catherine made a face and shrugged her shoulders. 'I had to go outside to the toilet *and* sleep in a box. Have you got a proper bed?'

'Yes, I have,' said Kay, 'But Jannie's old fashioned, never throws anything away. She can be a tyrant but you must stand up to her, not let her be boss.'

'That's if I stay ...'

'My dear, don't say that.'

'Well, I'm a square peg in a round hole. I don't fit.'

'But if you were to stay I'm sure Shetland would round off the corners.'

'I wonder if it would. Robbie didn't tell me what his home was like because he thought I wouldn't marry him if he did. But I would still have come.' Catherine looked at Kay and her lips lifted in semblance of a smile. 'I love him, you see.' Turning her head away she looked at the fire, at the peat glowing in the grate. 'It was the shock of seeing the squat little house,' she went on, 'I was expecting a bungalow and I thought his parents had a farm. I was wrong.'

Kay studied her, a pretty girl, too thin perhaps, but rationing could account for that. Would she stay and settle to life on a croft? Had Robbie Jameson chosen wisely? Leaning forward she took Catherine's hands in hers.

'Robbie grew up in this valley. He was an only child among adults. He would never have had to explain himself or his surroundings to anyone because it was the way we all lived.' Kay smiled and squeezed the hands in hers. 'Don't be too hard on him.'

Catherine didn't answer but slid her hands out Kay's and cradled them in her lap. Quietly as if speaking only to herself she said. 'He should have told me. I would have known what to expect if he had.'

'I have a nephew,' said Kay, 'who helps me out with things I can't cope with, but you've got Robbie; he'll take care of you, you'll be all right.'

'Maybe,' said Catherine, 'but I'd better be going or he'll wonder where I am. Thank you for the tea.'

'Come and see me any time,' said Kay. 'My door will always be open and don't give up on us.' As she was about to put her hand on the latch the door opened and Robbie was there.

'Hello, Kay,' he said, 'have you seen … ah, I see you've met.'

'We have,' said Kay.

'And now I'm going to take her away.' He turned to Catherine. 'Come with me, there's something I want to show you.'

FOUR

'WHERE ARE YOU taking me?' asked Catherine when instead of turning toward his home Robbie led her in the opposite direction.

'To look at this,' He pointed to the last house in the valley, 'it's mine.'

'Yours?'

To Catherine the house was a ruin. Grass was growing on the roof and springing up between the paving stones outside the door. The woodwork of windows and door was practically devoid of paint.

'Shall we go in?'

Why? thought Catherine, but said, 'Why not?'

The door creaked and groaned on rusty hinges as Robbie pushed it open. 'Take care where you step,' he said, 'the roof's been leaking.'

Catherine looked up. The ceiling, like a huge shelf, stretched only half-way across the room. The rest was open to the rafters. Tiny pinpricks of light shone like stars in the darkness of the roof.

'What happened to the ceiling?' she asked.

'Nothing, it's where the fishing nets were stored in winter, they have to be kept dry or they'll rot.'

Cobwebs festooned dirty windows, faded curtains hung limp. A shaft of light from a small window in the open roof space added feebly to that filtering through the curtains. A wooden chair, and others by a table on which crockery had been left, were covered in dust. A kettle stood on top of a stove like the one in Jannie's house. Pictures that dampness had buckled and blurred hung on the walls and there, skulking in the corner, was a box-bed.

'There are two more rooms here,' said Robbie as he disappeared through a doorway. Following him Catherine looked into a small room that was completely bare then walked into a bigger one. The only furniture here was a pair of wooden chairs. The ceiling was complete; there was a fireplace and one small window.

'Uncle Laurie left the house to me; he died not long after I joined up,' said Robbie. 'It's in a bad state because it's been left empty. But it's ours, it can be our home.'

'I thought we'd live in the town,' said Catherine, 'I'd rather.'

Robbie shook his head. 'Oh no, I could never do that.'

'But, Robbie, I'm not going to find any work here and neither are you.'

'Daa has given me his boat; I'm going fishing. Lobsters are making good money, I'm told.'

A sudden feeling of impending disaster flashed through Catherine's mind. 'Fishing's dangerous,' she said.

'Don't be silly, I've been going out in the boat with Daa almost since I could walk. I love being on the water. Please don't ask me to do anything else.' Robbie put his arms round her unwilling body.

She could feel his warmth; hear the steady beat of his heart. Was fishing something else that was secret? But lobsters were not found in deep waters, he would not be taking the boat far out to sea, all the same …'

'If you help me,' said Robbie, 'we can do the house up and you wouldn't have to share with Mam.'

'How long would that take?'

'Not long if I can get some more help.'

How long was not long? He was offering her a home, a wreck at the moment; maybe it could be made nice, but was it enough? When she showed a lack of enthusiasm he released her, put his hands on her shoulders, pushed her away from him and looked down at her.

'I know I was a fool to keep you in the dark,' he said. 'I know I should have told you what to expect, but I'm not going to keep on apologizing for it.' She had been looking into his eyes, now she hung her head. He put a hand under her chin and lifted it. 'It's up to you now, I love you, but do you love me enough to make a home and a life with me?'

The wind sighed in the chimney.

Jannie was knitting. Catherine, a book open on the table in front of her, abandoned her reading to watch. The piece of work under Jannie's hands seemed to grow visibly and Catherine was amazed at the way the Fair Isle pattern emerged. To her eyes it was extremely complicated, yet Jannie never once faltered or checked that the pattern was right.

'Where's Robbie?' said Jannie.

'He said he was going to help his father.'

Jannie merely nodded her head and made no reply. Only the click of knitting needles, the tick of the clock and the lazy grunts and quirks of a kettle on the hob disturbed the silence. Warmth radiated from the stove where a pot of broth simmered, but otherwise the atmosphere was one of ice.

It's up to me, thought Catherine; I have to try to get through to her. 'Are you making a jumper for yourself?' she asked.

'For me? No, no, it's for the merchant in Lerwick, he buys what I make.'

'Oh.' So did Jannie knit jumpers for pin money? 'I never learned how to knit,' said Catherine.

'Huh,' went Jannie as, her fingers never hesitating for a moment, she glanced at Catherine, 'then you'd better.'

'Why?'

'You has to do your share of gettin' money in, can't leave it all to Robbie.'

'I don't intend to. I shall get a job.'

'Ha, and what are you goin' to do wi' hands like yours?' Jannie's finger was pointing. 'Robbie needs a wife who can work wi' him, cuttin' peat, plantin' tatties and helpin' wi' the sheep. Not one that wants pretty clothes and time to read books. You'll be no use.'

Catherine snapped her book shut. What did she have to do to get through to the woman? 'You don't know that,' she said. 'I'm a state registered nurse. I worked full time in a hospital. I'm no stranger to hard work.'

'And what's a nurse,' spat Jannie. 'Anyone can bandage a finger.'

'You're right there, but it's much more than that. You don't train for years to bandage a finger.'

'But a nurse is no use on a croft.'

'I wouldn't be too sure of that.'

Jannie bent her head over her knitting again and muttered, 'You don't know anything about croft work. You should go home now, give Robbie a chance to find someone as would suit him better.'

'*What* did you say?'

Jannie stopped knitting and lifted her head. 'I said you would no way ever be a croft wife. You should go home. You'll only be a hindrance to the boy.'

Resisting the urge to throw her book at Jannie's head, Catherine, her eyes blazing said, 'If you think you're going to intimidate me and get me to leave you can think again. No one tells me what to do, least of all *you.*' As she spoke she leaned across the table and the anger behind her words made Jannie press back into her chair. 'Thank you very much for your *kind* words, Mrs Jameson. I am going to stay and if you want a battle you shall have one.'

FIVE

As HE WALKED Robbie cursed himself for his thoughtlessness in not telling Catherine what life in Shetland was like. He had been a fool to be so sure she would accept the way he lived without question. But why wouldn't she? He gave a wry grin as he remembered how she had wound her arms round his neck, said she loved him and that she would live anywhere with him. But her reaction to his home had made him see it through her eyes. How small the house seemed now, how old-fashioned and behind the times, but he had grown up with it and had seen nothing wrong with it. It was his home and while he had been away his thoughts had been full of the day he would be back. If Catherine could not accept his way of life and insisted on leaving he had no one to blame but himself. He had left her with his mother now and he wondered if that had been wise, for there was little doubt that she would not hesitate to show her displeasure at his choice of wife.

In spite of all the hassle it was good to be home, for this was the time of year he liked best. Though the earth was still sleeping there was an air of expectancy about it, soon it would be waking, terns and skylarks would return to nest along with curlews and golden plovers. Other birds would come back too and their calls would be music on the wind. Always there was the wind; thank goodness they had travelled up before the equinox and the gales that tended to come with it, which could sometimes be horrendous. The sea had been rough enough and he knew Catherine had not enjoyed being on the boat.

He was on his way to join his father and hadn't far to go; he could hear the snock of a hammer blow and the echoing knock, knock, bouncing off the hillside. There was his father's pony cart at the bottom of the hill. Robbie went up to it, ran his hand along the animal's back through the grizzled mane then down the animal's hard nose. He put his palm under the silky muzzle. 'Well, Flyn, old boy, you're still here then,' he said and was answered with a throaty rumble. Robbie smiled, patted the horse and left him while he climbed the hill to his father. 'Hi Daa,' he called.

John Jameson put down his hammer, waited for Robbie to join him, waited when he did and stood to recover his breath. 'You are not fit,' he said.

'No. Ships decks are flat, Daa, I've not been climbing many hills.'

'I hear you. How is Catherine today?'

'She's not in a good humour, in fact she's mad at me.'

'Why, what's wrong?'

'She says I didn't tell her what it was like here. Say's she'll leave.'

'Are you a fool, boy? You should have had more sense.'

'Ay, but I didn't. She didn't think much of Laurie's house either.'

'Likely she was used wi' somethin' better.'

'Yes, she was. Her da has a business and her folk live in a fine house. I've left her home wi' Mam now.'

John Jameson chuckled. 'And that was another fool thing to do. Jannie'll not hold her tongue and the lass had better be able to fight back. If she's still there when we get home, likely she'll stay. Now, let's get this done before dark.'

'Mrs Burnett, are you home?' called Catherine. When she got no answer she called again. 'Mrs Burnett, hello, Catherine here.'

'Oh, it's you,' said Kay, coming through from her bedroom. 'Just open the door and come in like everyone else. And call me Kay, my dear.'

'All right, do you have a local paper and could I borrow it? I've decided to stay, so I need a job.'

Kay opened a drawer and took out a newspaper. 'I'm so glad. It's time we had some young people in the valley,' she said. As she spread the paper on the table she added, 'Shall we look together, I can tell you who not to work for.'

'It might be difficult to find something,' said Catherine, 'I'm a nurse and I don't expect there'll be many jobs open to me, but I'll do anything.'

Heads together they studied the classifieds. There were no vacancies for nurses, but a cleaner was wanted at the doctor's surgery at Broonieswick.

'Would that do till something else comes along?' asked Kay. 'Dr Lumsden is an awful nice man; he's doctor to everybody round here and certainly all of us.'

'I know where Broonieswick is. When is the surgery open?'

'Today, two till four. You have to sit and wait your turn.'

'Right, I'm off.'

'You're not …'

Catherine didn't wait for Kay to finish, 'Yes I am,' she said. 'Bye.' Twenty minutes later she reached the surgery and was glad to take her place in the waiting room and sit down. 'And what can I do for you, young lady,' said Dr Lumsden when she was at last sitting opposite him.

'I'd like to be your cleaner.'

'Shouldn't you have made an application and come for an interview?'

'Why waste time on that? I need a job.'

'Really, and what makes you think this one's for you?'

'I've never worked as a cleaner before,' said Catherine. 'I'm a nurse, but there are no vacancies at the moment, which is why I've come to you.'

'A nurse. Where did you do your training and did you complete it?'

'In Southampton and yes, I did.'

'So you're state registered. Tell me more.'

Neil Lumsden held back the smile that threatened to spread across his face as he listened to what Catherine had to say. This was not just a cleaner, but pure gold, if not a diamond. He sat back in his chair, steepled his fingers together and looked at her. Catherine wondered if he was going to turn her down.

'I don't really think you're cut out to be a cleaner,' said Lumsden.

Catherine took a deep breath. 'But I need to work and I'll do anything.'

'I know, I appreciate that, but wouldn't you rather be nursing?'

'Well, it's what I trained for.' Catherine's heart sank. He wasn't going to give her the job, perhaps someone else had applied and beaten her to it.

It was then that Neil Lumsden allowed himself to smile. 'The health visitor for this district is about to retire. Wouldn't that suit you better?'

'But I would need extra training for that, wouldn't I?'

'Yes, I'm afraid you would.'

'Which would mean I'd have to go away,' said Catherine, 'because I don't suppose you do that here, do you?'

'No, it would be four months in Edinburgh, and you'd need to drive.' Shaking her head Catherine looked down at her hands, hoping to hide her disappointment. 'I can't drive either,' she said.

'That could be arranged.'

Being the health visitor would be ideal, but for the moment it was out of the question and, though that didn't mean for ever, she needed a job now. She looked up and smiled. 'I'd like to be your cleaner, please,' she said.

'You don't want to be the health visitor then?'

'Not now, perhaps later.'

'All right. No one else has applied so when can you start?'

'As soon as I can get a bicycle,' she said.

Lumsden stood up, shook Catherine's hand, and smiling down at her said, 'When you've got the bike come along and I'll show you what you have to do.'

Dusk had fallen and it was beginning to rain when Catherine got back to Deepdale. Lamplight gleamed in the window of the Jameson house, she looked in. Robbie was standing over his mother; he looked angry. She heard raised voices, Robbie's was loud. She hesitated a moment and listened.

'How long has she been gone?'

'Two hours, maybe,' said Jannie.

'Where did she go, did she say?'

'Never a word.'

'Mam, what have you been saying to her?'

'I said nothin'.'

'I don't believe that. I know you don't like her but you could try,' said Robbie. 'She's my wife. You'd better accept it.'

Catherine opened the door. 'Hello, I'm home.'

Robbie looked up when he heard Catherine's voice and his relief at seeing her was obvious.

'Where have you been?' he demanded.

'Thank you, nice to see you too, I've been for a walk.'

Jannie, a scowl on her face, bent her head and began to knit.

'I was worried about you,' said Robbie.

'Oh dear, did you think I'd run away? You don't have to worry, I'm here. It's starting to rain again.' She smiled at him. 'I'll put my coat away.'

John Jameson had gone out to the barn to feed his cow; Jannie was, as always, knitting; Catherine was reading a book and Robbie was studying the newspaper. Apart from the click-clack of Jannie's needles, the soft shush of pages being turned and the slither of ash in the ash pan, the room was quiet. From time to time Robbie looked over the top of his paper at Catherine. There was something different about her; she looked relaxed and happy, as though she were keeping a secret. Something had happened. Daa had said if she was here when they got home she would stay. She hadn't been, but she was now.

A rattle of stones and the sound of skidding outside the door broke the silence. Catherine started up. 'Whatever was that?' she cried. There was a crash then, as of something thrown down, which was quickly followed by the scrunch of boots on stone flags. The door opened and a face appeared round it.

'I heard you was home, Robbie.'

The lad who slid round the door, pushing it shut behind him, was a tall, gangling colt of a boy with arms and legs that seemed to have a will of their own.

Without turning her head, Jannie said, 'Sit down, Billie.'

Billie pulled a chair out from the table, sat down, stuffed his hands in his pockets and tucked his feet away beneath the chair. 'Mam said to come over and ask you to tea on Sunday, Robbie,' he said. 'And to bring,' he inclined his head toward Catherine, 'that one.'

' "That one" is Catherine,' said Robbie, 'and that one,' he said to Catherine, 'is my cousin, Billie.'

'I was thinking you would come to the meetin' house wi' me,' said Jannie. 'You can't do that if you're going to Rose's for tea.'

'Mam'll be going,' said Billie. 'They can go wi' her.'

'Thanks, Billie; tell your mam we'd like to come,' said Robbie. 'We'll go to the meeting' house wi' her and see you there, Mam,' he said to his mother. 'Now, Billie, would you like a job?'

'Doin' what?'

'I'm going to do up Uncle Laurie's house, and I need some help.'

Abruptly Jannie stopped knitting and sat motionless. When the needles stopped clicking Catherine looked at her and guessed that Jannie was not best pleased at what she was hearing.

'I'd have to ask my daa first,' said Billie, 'but he'll not say no. Why are you going to do it up?'

'Catherine and I are going to live there,' said Robbie. 'I've got to get stuff organized first, but when I have I'll let you know when to come over.'

'Fine that,' said Billie. 'Mam said not to be late, so I'd better be going.'

As Billie left John Jameson came in. 'It's no wonder that bike of Billie's is a wreck,' he said, 'the way he treats it.'

'Rose should buy him a new one,' said Jannie, 'That one is dangerous.'

'You know she won't do that,' said Robbie. 'She keeps her purse locked and barred, every penny's a prisoner as far as she's concerned.'

'You're not saying she's mean, are you?' said Catherine with a laugh.

'Mean? She'd put Scrooge to shame.'

'Now that's not fair,' said his father. 'Rose was only four when her daa was drowned. Her mam brought her and her brothers up on her own. Rose learned early that money doesna grow on trees.'

'Ay, but she's not short of a coin or two now.'

'Maybe not, but you never know when disaster will strike.'

'Is there a bicycle shop in Lerwick?' asked Catherine.

'Yes,' said Robbie. 'Why do you want to know?'

'I would like to have a bike.'

SIX

CATHERINE HAD TO admit that though there was not a lot of room in the box-bed it was comfortable and warm. They were lying there, he with his arm round her.

'I could get you a bike,' he said. 'Why do you want one?'

'I need it to get to work,' she said. She felt his arm tighten round her, his body tense.

'Work?'

'Yes. I got myself a job.'

'Where?'

'At the surgery, I'm going to be the cleaner.'

'But you're a nurse.'

'I know. This won't pay much, but Dr Lumsden asked me if I'd like to be the health visitor. That would mean training in Edinburgh and I don't want to do that. Not yet, anyway.'

For a moment or two Robbie maintained his grip, then with a sigh he relaxed. He said nothing, but pulled her round to face him and began to kiss her. Gently his lips touched her forehead then her cheeks, but when they found her mouth his kiss was full of passion. He held her tight, so tight that she knew how afraid he had been that he might lose her. She had been angry that he had not told her what to expect and had punished him; but the fault was as much hers as his; she should have asked more questions. She was here now though and going to stay. She put her arms round his neck and pulled him close.

'I do love you and I'm sorry I've been so horrid,' she whispered. 'Will you forgive me?'

'Hush,' he said as he ran his fingers through her hair, 'it was my fault and there's nothing to forgive.'

'You said once you'd give me anything I asked for. Did you mean it?'

'Of course.'

Well ... when the house is ready I would like a proper bed, one with a headboard and a footboard.' She sighed. 'Mm, and a nice mattress and cotton sheets and an eiderdown.'

'Anything your heart desires,' said Robbie. He had not lost her. She was here with him and she was going to stay. Tenderly he began to caress her body; cupping her breast he teased her nipple. With feather-soft touch his hand travelled down to stroke the roundness of her hip and the length of her thigh, arousing her desire as he did so. Parting her legs he fondled the soft cushion there; found the warm, moist, heart of it. Aflame now and eager for the completeness of being with him Catherine wound her legs round him, clasped him to her and enfolded him. As one they climaxed in a wild tumult of passion.

On that first night, when she and Robbie had slept in her father's house, making love with him hadn't been like that. Was this what their loving was really going to be like? Was this what she would have given away if she had left him? Without warning tears crept slowly down her face; as she wiped them away she turned her head to the pillow, glad that she'd changed her mind about leaving.

Shivering as she stood there, wearing only her bra and pants, Catherine poured a jug of hot water into the wash basin. Never had she had to wash herself in such spartan conditions. Not long ago Sunday morn-ings would have seen her luxuriating in a warm bathroom, but there was no bathroom in any of the houses in Deepdale. Neither was there anything in the way of heating other than the kitchen stove. Having a bath meant washing everything within reach and if possible finding someone to wash your back. She would have to forgo that pleasure this morning, for Robbie had gone to assess how much work had to be done to their house.

The piece of soap she had been given resisted all attempts to produce a lather. 'It's only fit for scrubbing the floor,' she grumbled. She washed quickly, it was too cold to do otherwise, and got dressed. She picked up her shoes, cleaned now and partly restored to their former glory; she decided not to put them on, but slipped her feet into a pair of flat lace-ups instead.

The wash basin emptied and returned to its place, she picked up her novel and went to the living room to wait for Robbie. Jannie was sitting at the table, the big family Bible open in front of her. She frowned when she saw the book in Catherine's hand. 'It is the Sabbath day,' she said. 'Do you not have a Bible?'

'No. Should I?'

'On the Lord's Day we read the Good Book. We don't knit or sew, we do nothin' that's not necessary and we go to the meetin' house to be led to salvation.'

'And what makes you think a preacher is going to help you do that?' asked Catherine. 'Surely practising your faith on a day-to-day basis is the right road to be on; you don't need someone else to show you the way.'

Clearly taken aback Jannie scowled. 'I thought you were a Christian? Well, wi' your heathen English ways you surely need salvation more than me.'

'That's a matter of opinion,' said Catherine, 'but a heathen I am not.'

At this Jannie compressed her mouth into a thin line and turned her attention to her Bible. 'I don't know what Robbie was thinkin' about when he brought you home,' she muttered.

'What don't you know, Mam?' said Robbie as he opened the door.

'Doesn't matter,' said Jannie.

'Your mother thought I ought to be reading the Bible and when I said I didn't have one she seemed to think you'd married a heathen.'

'Catherine's not a heathen, Mam.' Robbie pushed the door shut behind him. 'And you've no reason to say she is.'

'I was taught to respect the Sabbath,' said Jannie, a scowl on her face.

'And who says we don't?' said Robbie, 'we're going to the meeting house wi' you, aren't we?'

'Ay, well.' Jannie bent her head to the pages of her Bible again, muttering something under her breath as she did so.

'Put your coat on, Catherine, and come with me,' said Robbie. When they were outside he spoke again. 'I don't know why they haven't been in, but we're going to see my aunts. I'm not sure what you'll make of them. They're a bit old-fashioned; still living in the past, you might say.' He stopped at the door of his aunts' house and, taking Catherine's hand, opened the door. 'Is anybody home?' he called.

'Come in, Robbie,' said a disembodied voice.

'I've brought someone to see you,' he said as his aunts came forward to greet him. 'This is Catherine, my wife. You'll not have to speak Shetland to her, she'll not understand.' He turned to smile at Catherine. 'This is Mina,' he said, indicating the elder of the two women, 'and this is Laura.'

Mina Williams was tall; lean of build, she stood ramrod straight, black hair parted in the middle was pulled severely back into a bun.

'Welcome to Shetland, lass,' she said. 'Jamie told us you were here.'

'So why did you not come along to say hello?' asked Robbie.

'She said yon wife was not happy, so we thought we'd wait.'

Laura stepped forward. 'So nice to see you, dear,' she said.

Laura was as short and round as Mina was tall and lean. Her soft grey hair, also pinned into a bun, rebelled at its confinement and sprouted stray wisps.

'What are you doin', Laura? These folk will be wantin' tea,' snapped Mina.

'Oh, yeh, yeh,' said Laura as she ducked her head and scuttled away.

Catherine had warmed to Laura and a smile had started to light up her face, now it faded away. Why had Mina spoken to Laura in such a domineering way?

'Thanks, Mina,' said Robbie, 'but we'll not be stopping long. We've promised to go over to Rose's for tea and Mam will be putting our dinner on the table soon. We'll come by another time. I just wanted you to meet Catherine.'

'Ay, it's fine to have you back, Robbie, but you can sit for a minute, tell me what you've been up to.'

The chair Catherine was invited to sit on was as hard and uncomfortable as those in Jannie's house. She sat opposite Mina and while Robbie was being quizzed she studied her. The woman sat bolt upright. A shawl round her shoulders was pinned together with a brooch. A long black skirt reaching down to her ankles, stopped short to reveal feet in lace-up boots, placed neatly side by side.

The room, as austere as Jannie's, was as neat as a new pin. It too was plainly furnished and there against one wall was another large box-bed. On the hearth a peat fire glowed, and hanging from a hook in the chimney a kettle puffed steam. But no cat sat on a chair or the floor here.

Robbie was right: the aunts had not kept up with the times. But neither had Deepdale it seemed, and if the clock could be turned back fifty years everything would be in its proper place.

'Excuse me, dear,' said Laura as, teapot in one hand and a pot holder in the other, she reached for the kettle. Tipping it forward she poured boiling water into the pot. As she turned away she hesitated, once again her eyes met Catherine's and a warm smile lit her face.

Laura's clothes were almost identical to Mina's, but the face that peeped out from the unruly hair was as round and pleasant as Mina's was lined and stern. What had Laura done to deserve such a sister? The saying, 'still waters run deep' came to Catherine's mind and she wondered just how deep the emotions might be that ran under Laura's pleasant exterior.

'Tell me about yourself now, Catherine,' said Mina when tea had been handed round. 'What did you do during the war?'

'I was a nurse in a hospital in Southampton,' said Catherine.

'We were overrun with soldiers and airmen,' said Mina. 'Local lasses behaved in a disgusting way, getting with child with no idea who the father might be. God will wreak his vengeance.' She slapped her hand on to her thigh.

Oh dear, thought Catherine, another Jannie.

'They violated the teachings o' the scriptures,' Mina went on. She looked at Catherine, 'You must be a God-fearing young woman, for you married in church. What is your religion?'

'Aagh … Church of England,' said Catherine, mentally crossing all her fingers. Although she was still a believer her faith had suffered a severe shock when she had seen pictures of what man had done to man in the concentration camps in Germany. She had questioned why a loving God had allowed that to happen and had found no answers. She believed that Christianity should be practised daily, and attending church on a Sunday was no proof of adherence to that. Church of England, she had said, hoping that there wasn't one on Shetland.

'Ah well, it'll no matter, you can come to the meeting house wi' us.'

'We're going tonight with Rose so we'll see you there, but we've got to go now or Mam'll be fretting,' said Robbie. 'Fine to see you, you're looking well. Thanks for the tea. Bye.' As he closed the door behind them he said to Catherine, 'Well, now you've met all the inhabitants of Deepdale, what do you think?'

'How do those two survive? What do they live on?'

'They get a share of tatties and neeps, potatoes and turnips to you, because they help with planting and harvest, and I guess they've got some savings.'

'Why did Mina speak to Laura the way she did? And why did she change her speech when she spoke to me?'

Robbie laughed. 'Mina was 'talking proper' to you, "knappin" we call it.' He pronounced it k-nappin.

'You'll have to teach me the dialect so I can understand.'

'Don't worry, you'll learn.'

SEVEN

ROBBIE AND CATHERINE were on their way to the Hayfield croft, home to Rose and Bobbie Robertson and young Billie. They had left Deepdale and were climbing the hill to the moor when Catherine asked why they were going that way.

'Because it's a fine day,' said Robbie. 'We could have gone by the road, but that would have taken longer.'

It was a steep climb. At the top Catherine said, 'I can't go any further.'

Robbie put an arm round her shoulders and turned her to look back the way they'd come. She slipped an arm round his waist and leaned against him.

'You can't see anything of home except the bay,' he said, then, putting his head close to hers, he pointed at a wave-washed rocky outcrop topped with sparse green turf beyond the headland, 'but see that island out there? That's Mouat's Craig. I'm going to set pots there and hope that I'll get a fine catch of lobsters.'

'Do you know how?' asked Catherine.

'No, not exactly, but I'll learn. I know they like to be near rocks and on a sandy sea-bed. Round Mouat's Craig should be just the right place.'

'You will be careful, won't you?'

'Of course. Have you got your wind back? Are you ready to go on?'

They walked on, Catherine behind Robbie as he followed one of the narrow winding paths made by the hill sheep that skirted patches of bright green moss and pools of water. They stopped to watch as a hare, its coat patched brown where it was losing its winter white, leapt up from almost under their feet to bounce away, leaping, running and zigzagging till it was out of sight. Keeping to the sheep trails they crossed the moor and, wending their way through the humps and hollows of the peat banks, were at last on the track made by the ponies and carts used to carry home the cured peat. The way was downhill now and they walked side by side.

Billie saw them coming, and when they reached the Hayfield croft Rose came out to meet them. She put her arms round Catherine, 'You're a bonnie lass,' she said. 'I see why you wed her, Robbie. Come in.'

Pretty curtains hung at Rose's windows and her house was brighter and more comfortable than Jannie's or the aunts' and to Catherine's relief there was no sign of a box-bed. Billie had followed them in; now, hands in pockets he lolled against the wall and stood looking at her.

'Don't just stand there,' said his mother. 'Get your father.' Without a word Billie went out. 'He tells me you're going to do up Laurie's house, Robbie.'

'That's the plan.'

'What will you do, Catherine, when Robbie's at work?' said Rose.

'I'm going to be Doctor Lumsden's cleaner.'

'Are you? What about his wife? I thought she did that.'

'He told me she's not in good health and Kay said she was a sickly body.'

'Ay, maybe.' Rose smiled, but did not enlarge on her comment. She looked at Robbie. 'And have you got a job yet?'

'I'll be fishin' for lobsters; Daa's give me the boat. Ay, here's Bobbie.'

Bobbie Robertson had spent a life at sea, and wind and salt water had tanned and weathered his face till it was nut brown. His blue eyes twinkled as he clapped a hand on Robbie's shoulder, then smiled at Catherine and wished her welcome.

Catherine listened as Bobbie and Rose plied Robbie with questions about his time in the navy. When they lapsed into the dialect she understood nothing.

'Come, sit down and eat, all of you,' said Rose when she had piled the table with food. 'We don't want to be late for the meeting.'

The little chapel at Norravoe was filling rapidly when they reached it. Jannie, Daa and the aunts were already there. Robbie ushered Catherine to sit with them and took a seat beside her.

The interior of the building was very plain: whitewashed walls, benches and pulpit of varnished wood. On a table in front of the pulpit was a small font flanked by a pair of brass candlesticks. There were no flowers. Oil lamps hung from the ceiling. A cool, slightly damp, unlived-in smell tainted with a faint aroma of pine filled the air, mixed now with the varying odours of warm bodies.

The congregation ranged in age from the very old to the extremely young. Conversations went on in whispers. Children fidgeted. All came to a stop when a door opened and a woman carrying a book and a sheaf of paper walked through. She was followed by an elderly man, small and thin, so thin that his clothes flapped about him as he walked. He wore a black suit, in contrast with which his shirt was startlingly white. A fringe of sparse hair ringed his scalp. He climbed the stairs to the pulpit and as he did so, despite his meagre weight, each step creaked in protest. He sat down, then leaned forward to put his head in his hands and disappear from sight. The woman sat at a harmonium and began to play.

Winter had not been kind to the instrument; damp had crept into the fabric of its bellows as well as its internal workings, which made its performance somewhat erratic. As she pedalled manfully in an attempt to get it to produce something more than an asthmatic rendering of the piece she was playing, the organist's face was flushed, and, due to the fact that she shook her head whenever a note was off key her hatpins began to come loose, which set her hat adrift.

It began first as a smile, just a small quirk of the lips as Catherine, in an effort to take her mind off the organist, studied the bare pate of the preacher who was now sitting upright, his eyes closed. But then the smile broke into the suspicion of a giggle when the harmonium went into top gear to bellow out what should have been played pianissimo. The giggle was quickly smothered, but it would not be completely still and Catherine, hand clamped over her mouth, bent her head and prayed that the preacher would announce the first hymn while her shoulders shook and the chuckle persisted, bubbling up and trying hard to be free.

Beside her Robbie was hardly able to suppress a smile himself. He looked at his mother's stony face, shook his head and mouthed, 'Something's gone the wrong way,' while he patted Catherine's back.

The preacher stood and in a deep bass voice, boomed, 'We will open our tervice today wit hymn number tix hundred and tixty-tix.'

Catherine buried her head in her hands, laughter threatened to burst forth again. Robbie thumped her hard on the back till she coughed and spluttered and wiped her streaming eyes.

No one in the chapel or anywhere between it and Lerwick could have failed to hear that voice. Where on earth had it come from? The harmonium wheezed, the organist played the opening bars and the congregation stood, opened their hymn books and burst into song.

Catherine stood too and after a while began to sing as well. After the hymn and when the congregation were settled in their seats again the organist played softly while the collection was taken up. A chapel worthy, wearing a tweed suit and conker-bright boots, carried the offertory box. With every step he took his boots squeaked. Was there to be no end to this farce? In an effort to contain a laugh Catherine snorted, clapped her hands across her face and bent her head to cover her embarrassment.

There was to be no more cause for merriment however. As the service proceeded the lessons read were gloomy, the hymns in minor keys were, too. By the time the preacher began his sermon Catherine's expression was grim.

For a man with such a wasted frame the power of his voice was amazing. His enthusiasm for the scriptures knew no bounds; fanatic in his delivery he beat the top of the pulpit with his fist to drive home a point. Hellfire and damnation was his theme and he promised nothing but eternal misery if the commandments were not obeyed to the letter.

Catherine's mood grew dark, then darker. Where was the God of love? Obviously not to be found in this chapel. Beside her, Jannie nodded her head and murmured her agreement with what the preacher was saying.

Still the little man went on. Waving his arms he sobbed, mopped his brow and streaming eyes, lapsed into near silence, then, as he gave one last exhortation, he seized the sides of the pulpit and threw himself forward. There was a concerted gasp from every member of the congregation as they, like Catherine, took a metaphorical step back, fully expecting him to shoot out of the pulpit and land on the floor at their feet. Not so; with a sigh he stood back to breathe, 'Amen', which was resoundingly echoed from all corners.

The last hymn sung and the closing prayer said, to a shuffle of feet the chapel emptied. Little groups formed on the path outside to exchange news and gossip. Robbie's hand was pumped, his shoulder patted. Catherine was introduced to those whom Jannie thought mattered, while others were ignored.

'And what did you think of our chapel, Catherine?' asked Jannie when they were on their way home.

'Chapel was fine,' said Catherine, 'but I won't be going there again.'

'You'll not be coming to the meeting? exclaimed Jannie.

'No. I've seen too much of life to go to church and be condemned to hell by some skinny little runt of a man.'

With a sharp intake of breath Jannie stopped walking and stood stock still, shock evident in the expression on her face. 'You can't say things like that about our preacher, and what do you mean, you've seen too much? Why, you're no more than a child.'

'That's what you think, is it?' The two women stood facing each other. The aunts, aghast at what was happening, stood behind Jannie and stared. Daa looked everywhere but at them. Robbie, anxious to intervene, began, 'Listen, Mam,' but Catherine placed her arm across him to keep him behind her. 'Shut up,' she said. Robbie silenced, she went on, 'I worked in a hospital throughout the war, saw people with terrible injuries as the result of German bombs. Some died, often in great pain, children too.' She spoke vehemently and passionately. 'I did everything I could to comfort them and tell them of God's love. It would have been very cruel of me if I had talked to them the way that preacher did. The Bible tells us that God is love, but there was no love in that chapel today.' Now, her voice lowered, she said, 'No, I will *not* go to chapel to be threatened.'

She turned away leaving the rest of the family speechless.

'Come on, Robbie,' she said, 'we'll walk on.' Taking his arm she marched him forward, stepping out till they were well ahead of the others.

'You didn't think much of the preacher then?' said Robbie.

'What was that man trying to do? Where were love and compassion?' Catherine's anger was plain to see, its force made clear by the way she strode along.

'Hey, slow down,' said Robbie.

'Slow down?' Catherine stopped abruptly and turned to look at him. 'According to that man God is a monster to be afraid of. That's not the Christianity I know. You'll never see me in church again.'

Robbie laughed. 'Bet we do.'

EIGHT

T HE BICYCLE WAS not new, but was in better condition than Billie's. With the wind in her hair Catherine flew down the hill toward the surgery. Neil Lumsden was delighted to see her. 'I don't think I need to tell you much about cleaning,' he said as he showed her round. 'No doubt you had some dragon of a matron at the hospital where you worked, but you might answer the phone and take messages.' Then, wagging a finger at her, 'But you won't steal any of my patients, will you?'

'Wouldn't dream of it,' said Catherine.

'How are you settling in?'

'Well … it's a bit different from home.'

'Mmm.' The doctor looked sideways at her. 'I'm not surprised you said that, but I'm sure you'll weather it. I'm off now, I may see you tomorrow.'

The surgery, occupying a couple of rooms on the ground floor, contained a desk, a couple of chairs, an examination bench and a locked cupboard. The waiting room was furnished with an odd assortment of chairs. A few magazines were laid on a coffee table. A fire had been lit and slabs of peat still burned in the fireplace. Catherine imagined Lumsden's patients sitting there discussing and comparing ailments. A visit to the doctor here might almost be classed a social occasion, far removed from the sterile qualities of the waiting-room in casualty at St Margaret's in Southampton.

Catherine was happy to be away from Jannie, who, since the words they'd had coming home from the chapel, had grown even colder toward her. She concentrated on her work and when she thought the rooms would pass the strictest of matron's inspections she locked up, got on her bike and rode off in the direction of Deepdale.

Robbie was on the roof of their house with Billie when she got home. 'We'll soon have it finished,' he said as he came down the ladder. 'It's not as bad as I thought, only had to replace a couple of bits of timber. We're tarring it now.'

'I've never seen a tarred roof. Why don't you put slates on it?'

'Probably will later on, but we've got other stuff to spend our money on, furniture for instance,' said Robbie.

When the roof had at last been declared watertight and the floor in the living room made sound Catherine took the table and chairs outside. With a bucket of soapy water and a scrubbing brush, borrowed from Kay, she scrubbed and rinsed and dried. She also borrowed a dustpan and brush and a long-handled broom and went to work indoors. She took down pictures and curtains, destroyed cobwebs, cleaned the stove, swept walls and floors. She had already colour-washed the bedroom. Propped against the wall there, waiting to be put together, was a new bed. A bed that had been ordered, waited for, and welcomed when it came. The box-bed in the living room would have to go. She was looking at it when Kay walked in.

'How are you getting on?' asked Kay.

'Not bad,' said Catherine. There was dust in her hair and the remains of a stray cobweb highlighting her curls.

'Is there anything I can do to help?'

Catherine laughed. 'Only if you've got an axe.'

'An axe? Oh, the bed. My dear, you can't chop it up, it's good wood.'

'Robbie said I could have anything I wanted. I ached for a proper bed. I've got one. This one has to go and if you won't help then I'll smash it up myself.'

'I would have thought that by now,' Kay's voice was stem, 'you would have realized there's a shortage of timber here. The wood in that bed is valuable.'

Valuable! Catherine looked at Kay, who went on, 'Every piece of wood has to be brought in by boat; surely you've noticed that what trees do grow here are very stunted and that there aren't many of them.'

'Well … yes … but I never thought …'

'No, I don't suppose you did. Let Robbie take the bed to pieces and use it to build something else.'

'Mm, I suppose you're right,' said Catherine.

The rain and wind of April gave way and May came in with fine cold days. Catherine, on her way home, stood at the top of the road and looked down into the valley. The aunts in their long skirts and shawls were throwing scraps out for the hens. Jannie had come out too and the three old women stood there gossiping.

A shaft of sunlight drifted across the ocean, highlighting the restless waters of the bay and making them shimmer with a brightness that was painful to see; the beach glowed. Sunshine spread to the valley and brought it to life. It chased shadows across the land over the houses and away up to the hills. It made mirrors of windows, heightened the colours of all it touched, and Catherine saw the valley in a different way. It was a little world on its own, far apart from the hustle and bustle of life away from the islands; now she could begin to see why it was where Robbie wanted to stay. She stood to take it in for a few minutes more, then, pushing the bicycle, went down the hill.

They watched her as she drew near, the aunts and Jannie, and she was sure they had been talking about her. It was obvious from the way they nodded their heads and smiled at one another.

'Hello,' she said. 'It's a lovely day, isn't it.'

'Not bad,' said Jannie, and, 'So it is,' said Mina, while Laura just smiled.

'And how are you getting on with our good doctor?' asked Mina.

'I like him.'

'He'll not work you too hard. Do you see the wife?'

'I haven't seen her yet. I gather she's not too well.'

'A likely story.'

Oh dear, what piece of gossip was Mina wanting to tell? Catherine didn't want to hear. 'Please excuse me,' she said, 'I must get on. I have things to do.'

Standing on the floor in her house was a rope-bound box. When Robbie had complained about the weight of it, when he had to drag it on and off trains and on to the ferry, she had wondered why she had bothered to bring it with her. But it contained all her treasures and at last it was going to be opened. The house was cold, but she soon had a fire going and in front of it, kneeling on a rug that Kay had given her; she pulled the box towards her and began to unfasten the ropes that bound it. She didn't hurry, but eased every knot apart and rolled the rope into a ball. Then she lifted the lid.

She lifted out sheets then pillowcases. There were more pillowcases, but these were embroidered. As she opened them out she was taken back to when she sat with needle and thread, dreaming as she stitched, of the day they would be on the bed she would share with Robbie. She put them aside and took out more linen, tablecloths and towels. There were some wrapped bundles, a clock, ornaments, a set of saucepans and a kettle. From the middle of it all she lifted a package wrapped in a towel; when it was unwrapped a doll with blue eyes in a china face stared at her. 'You made it then,' said Catherine, 'I was afraid you might get broken. One day I'll give you to my little girl. That's if I'm lucky enough to have one.' She put the doll on the chair behind her and turned again to the box.

Another package contained a framed photograph of her parents. She held it up and looked at them. 'You would never believe me if I told you what it's like here,' she said, 'and for that reason I never shall. But I love Robbie and "better or worse", that's the way it shall be.'

She was surrounded by the contents of the box which she had spread out on the floor when Robbie came in.

'What are you doing?' he said.

'Diving into my treasure chest. We've got plenty of sheets and pillowcases, but no blankets or pillows. We've got saucepans and cutlery but no plates. What are we going to do?'

'Go and see Kay, she'll know.'

It was a fine morning. One of those rare days when the sky was a bonnie blue and the sea looked up and swallowed it whole. One of those days when wind fled away and peace settled over all, a day too tranquil for anything but pleasure.

'Leave what you're doing,' said Robbie. 'We're going out in the boat.'

Catherine needed no second bidding. As they pulled away from the shore in the dinghy she looked into the crystal-clear water. 'I can see right to the bottom,' she said, 'and there's a fish.'

'I'll get you a line so you can fish for your own supper then,' said Robbie.

Aboard the *Deepdale Lass* Catherine stood beside Robbie as he sailed out of the bay. 'It seems bigger now we're on it,' she said. 'Are you sure you can manage it and set the pots by yourself? Shouldn't you take Daa with you?'

'No. He wouldn't want to come, that's why he gave the boat to me.'

The sea was like glass with hardly a ripple to disturb its surface; its only turmoil was in the wake of the boat. Catherine was thrilled with the sound of water lapping the sides of it, the purr of the engine and the lazy mewing of a gull.

'This is lovely,' she said. 'I'd like to do it again.'

They sailed up the coast, Robbie pointing out and naming places. Then he turned the *Lass* and headed out to sea. When he turned towards land again Catherine could see how secluded the valley was; she could also see way up the hill to where sheep were grazing. With the engine slowed Robbie took the boat round Mouat's Craig. 'There's no way to land on it,' he said. 'It's just a skerrie, a lump of rock. I'm going to set my pots here. We'll go home now.'

With the engine idling he eased the *Deepdale Lass* through the entrance to the bay, anchored her and helped Catherine down into the dinghy. As he rowed ashore he asked her if she was going to be busy that afternoon.

'I've got to start cutting peat,' he said, 'I wondered if you'd come with me?'

Jannie was at her sister's house and she, along with Mina and Laura was busy with a piece of knitting.

'What does du think of Robbie's wife, Jannie?' asked Mina.

'Well, I thought I might have made her go home, but she's going to stay.'

'And are you not pleased at that?'

'No. I know she'd be no use on a croft, you only have to look at her hands, fine and soft they are. I cannot see her working wi' the peat or the sheep. My poor Robbie's gotten himself the wrong wife.'

Laura listened to her sister's conversation, but said nothing.

'She didn't take long to get a job,' said Mina.

Jannie muttered, 'And how long do you think that'll last? She says she's a trained nurse. You don't have to train to clean a house.' Turning the work in her hands she inserted the spare needle into the knitting-belt on her waist and set her fingers flying again. 'Wait now till she has to help Robbie wi' plantin' tatties and clippin' sheep. Hard work'll be too much for her.'

'And what would she do if she had a bairn?'

'A bairn?'

'Ay, did you not think she would?'

For a moment Jannie's fingers stopped. 'Well, I know it's likely, but I was so sure she wouldn't stay I hadn't thought about it,' she said.

'Likely you should,' said Mina. 'If she can't cope wi' the work now, how would she do wi' a little one to look after?'

'Ach,' Jannie shook her head, 'it'll not happen, she'll be away before the year is out. She was never made to work hard.'

Laura stopped knitting, lifted her head and looked straight at Jannie. 'That's not right. Catherine cleaned out her house all by herself. She painted all the walls and the wood round the windows and the door. Robbie didn't help at all; he was busy on the boat.'

The clicking of needles had stopped. Jannie and Mina stared at Laura. Suddenly Mina's jaw snapped shut, 'You don't know what you're saying, Laura. Go and put the kettle on.' She turned her attention to Jannie. 'Never mind her.'

Catherine carried a bag containing a flask of tea and some bannocks. Resting on Robbie's shoulder were his tools. In the valley the air had been still and warm, but as they climbed the hill it grew cooler; when they reached the top there was a soft breeze.

'Just the day for what I have to do,' said Robbie.

'How do you know which bank is yours?' asked Catherine.

'These have always been dug by Deepdale folk. This is the one for us.'

For a while Catherine watched as Robbie sliced off the tough heathery turf to expose the peat beneath it.

'You don't have to dig for everybody, do you? What do your aunts do?'

'Daa and I dig for them, but they and Mam have to come up to raise it. You'll have to come and do ours.'

'Raise it?'

'Turn it and dry it. I'll show you what to do.'

They were not the only ones on the moor, among others who had come to win their peat was Billie. He saw them and came loping across.

'I hear you have the boat in the water,' he said. 'Will you take me fishin?'

'I likely could.'

Robbie stood holding the handle of his spade. He looked at Billie, who had hung his head and was looking sideways at Catherine. He laughed. 'Aren't you going to say hello to Catherine?' he said.

'Oh, ay,' said Billie and with a fleeting smile looked at Catherine. 'Hello,' he said; then, 'I'd better get to me work or Daa'll be at me if I've not done.'

He was off as he had come, bounding and leaping from tussock to tussock.

'He's awful shy,' said Robbie with a grin on his face, 'but I'd say in a year or two, when he gets a fancy for a lass, he'll lose that.' He went back to his work and watching him, Catherine thought what a hard job it was. How much longer would it take?

And then Robbie had done with the turf and the length of the peat bank had been exposed. 'I'll have that bannock and a drink now,' he said and sat himself down on the turf beside Catherine.

'Do you have to do all this hard work?' she said when they had eaten and she had poured out mugs of tea. 'Couldn't you burn logs or coal?'

'Yes, that would be very nice,' said Robbie, 'but where would we get them? Coal comes by boat, is expensive and there are no trees to provide logs.'

'I should have known that,' admitted Catherine. 'I wanted to chop up the box-bed, but Kay wouldn't let me. I've got a lot to learn.'

'She was right. Peat is free,' said Robbie, 'but wood is expensive.'

He drained his mug and put it down. Then, hands behind his head, he lay back on the turf and closed his eyes. Catherine sat and looked around her. A skylark rose up out of the heather and, trilling its song, climbed the sky. In the distance the sea was blue and sparkling. There was no rush of traffic here, no one was in a hurry, no get to work on time and can't be late. Life went on in a different way.

'Robbie,' she said, 'why does your mother boss everyone about?'

'She's always been the same. I don't take any notice.'

'You do. I heard you shouting at her when you didn't know where I was.'

'Ah … that was different. I thought she'd said something to make you leave and I wasn't going to let her drive you away.'

'Why do you let her get away with it? Why don't you answer her back?'

'What good would that do? It would only make her more mad.'

'She's not going to boss me.'

Robbie gave a deep throaty chuckle and said, 'I'd already gathered that.'

'Would you like to know what decided me to stay?'

At that he sat up and looked into her face. 'I most certainly would.'

'It was your mother.' Mimicking Jannie, Catherine said, ' "You'll be no use. You should go home, give Robbie a chance to find someone as would suit him better." Well, I wasn't going to have that. I may not know how to milk a cow or look after sheep, but I can learn.'

A smile spread across Robbie's face. He kissed Catherine. 'I love you, my little firebrand. I think Mam has met her match, but I'd better get on with the cutting.' He picked up one of his tools and began to slice into the peat.

'That's a funny-looking spade,' said Catherine.

'It's called a tushkar.'

Cutting down, then lifting and turning the dark wet slab to lay it on the turf at the top of the bank, Robbie worked slowly backwards. Side by side the slabs lay the length of the bank. When he reached the end Robbie paused to rest.

'When you've finished will you have some time off?' asked Catherine.

'Ha!' snorted Robbie. 'Maybe at the end of October. Summer is when the work has to be done. Winter is dark, but I shall take you dancing then.'

'I shall look forward to that,' she said.

Robbie began to cut again. This time the slabs were laid crossways on the first ones; once more he cut a length of the bank. When several rows had been cut and he had once again reached the end he looked up at Catherine and said, 'That's it then, enough for today.'

NINE

'I'm sorry if I've been a disappointment to you, Mrs Jameson, and that you've had to put up with me,' said Catherine, 'but I'll be out of your way now.'

With her back to Catherine Jannie busied herself with the pots on her stove. 'Yea, yea,' she said, not bothering to turn round.

Catherine stood and looked at her mother-in-law, at her untidy bun of hair and the knot of apron strings at her waist. She had lived with Jannie for two months; eight long weeks in which Jannie lost no opportunity in letting her know she was not welcome. The snide remarks were always made when neither Robbie or his father were there. Was Robbie right when he said that to fight back would only make his mother worse? It was not true that 'the soft answer turneth away wrath', for she had tried that and it had made no difference.

The house at the far end of the valley was ready and she and Robbie were moving in. They had bought blankets and some pieces of furniture. Kay had given them an eiderdown and pillows. Rose had sent Billie over with a box of china. 'Call it a belated wedding present,' she had said. Robbie had already taken their clothes and her suitcase along. Now Catherine carried her overnight bag.

There was no sign of the aunts or Kay as she walked along the path and Robbie was out in the boat, checking his lobster pots. Catherine was glad of that, for this was to be the very first day she could really call herself a wife, the first time she could cook a meal instead of having to eat what his mother provided.

She opened her door, went in, walked through to the bedroom and put her bag down on a chair. Robbie had put the bed together: her 'proper' bed, and now it took up most of the room. There was a chair on one side of it, a small chest of drawers on the other and a larger chest against the wall. It was enough.

In the living room Catherine lit the fire and began to prepare a meal. Her supply of pots and pans being limited, a one-pot meal would be easiest, so it would have to be stew. When the fire was going well she shut down the dampers, put the pot on the back of the stove and left it there to simmer while she went to the bedroom and made up the bed. That done she went out to watch Robbie coming home.

Her vantage point was a little way up the hill beyond Jannie's house. She had gone there to watch for him several times, because she could see beyond the headlands and as far as Mouat's Craig, where he had set some of his pots. If Robbie's boat was on the far side of it she was not able to see it.

She scanned the ocean. White-topped waves rose and fell. Though from the distance they did not look big she knew they were; only the top of the wheelhouse of a fishing-boat further out to sea was visible when it sank into a trough. A raucous crowd of seagulls flew over it; obviously there was a catch of fish on board and the crew were gutting and throwing the offal to the birds. She pulled her coat closer round her, for though the day was fine the wind was keen. Huddled on her perch, she hoped Robbie wouldn't be long.

The fishing had been good and the lobsters Robbie had caught had brought good money. They had put some aside to make improvements to the house later on for there was talk of electricity coming to Lerwick and sooner or later it would come to Deepdale. Not only was there talk of electricity but of piped water too.

'I told you things would change,' said Robbie. 'You'll have your electric cooker and your washing-machine.' She had laughed and said she couldn't wait.

Water on tap was more important than electricity, she thought, for drinking water had to be fetched in a pail from a spring halfway up the hill. Why couldn't it have come to light somewhere in the valley? Washdays meant rainwater dipped out of a water butt and heated on the stove. Water that could be had by the turn of a tap would be a boon.

She scanned the ocean again and was rewarded with the sight of the prow of the *Deepdale Lass* nosing out from behind Mouat's Craig. She would watch till it was coming into the bay then go down. Robbie would have to put the lobsters he had caught into the keep tank till he had enough to take them to the fish market. She would have time to get his meal on the table by the time he came in.

'Well, she's gone,' said Jannie.

Daa was washing his hands. 'You mean Catherine?' he said.

'Ay.'

'But not far enough for you … obviously.'

'That would be right.'

'Do you not think that however far she went Robbie would not go wi' her?' Daa dried his hands then picked up the bowl of dirty water.

'Well, I couldna stop him,' said Jannie.

Opening the door Daa threw the water on to the grass beyond the path. 'Then be thankful she stayed,' he said. 'You might be glad she's here yet.'

'I cannot think why.'

What was it that had turned Jannie into a sour old woman, thought Daa, or had she always been that way? 'I shall be away all day tomorrow; if I'm late home will you milk the cow?' he asked.

Now that he had handed the boat over to Robbie, John had taken work on road maintenance with the council in order to supplement his meagre income from crofting. But sometimes the work took him far from the valley and there were jobs at home that had to be done. With bad grace Jannie agreed; she and the cow did not have a good relationship.

'You'll be glad you only have the two of us to cook for now,' said Daa, hoping to placate his wife.

'Ay,' she said. 'Them from south don't eat like us. I canna think what Robbie's going to get for his tea.'

'We don't have to worry about that,' said Daa. 'Ah, here's Mina.'

'I'm come to see if you have anything for the merchant, Jannie,' said Mina as she stepped in. 'I'm going to Lerwick tomorrow with Laura's and mine.'

'Yea, I have some. You'll take tea?' said Jannie.

Mina had already settled herself on a chair. She nodded her head in answer to Jannie's question. 'I see the lass has a fire going, her chimney was smokin'. Has she gone from you now?'

'Ay,' said Jannie.

'She was sitting up the hill waiting on Robbie coming home. I saw her.' Mina grunted her disapproval. 'You would think she'd have a piece of work in her hands, would you not'? But no, she was idle.'

'She can't knit.'

'Can't knit? Did her mam not teach her?'

'She's a nurse, maybe she thinks she doesn't have to.'

'She would need to know somethin' more than nursing to be a wife.'

'Yea,' said Jannie. 'I was just wonderin' if she could cook, for a man must have his meat.'

'You would wonder—' began Mina.

'Could you not leave the lass alone?' Daa looked from one to the other of the two women. He rarely raised his voice and neither did he now. 'You should be good to her and not the scheming old wives you are. You've given her no peace since she got here. She needs time to settle in.'

Two pairs of eyes turned on him, stared then turned away. 'I should be going,' said Mina. 'I'll not bother wi' the tea. Where's your stuff, Jannie?'

The latch clicked and the door opened and Laura, still holding the door handle, stood there. 'I'm brought you some eggs, Catherine,' she said. 'The hens is laying well.'

'Thank you,' said Catherine. 'Come in.'

'I'll no' stay. Mina is gone along to Jannie's. I'd best get back.'

'Wait though,' said Catherine. 'Should I not pay you?'

'No, no, we have too many, dey is for you.' As suddenly as she'd opened the door Laura closed it and was gone.

Catherine, holding a paper bag full of eggs, turned to Robbie.

'What goes on there? Why does Mina treat Laura the way she does?'

'Don't underestimate Laura; she knows all too well how to cope with Mina,' said Robbie, 'but Mina, well, I think she's worse than Mam. If there was no one else in the room she'd quarrel with the poker.'

'Robbie, you exaggerate.'

'No, I don't. She's the eldest and I think she brought the other two up. She had to take charge and it's become a habit she can't stop.'

Catherine had been about to dish up. She had laid the table, made tea and cut thick slices of bread; now she began to ladle out the stew. 'Now we're on our own,' she said, 'I want you to tell me what life is all about on a croft.' She had filled Robbie's plate. 'There's plenty,' she said. 'You can come back for more when you've finished that.' She put the pot back on the stove and sat down.

'What do you want to know?' asked Robbie.

'Where my place is and what you expect of me.'

Between mouthfuls of stew Robbie explained and as he did so Catherine grew quiet. At last she said, 'It seems as though I have to be a Jack-of-all trades. But I can't knit and I can't make butter or bannocks. I can't milk a cow and I know nothing about sheep. I grew up in town so I know nothing at all about gardens or animals, or how to fillet fish or salt mutton. In fact, the only thing I'm good at is nursing and I can't even get a job at that.' She took a long deep breath, then looked straight at Robbie. 'I'm beginning to think your mother was right when she said I should leave and let you find someone better suited to you.'

With a roar Robbie jumped up. 'She had no right to talk to you like that. I've a good mind to—'

'Sit down; I'm here, aren't I? If I'd been going to leave it would have been then. In fact, it was what made me stay. I wasn't going to be pushed out by her, but … well … it looks as though I'm going to have an uphill task.'

Across the table Robbie took Catherine's hands in his. 'I'll teach you. You don't have to learn it all at once. It's a hard life now, but when Mam grew up it was harder. The family had to pull together; things always worked that way.'

'Have I judged her too harshly, then?'

'No, she's always been crabby. But she knows what living on a croft is like and likely she thinks it would be too much for you.'

'Do you think it would?'

'It's getting better, I think you'll manage. I told you I want to breed pedigree Cheviots, improve our sheep.' He squeezed her hands tight. 'I saw so many things while I was away, better sheep, tractors, green fields, and it'll happen here, the hills will go green and crofters will be better off.' He gave an exultant little laugh. 'It's going to be good. So don't take any notice of Mam.'

Catherine could see the gleam in his eyes, heard the passion in his voice. 'I shall be with you all the way. Now I'd better wash the dishes …'

'Leave the dishes, let's go to bed.'

'But it's …'

'Early, I know, but I want to make love to you.'

Catherine had fantasized about the bed, imagined sliding her naked body between cool cotton sheets, resting her head on soft down pillows and turning to see Robbie's head on the pillow beside her. They would talk, whispering in the dark before making love and curling up to sleep wrapped in each other's arms.

But the bedroom was cold and as she took off her clothes she began to shiver. Could she do this? The sheets would be cold too and to her mind came the memory of her warm body diving into an icy sea. Wouldn't the shock dull Robbie's ardour? And wouldn't it be better if she put her pyjamas on? No. There was nothing for it but to take the plunge. Pulling back the covers she jumped in. 'Aagh,' she gasped as ice cold cotton came in contact with her skin.

'I thought you told me you were tough.' Robbie laughed as he lifted the bedclothes and slid between the sheets. His indrawn breath went on for several seconds before he let it out in a long moan.

Catherine laughed. 'It's not cold, is it?'

'You'll get a hot-water bottle somewhere tomorrow,' said Robbie as he put an arm round her to pull her close, 'or you'll sleep alone.'

'Never,' said Catherine. 'I will not share my bed with anyone but you, nothing and nobody, not a teddy bear, or a cat and not even a hot-water bottle.'

'You talk too much,' said Robbie as his mouth closed on hers.

His body was warm and pressed against him she could feel the soft curling hair on his chest against her breasts. They were alone at last, no thin walls through which others could hear the cries and moans she could not suppress when she and Robbie made love. Free of those restrictions and longing for the completeness of being one with him she snaked her arms around his neck, leaving her body for him to explore and tantalize. With his tongue he parted her lips. 'Aah,' she moaned. She pressed closer to him. His fingertips brushed lightly on her skin. With gentle hands he traced the length of her spine, the outline of her hip, her buttock, the back of her thigh. When he lifted her leg to lie over his, she gasped. So close, so close, she could stand it no more, rolled on to her back and, reaching for the heights of ecstasy, welcomed him into her. Lifting her legs she wrapped them tightly round him, soared to the very summit of delight at his thrusts and cried out as she climaxed.

When it was over and he lay limp and heavy on her, she relaxed and lay supine. She traced the line of his breastbone with a finger, then laid her hand flat against his chest. Under her palm she could feel the steady beat of his heart. 'I love you so much,' she said. 'I would have been a fool to walk away from you.'

He kissed her tenderly, then laid a finger on her lips, 'You talk too much,' he said, then rolled away and lay beside her. 'I love you too. Now go to sleep.'

TEN

A shaft of sunlight poking its finger between the curtains shone on Robbie's face and woke him. He raised himself on one elbow and looked down at his sleeping wife. Catherine's long dark hair was spread across the pillow, a smoky curve of eyelashes rested on soft cheeks; red lips parted as she breathed gently in and out. He kissed her temple. She stirred, opened her eyes, turned and looked up at him.

'Good morning, Mr Jameson,' she said.

'Good morning, Mrs Jameson,' he replied.

She laughed and reached up to kiss him, 'And how are you today?' she said.

'I'm very well,' he replied.

She was so close, warm and soft, that desire stirred in his loins. But he had work to do, pots to set and fish to take to the merchant. He thought about it for a moment, considered it for another, abandoned the thought and drew her close.

'I love you, Robbie,' she said. 'Don't ever leave me.'

'How could you even think such a thing? You know I never would.'

When Robbie eventually opened his front door Jannie Jameson stood there, hand raised, about to knock. 'What are you doin' here?' he said.

'Why do you lock your door?' said Jannie. 'You're late.'

'What do you want?'

'I ah … I … I was thinkin', if you were takin' the catch to the town, while you were there could you get somethin' for me?' stammered Jannie. She was looking behind Robbie at Catherine, who was wearing a dressing-gown.

'Is anything wrong?' said Catherine. 'Is somebody ill?'

'No,' said Robbie, ignoring the way his mother was looking at his wife, 'Mam wants me to fetch somethin' from the town for her.'

'Well,' snapped Jannie, 'hadn't you better get a move on?'

'I am.' Robbie closed the door and turned to Catherine. 'Take no notice of her, she was just being nosy. What are you going to do today?'

'I shall come and watch you away, then see if I can coax the stove to heat the oven and let me bake a cake. Maybe I'll look for you coming home.'

Little ripples lapped the shore. Catherine stood on the beach and watched as Robbie pushed the dinghy into the water to row out to the boat. When he was aboard the *Deepdale Lass* and sailing out of the bay she went back to her house.

Coping with a temperamental stove was a new experience for her. Kettle and pots on the top were easy to manage, but how was she to keep the oven temperature constant? Somehow she did and the cake she took out of it some time later looked good to her. She stood it on a rack and when it cooled, put it on a plate and spread a cloth over it. They would have it with a cup of tea when Robbie came home. And now she would go and watch for him.

It was one of those days when it was warm and the wind had gone away to worry someone else. Mina and Laura sat on a bench outside their house. They were there to take advantage of the better light for, as always, they were busy knitting. They nodded as Catherine passed and asked where she was going.

'Robbie should be home in a little while. I'm going to sit up there,' she pointed to the hill, 'and look for him.'

'Do you not have a piece of knitting to do?' asked Mina.

'No,' said Catherine, 'I don't knit and don't want to learn.'

Jannie was just stepping out of her house when Catherine drew near; she stopped when she saw Catherine. Knitting in hand, she pulled at the ball of wool lying in the pocket of her apron, then without a word turned and went back inside.

What have I done now? Oh, I know, I wasn't up at the crack of dawn, so I made Robbie late for work. It has to be my fault, of course.

Reaching her perch Catherine took in the day. It was June and the kind of day she would have taken for granted back home. But here it was definitely 'a day between weathers'. The sun shone down out of an endlessly blue sky with never as much as a wisp of cloud to mar its face. The wind had died away which left the land unruffled and the sea calm. Catherine had never seen it in such a good mood since Robbie had first brought her home. Oh, there had been the odd day when the weather had promised to be kind, but as it often did it changed its mind and the wind whipped the sea till it was angry and the waves were high and white topped. She had seen the ocean rage and she'd seen it rough.

She'd worried when Robbie had gone out when it heaved and rolled into peaks and troughs and appeared to swallow boats much bigger than his, but he had always come home to smile and say, 'You don't need to worry, lass.'

He'd taken a rod and line with him today and had said that when he had slipped the pots he would fish and bring home a fine fat one for their dinner. She looked at the watch on her wrist and counted the hours since he'd left. He'd been gone a long time and he'd said he wouldn't, but maybe he'd been delayed at the town. She put a hand to her forehead, shielded her eyes from the glare of the sun on the sea and scanned its surface. Nothing … there was nothing but a few gulls circling over its broad expanse.

A frown creased her forehead. Even though he was late he should be in sight, for she could see a long way up the coast. Again she searched the ocean for sight of him but there was nothing, not even the smallest boat in that flat blue stretch of water. She was beginning to worry now.

Voices drifted up to her from below, and looking down she saw that Jannie had come out to join her sisters. Skinny black-clad legs ending in feet encased in sensible shoes stuck out from under her floral wrap-round overall. It was what she wore every day, and apart from the coat and hat she had worn to the chapel Catherine had never seen her in anything else. Even in a crowd Jannie would be unmistakable, whereas the aunts in their black skirts and grey shawls reminded her of nothing else but the hooded crows that sat on fence posts and cawed.

The aunts were fussing about the chickens, making clucking noises and throwing down scraps while they gossiped, Jannie's fingers were as always flying over the wool and needles in her hands.

A rattle of stones on the track made Catherine turn her head to look. She wasn't surprised to see that it was Billie flying down it on his rackety old bike. His feet were stuck out at an angle, his coat tails flying, and she was afraid he was going to have an accident. But then his feet found and controlled the madly circling pedals, his hands pulled up the brakes, he skidded to a stop and laid the bike down on its side only a short distance from the three old women. She watched as he spoke to them, waving his arms about as he did so. The women looked at him, huddled together and leaned towards him, as if eager to hear what news he had to impart.

Sitting on a mossy patch, the sun warm on her back, Catherine smiled. She could imagine the excitement with which they would listen to any piece of gossip Billie was bringing; and gossip it would be for what else was there to tell? Although they treated her with such disdain she felt sorry for them, sorry for the apparent unending monotony of their lives, sorry for the perpetual round of cooking, cleaning and knitting, always the knitting, the day-to-day routine that seemed incapable of change. She was never going to let her life become as theirs.

Then they were falling apart, throwing up their hands and the screech and wail of them carried up to her. What was that all about? They came together again, clutched and clung to each other while poor Billie just stood and watched. Kay came out of her house to see what all the noise was about.

Gradually, the weeping and wailing subsided. When it had the women drew a little apart and turned their faces up to look at Catherine. In spite of the warmth of the day a chill ran down her spine and she shivered. Lowering her head she began to pleat the hem of her cotton skirt between her fingers. 'Don't look at them, don't look at them,' she whispered, 'it's nothing to do with you. Robbie'll be home soon; he'll tell you what it's all about.'

But then the wailing began again and she lifted her head to look. Mina and Laura had wrapped their arms round one another. Jannie sat on an upturned pail, clutched her face and rocked back and forth. Kay was wringing her hands. Billie was climbing the hill towards her;

'What's going on?' she asked.

'You'll have to come,' he called. 'You're needed.'

'Why, what's happened?'

'They'll tell you,' Billie replied as he turned away.

Down the hillside they went, Billie always a bit in front of her. It was no use trying to talk, she needed her wits about her not to slip on the dry wiry grass. When they reached the yard in front of the house and Billie's boots clattered on the stones Jannie leapt up, seized Catherine by the arms, shook her violently and cried, 'I kenned fine it was an ill day you walked through my door.'

Shocked at Jannie's blotched and tear-stained face Catherine cried, 'Something terrible has happened, hasn't it, is it Dad? What is it? Tell me.' She pushed herself free of Jannie's grasp, looked from one to the other of the women clustered round her. 'Tell me what's happened, please.'

Mina had covered her face with her hands; slowly she pulled them down her cheeks. 'It's Robbie … he'll not be coming home,' she moaned.

A great stillness filled Catherine, the calmness of disbelief. 'Not …

coming home … Why not?' No one answered and all eyes except Billie's, looked away from her. Why were they doing this to her? 'He's taken the catch to Lerwick, hasn't he?'

Still no one answered. They were hiding something from her. She grabbed Billie by the arms, dug her fingers in till she could feel flesh through the stuff of his jacket. 'Speak to me,' she demanded. 'You tell me.' Billie leaned away from her, but continued to look her in the eye.

'He … he …' twisting up his arm he covered his mouth with his hand then, letting it fall said, with a sob, 'he's drowned, the sea took him.'

For long moments she held him, fingers flexing, biting into his arms, but still Billie held her gaze. Billie wouldn't lie, not about something like this, would he? Would he? No, she wasn't going to believe him.

'No,' she said at last, 'how could it, look at it.' Her voice was calm. She twisted him till he was facing the sea. 'It's peaceful, not angry. You're wrong.'

'I'm right … he was slippin' pots,' sobbed Billie.

Letting go of him Catherine covered her ears with her hands; an angry roaring sound filled them. 'No, no, I don't want to hear,' she shouted, but through the roar she heard some of Billie's words: 'ropes … foot … overboard.' She stared at him, her face twisting and twitching. 'Noooh,' she screamed and slapped his face right and left. 'You lie. I don't believe you, I *don't* believe you.'

The women had been forgotten; now she turned to them. Perhaps they would tell her the truth. Her heart sank. Jannie sat on the bucket again, mouth open, eyes staring, hands rolling one over the other as she rocked slowly back and forth. Laura hung her head and wept, but Mina looked back at her stony faced. Kay, her face stricken, reached out to her, but then mutely pulled back her hands.

None came to comfort her.

With a roar of grief and anger at their lack of compassion, Catherine screamed at them. 'God blast all of you, you're nothing but evil old witches.' Then she ran, blindly, heart pounding, across the yard and the back green and away up the hill towards the cliff. Billie, afraid of what she might do, followed.

Sobbing, feet slipping, grabbing at the wiry stalks of heather Catherine climbed until at last she reached the fence that stood at the top of the cliff, a flimsy barrier between her and the water hundreds of feet below. She clutched at the fence, at the cruel barbs of the top wire.

Billie, seeing that she had stopped running and was standing still, sank down to watch and wait.

Catherine looked out to where sea met sky and the two blended into one, then brought back her gaze to the foot of the cliff. Looking down she watched as the water churned and ate the rocks, fell back then reached up to swallow them again. The sea was not to be trusted. It was greedy. The wicked sea had stolen Robbie when German bombers and U-boats had failed.

She had to believe it. Billie would never make up a story like that. Robbie was gone from her and she would never see him again. She gripped the wire so tightly that the barbs pressed into her tender flesh, but the pain was as nothing compared to the pain in her heart.

'Noo,' she moaned. 'Noo,' as a flood of tears filled her eyes. She lifted her head and from somewhere deep in her gut, a raw primordial cry arose, a howl, a desperate animal sound, torn from the black abyss of her sorrow, a primitive outpouring of grief, thrown to the four winds, on and on and on.

When it was spent, desolate, her spirit broken, she sank to earth, her face twisted into a grimace as she wept the pain of loss. Little by little her agony subsided; when it had she folded her arms about her and whimpered softly as the tears continued to flow.

Lying on the ground, Billie listened to her voice borne on the air, heard it taken up by the plaintive cry of gulls, the sigh of a breeze through dry stalks. He wanted to comfort her, knew it was not his place to do so, but her pain was his pain, and burying his face in his hands he wept too.

ELEVEN

THE SOUND OF knocking slowly filtered through the haze that filled Catherine's head. She looked at her bedside clock; no, that couldn't be right: ten o'clock, the sun streaming through the window and she lying on the bed, still dressed.

Then she remembered.

There was the knocking again and someone calling her name, it sounded like Billie. She got off the bed. 'I'm coming,' she called.

'Mam sent me over,' said Billie when she opened the door.

'That was kind of her.' Catherine put a hand to her head and realized that her hair was in a tangle. 'Sorry, Billie, I haven't combed it. You'd better come in.'

Billie watched as she stirred the fire. It was out.

'What did your mother think I might need?'

'Someone to talk to … ken … she knows … Jannie would'na … Mam said would you come and stay wi' us for a while. She'll look after you.'

Unbidden, Catherine's eyes filled with tears. 'That's very kind of her, but there will be things to do here and I'd rather be on my own.'

'Are you sure?' said Billie. Catherine nodded. 'I'd best be getting home then, but … you only have to ask. I'd do anything for you, Catherine.'

When Billie had gone away Catherine sat down and ran a hand across her forehead; her head throbbed. She felt empty, devoid of feeling. She was a knitted toy and someone had pulled out the stuffing. But Lumsden had given her some sleeping pills. 'You may feel drowsy next day, but do take them, they will help,' he had said. So she would blame him. He had told her they would manage till she was ready to come back to work, but considering the harshness of island life and the fact that she was now alone, didn't she think it might be better if she went home? No, she had said, this was her home.

She had been through all that yesterday, but, 'accept what you can't change and work at what you can' had been her mother's motto and now it could be hers. She would have to face Jannie's accusations and Mina's acid remarks, but she would not let either of them get to her, would not shed tears in their presence, they could think what they liked, she would grieve in the privacy of her own home, and grieve she would, for even now tears filled her eyes. She dashed them away; she needed to wash and dress, for there would surely be more visitors.

The room was cold for the fire was still unlit. Listless and unmotivated Catherine was sitting by the table when Daa walked in. Grief, cold and stark lay on his face. He gathered her into his arms. She clung to him and drew strength from his quiet comfort.

'Oh, lass, that this should come upon you and you so far from home. Whatever you want, you only have to ask. And never mind the old wives,' he said, 'they'll be along to see you.' He loosed her and looked down at her. 'They'll surely want to tell you what to do.'

He left her then and as he went out Kay came in.

'Has Jannie been along yet?' asked Kay.

'No.'

One quick glance round the room told Kay that Catherine had done nothing. 'Then we'd better light the fire,' she said, 'because she'll be here.'

While Kay busied herself Catherine walked to the window and looked out. 'The dinghy's there, but where's the boat?' she said. 'It should be home.'

'Do you have enough milk?' Kay's voice was sharp.

Turning to look at her, Catherine said, 'Of course I've got enough, Daa gave me some yesterday. But I want to know where the boat is.'

'Jannie'll be along later,' said Kay, 'and Mina and Laura will come with her. They'll expect some tea; that's why I asked if you had enough milk.'

'What are they coming for?'

The fire was burning nicely. Kay set the kettle on the hob. 'Come and sit down,' she said. 'I've brought you some fresh bannocks; help me butter them, they'll want something to go with the tea.'

Catherine sat down and, looking at her hands, began to trace the lines on her palm. Then with finger and thumb she took hold of the gold band she wore and began to turn it round. Round and round it went, round and round; there was no end to it, it went on for ever. Why then didn't loving and being together go on for ever? She and Robbie had had so little time; why had it to end?

'Catherine, my dear,' said Kay, 'I'm going to stay; you'll need me.'

'Why?'

'Because you're going to have more visitors and there are plans to make.'

Catherine showed not the slightest hint of interest or care and Kay worried for her. 'Come on,' she said, 'you have to face up to this. I'm here to help.'

'It's all right, Kay. Lumsden gave me something to help me sleep; now my head feels fuzzy.' Catherine got up and went to the window again. 'But where's the *Deepdale Lass?* I want to see the boat; it ought to be out in the bay.'

'Oh, darling, I expect they took it away in case it upset you. We'll have to ask Daa,' said Kay. 'Don't worry, we'll find out where it is.' Her tone was conciliatory, but knowing that Jannie Jameson would try to impose her will on the girl when it came to funeral arrangements her manner became brisk. 'Now then,' she said, 'Jannie and the others will be here soon.'

'Why? They never visit me.'

'There are arrangements to be made. Can't get away from it, so let's get ready for the advance of the old wives.'

At that Catherine smiled. 'All right then,' she said.

The murmur of voices and the sound of feet on the flagstones outside the door announced the arrival of Jannie and her sisters a short time later.

'Oh, you're already here,' said Jannie when she saw Kay.

'I thought it would not be right to leave Catherine alone,' said Kay. 'Losing someone dear is hard to cope with, as I know only too well.'

'Ay,' said Jannie, 'but we're here now.' Dismissing Kay with a nod she turned her attention to Catherine. 'Now, lass, I'll see to the funeral, you don't need to give that any thought.'

No, thought Catherine, as the fuzz in her head began to clear, you're not going to treat me like a child and push me into the background. 'Would you please sit down, Mrs Jameson,' she said, 'and you Mina … Laura. Will you take tea?' She took the teapot from Kay who had made tea when they heard the women coming in. 'Kay has kindly brought me some bannocks.'

For a moment or two Jannie stood looking at Catherine, then she sat down. Catherine poured tea, asked if they took sugar and how much milk. When they had been served she turned to Jannie.

'It is my husband who is to be buried,' she said in a voice that was now calm and controlled, 'and I think it is my duty to make the arrangements. It's very kind of you to offer to do it for me, Mrs Jameson, but no thank you.'

The passage of teacups from table to mouth stopped abruptly. All eyes were fixed on Catherine, then Mina and Laura's switched to Jannie. Jannie was looking at Catherine in astonishment. She put her teacup down, swallowed, and looked round the table at the others.

'Well … well …' she said, 'I never—'

'Can I say something?' interrupted Kay.

'If you must,' said Jannie.

'I'm sure Catherine wants to do right by Robbie.' Standing by Catherine, Kay put a hand on the girl's shoulder. 'But the rest of us know what happens at a Shetland funeral. She would probably welcome your help, Jannie, when she knows too.'

'What are you talking about?' said Catherine. 'How could it be different?'

'Well, you would not be going to the kirk,' said Mina.

'Not to the church? You must be joking.'

'No, it's no joke, the women all bide at home,' said Laura.

'That can't be true,' said Catherine. 'Surely you're not telling me I can't go to my own husband's funeral?'

'Ay, that's right,' said Jannie, 'it's the men that follow the coffin, we all bide at home to get the food and the drams ready for them when they come back.'

'It's traditional,' said Kay. 'Done that way for as long as I can remember.'

Catherine jumped up and thumped the table with her fists, making teacups rattle and bannocks jump on the plate. 'Ha,' she spat, 'that's one tradition that's about to bite the dust, because I shall be right there behind my Robbie.'

Jannie and the aunts, Mina with a mouthful of bannock, Laura just picking up another, gazed at Catherine in amazement at this outburst.

'How could I not,' cried Catherine, 'I would never have a moment's peace for the rest of my life if I failed to be with him on his last journey.'

Jannie sighed and shrugged her shoulders. 'But … but …' she began.

'Don't you "but but" me, Jannie Jameson,' snapped Catherine. 'Tradition or not my place is with Robbie right to the end.' Defiantly she stood and glared at her mother-in-law. 'You can do what you like; stay at home and make tea if you want, but I … shall be at the church. Just you try and stop me.'

'I don't think anyone would want to do that,' said Kay, 'but perhaps it would be better to get someone to help you with the arrangements.'

'It's the last thing I can do for him, Kay.'

'Yes, I know, but he had a mother too. Could you not consult the undertaker together? Share the burden?'

'I would do that wi' you,' said Jannie.

Catherine sat down; her shoulders sagged as she slumped in the chair. She had made her point and now Jannie was softening and offering to help. This was too much. Putting her elbows on the table she rested her head in her hands and thought about what Kay had said. Perhaps she was right. It was not for her to deny Jannie the chance to help with the arrangements for Robbie's funeral. She sighed, looked at Jannie and said, 'All right then.'

As they went home, Mina, walking beside Jannie, said, 'Well, you have a viper in the nest. What else is she going to change?'

'I'm thinkin' that she'll not change anything, for she'll go home to her mam,' said Jannie. 'There's nothing to keep her here now.'

'That would suit you, would it not? But you cannot be sure; there's no tellin' what yon wife will do, so I wouldn't count on it.'

'Then you don't know me,' said Jannie. 'I don't want to see her here.'

Jannie's wrong, thought Laura, Catherine isn't going to be bullied, for that's what Jannie is, a bully; but now, someone is going to stand up to her. A little smile crept across Laura's face. What will Jannie make of that?

TWELVE

IN THE CHAPEL the pews were filled with men, not one jot of colour amongst them, hats, coats and ties were all in unrelieved black; only a brief glimpse of shirt front now and then revealed a dash of some pale colour. They looked at her, some with quick glances, some stared and all were obviously thinking she shouldn't be there. John Jameson held fast to Catherine's little black-gloved hand.

Thankful that the minister was not the fanatical little man who had preached at the meeting-house, she watched and listened to this one, stood automatically when hymns were announced; let the deep, resonant sound of men's voices wash over her. And all the time there was the coffin in front of her, containing Robbie, her friend … her lover … her husband. The sweet perfume of the simple bouquet that rested on it, the freesias and carnations that had been her choice, scented the air. Grateful for the occasional squeeze of Daa's hand, which told her he was hurting as much as she was, and mindful of the closeness of tears, she retreated into herself, put on a fragile armour in order to be strong for the man at her side.

Then they were leaving, going out, following Robbie as he was being carried to his last resting place and the swarm of black crows were behind them. The mourners came forward, one by one, to throw the symbolic handful of dirt. They had looked at her then with eyes that were sad and mirrored her own.

Then it was over and they were back at Jannie's house. It was filled with mourners, the minister, the doctor and the black-clad men who tossed back the whisky, drank tea and ate the food that had been prepared. They came to shake her hand, murmur a few words of condolence, then drifted away.

When those they had served were gone she sat at the table with Jannie and Daa, Mina, Laura and Kay, taking their own refreshment. Conversation was desultory, faltered and little by little failed and came to a stop. An air of quiet descended.

Catherine looked round at Robbie's family and wondered if she would ever be recognized as part of it. She had lost the key to open the door; now it was closed and she realised life could never be the same. She stood. 'Thank you, Mrs Jameson, and thank you Mina, Laura and you too Kay, for all you've done,' she said, 'and especially you, Daa, for being at my side. It's time for me to go home.'

There were murmurings from the aunts and Jannie as Catherine pushed her chair under the table and prepared to leave.

'I'll come with you,' said Kay. 'It's time I was off too.'

They walked together till they came to Catherine's house. Kay took the girl in her arms and held her. 'I'm here for you any time of day or night,' she said.

Catherine went in and shut the door; it was her house now, not hers and Robbie's, but hers. Her breakfast cup and saucer were still on the table and there too, on the sideboard, was the cake that she would never eat because she had made it for Robbie. The house was quiet; standing still and waiting for her. There was no one to welcome her, no one to kiss her. The brave face she had managed to maintain throughout the day suddenly crumpled. Stumbling through a mist of tears she ran to the bedroom and threw herself on the bed, the wonderful proper bed she and Robbie had shared for one deliriously happy night. Then she wept, beat the pillow, cried, sobbed and moaned till she was completely drained. Exhausted, she lay there clutching the sodden rag that was her handkerchief till at last sleep stole silently in to gather her in his embrace and carry her away.

She woke to the sound of a gull on the roof, looked to the window; it was still light, still day. She pulled herself up, slid off the bed, stood and stretched, then went to look in the mirror on the wall above the chest of drawers. The face that looked back at her was blotched and red, eyes swollen, hair tousled.

'Oh my God,' she whispered, 'you look awful. You need a bath.'

In her kitchen she raked out dead ashes, rebuilt the fire, then put her kettle and all her saucepans, filled to the brim with water from the rain butt, on to the stove to heat. She fetched the wash tub and put it on the mat in front of the fire.

Sitting down to wait for the water to boil she began to think about what she was going to do with her life. Robbie had told her his plans and she had promised to help him. He wasn't here now. Could she do it for him?

When the rattle of a saucepan lid caught her attention she got up and went to the stove. The smallest pan was boiling so she set it back and pulled a bigger one forward. It would be a while yet before the water was hot enough for her bath. She pushed more peat in the stove, then sat down again.

On the table in front of her lay her work basket. It had been given to her by her mother. 'You'll need this,' she had said. 'Men always need a button sewn on or a tear mended.' Catherine began to examine the contents; amongst the needles and cotton, elastic and sock-mending wool was a pair of scissors. She picked them up; they had been her grandmother's. Holding them with finger and thumb she opened and closed the blades, heard the sound that mirrored the word. Scissors, scissors. They were sharp. Would they cut hair as well as cloth?

In the bedroom she looked in the mirror, pulled a lock of hair forward, positioned the scissors either side of it … then cut … crunch … the blades came together and chopped it off. Holding the severed curl she looked at it, then put it down. Methodically and deliberately she cut and cut again until her long dark mane had been reduced to a crop of curls. She smiled at her reflection. 'New me,' she said. 'Catherine Jameson, new model ready to face the world.'

Pan lids rattled with escaping steam when she returned to the kitchen. She poured hot and cold water into the tub and when the temperature was right stepped out of her clothes and into it. With her knees almost under her chin she soaped her flannel and began to wash.

THIRTEEN

A BROWN-PAPER parcel tied with string was strapped to the carrier on the back of Catherine's bike and on each handle bar hung a shopping bag. Though not as rough as the track down into Deepdale the road from the town was by no means smooth. It had been tarred in places, but the stretches in between were potholed and the bags on the handlebars made steering difficult. Not only did she have to concentrate on steering, but be prepared to brake hard at a moment's notice. Why was it the silly sheep always seemed to wait until the last moment to dash across the road in front of her? She shouted at them and rang her bicycle bell but it made no difference. They seemed hell bent on suicide.

Suicidal sheep and potholes apart, the road down into the valley was the most hazardous part of her journey. Its steep descent combined with loose stones required more courage to ride down it than she possessed so she got off to walk.

Knitting in her hands, Jannie stepped out of her house as Catherine drew level. 'You've never been to work,' she began, then gasped. 'What have you done to your hair?'

'It was too long so I cut it,' said Catherine.

Jannie eyed the shopping bags and parcel. 'You've been shopping.'

'That's right.' Not willing to divulge what she had shopped for Catherine walked on. She knew that Jannie, still knitting, would be watching her and wondering what she had bought.

'Daa,' said Catherine, 'you said I had to ask if I wanted anything. Well .. . will you teach me how to be a crofter?'

Daa was unharnessing the pony. He laid his hands on its back, looked at and studied her. 'Do you know what you're asking?' he said.

'No, but I want you to teach me.'

'Why.'

'Robbie told me his plans and I promised to help, but I don't know how.'

Daa turned his head away; softly he said, 'But Robbie's not here.'

'I know,' said Catherine, 'but I promised and I'd like the chance to make his dreams come true … or at least try.'

Daa took his pipe from his pocket and some tobacco from a screw of paper and began to fill the bowl. Catherine watched as he struck a match, put it to the pipe and drew on it. He would be thinking and wouldn't answer till the pipe was well and truly alight. With it clamped between his teeth Daa went on taking the harness off the pony. Catherine waited.

'Crofting's a hard life with very little return,' Daa said at last, 'and you're a nurse and that's an important—'

'No,' protested Catherine, 'I've made up my mind; please don't tell me I ought to go home and take up nursing again because—'

'Lass,' Daa butted in, 'I'm not going to tell you what to do, but croftin's …' he shook his head. 'You would have to be out in all weathers and you should know what you would be takin' on.'

'But other women do this, Daa. Surely I could too?'

'Shetland bairns start to learn as soon as they can walk, if not before.'

Catherine stepped forward, put her hands on the pony's flank, then looked up into Daa's face. 'I've made up my mind,' she said. 'Somehow or other it's what I'm going to do. Robbie said I could get books from the library and he would teach me.' She paused, pleaded, 'Could you not teach me, Daa … please?'

Daa took his pipe from his mouth and looked at her.

For what seemed an age he said nothing. Returning his gaze Catherine willed him to agree to her request. Then to her relief a slow grin spread across his face. 'You're a brave girl,' he said, 'and a very stubborn one. Go home, I'll come along to see you and we'll work something out.' Clamping his teeth on the stem of his pipe he chuckled and led the pony into the barn.

It was a pleasant day; cool with some wind, just the sort of day to be out of doors. Catherine was going to the moor to work at her peat bank. When she came out of her house the aunts were feeding their chickens. Kay had joined them and Jannie was there too, knitting as always. As Catherine approached them Jannie was first to speak.

'Get back in your house and dress decent, you cannot be seen like that.'

Laura giggled; Mina silenced her with a stern look then turned to Catherine. 'Have you no shame?' she said. 'You a widow and dressed like that?'

'What's wrong with what I've got on?' asked Catherine, spreading her arms wide as if to show herself off. She was wearing a jumper over a cotton shirt, a pair of trousers and boy's boots. Her boyish look was accentuated by her short-cropped hair. 'I'm going up the hill to work with the peat,' she said. 'You've got to agree that trousers are much more sensible than a skirt.'

'But you're a woman,' snapped Jannie.

'So what?'

'Who cut your hair?' asked Kay.

'I did.'

'Mm. You'd better let me tidy it up. It could do with a little help.'

Jannie's expression was dark and disapproving, Mina's too, but Laura, who stood behind Mina, had a smile on her face.

Catherine smiled at them all. 'Well, from now on when I'm working outside this is what I shall be wearing,' she said, 'so you'd better get used to it.'

As she walked away she chuckled, knowing that Jannie and Mina, but not Kay or Laura, would be tut-tutting and muttering their disapproval. Didn't they know the war had changed the role of women? Or had these women been so isolated in their little valley that life had virtually passed them by?

There was no one else on the moor when she got there. The sea was visible to east and west. Some distance out from the shore a fishing boat rose and fell on the heave of the water, up it went to ride the wave then down to disappear in a trough. Sometimes the wheelhouse remained visible; sometimes it was out of sight, but however deep it went the little boat always rose up again.

Wind and weather had combined to start the drying process of the peat laid out on the turf above the bank that Robbie had cut; such a long bank, such a lot of peat. It was going to take some time to get it all raised up. And that was only the beginning; later on she would have to get it home and then it would have to be stacked again.

She had brought a bottle of water and some sandwiches with her. She took off her jumper and put it down with the bag. She had to build pyramids, but how? Copying someone else's she set to work. She had been busy for some time when she heard her name being called; she looked up and saw Billie.

'Hello, Catherine,' he said. 'Ah my, what have you done to your hair?'

'It was always getting in my mouth and eyes so I cut it and now it doesn't.'

'Looks all right. How are you getting on wi' the peat.'

'It's a back-breaking job, isn't it?'

Billie laughed. 'Ay, but if you don't count the work, it's free.'

'I guess you're right,' said Catherine. She folded her jumper, laid it on the bag, then sat on it. 'It's time for lunch. Would you like a sandwich?'

'I'm had me dinner. I see you're wearin' breeks and boots. Bet Jannie doesn't like that.'

'No, she doesn't and neither will she like me being a crofter.'

Billie's mouth opened and shut several times before he could say, 'Crofter?

'Yes. Daa is going to teach me how to run Robbie's croft.'

'Are you out of your mind?' said Billie, hesitating before going on, 'You're a woman and,' he looked at her and paused before saying, 'you're English.'

'What's that got to do with the price of fish?'

Billie looked uncomfortable. 'There's some that don't like the English.'

'Oh. Do you think that's why Jannie doesn't like me?' asked Catherine.

'I don't know, it might be. She didn't know you were comin'. She was mad at Robbie for not telling her.'

'But he wrote her a letter. I know because I posted it myself.'

'Ay, well, sometimes things go astray.' It wasn't only the letter that had gone astray, thought Catherine. 'What's it like south?' asked Billie. 'The men from the fishin' tell stories of it, but … I'd like to go some day.'

'Why would you want to do that? Aren't you happy here?'

'Just want to see it for myself.'

'I don't think you would like it.'

'But it's …' he looked disappointed.

'Where it all happens?' said Catherine.

'Yea, that's what the men say.'

'You don't want to take too much notice of them,' said Catherine. 'Fishermen are notorious for telling tales. You don't want to go, you really don't.'

'Well … well … I just would.' Billie scrambled to his feet. 'I'd better get on wi' our peat.' He stood and looked down at her. 'You'll not say anything to Mam, will you? She'd not be pleased.'

'No, of course I won't.'

Billie loped off. Catherine watched him go. Was he lonely, living on that isolated croft with only his mother and father for company? Was that why he wanted to get away? Who could blame him? Their lives probably followed the same routine as the folk in Deepdale, planting and growing crops, working with animals, and trying to wrest a living from a land reluctant to give.

FOURTEEN

A SUDDEN SCUD of rain beating on the window woke Catherine. She opened her eyes, stretched, yawned then looked at the clock by her bedside. Eight o'clock; she'd overslept. She swung her legs out of bed and stood up. Suddenly a desire to be sick made her cover her mouth with her hand. She sat down heavily, but when it happened again she slid off and reached for the chamber pot beneath it. Down on her knees, hands flat on the floor she vomited, retched again and again until she spewed nothing but clear liquid and her stomach was sore. When there was no more she sat back on her heels and reached under her pillow for a handkerchief to wipe her mouth and mop the sweat from her brow.

And then the tears came but, like the rain in a summer storm, hard but fleeting, the storm of her weeping was soon over. 'Oh, Robbie,' she cried, 'I'm pregnant. I should have known.' She had missed a couple of periods, but the shock of losing him could have done that.

She looked at the clock again. She was going to be late for work, but no, surgery was held in a cottage at Norravoe today; there was no need to rush, no need to think of excuses, it was her day off.

She sat on the bed and placed her hands on her stomach, the flat stomach destined to swell with new life. Where and when had the seed been planted? She had hated the box-bed and hadn't wanted to make love in it, so she and Robbie had lain in the soft hay in the barn. They had laughed, felt like naughty children, and, freed from the knowledge that ears might be listening, their lovemaking had been passionate and wild. It must have been there that she had conceived, for sometimes, with no condom in Robbie's pocket they had taken a chance. A smile spread across her face. 'Whatever you are,' she said, 'boy or girl, you were conceived with love and I shall see that you are surrounded with it all your life.'

In the kitchen she poured water in a bowl and splashed it on her face, the coldness of it refreshed her. She filled the kettle and put it on the stove. The wind that rarely ceased sucked at the chimney and pulled the fire to life, the stove glowed and the kettle sang. Catherine made tea and ate a plain biscuit, looked out of the window and saw that the rain had cleared. She would go up to the moor and get some peat.

She picked up a couple of shopping bags then, from the shed at the back of her house, fetched some hessian sacks, rolled them up and tucked them under her arm.

'Hello, Catherine,' said Kay, 'where are you off to?'

'I thought I'd bring home some peat.'

'With shopping bags?'

'Yes, I haven't got anything else.'

'Daa will bring it home in the cart, surely Robbie told you that?'

'Well, yes … that's what I thought, which is why I've got these sacks. I'll fill them anyway, but Jannie told me I had to fetch it myself.'

Kay gave an exasperated sigh. 'Oh, that woman.'

'Well, it's a nice day,' said Catherine, 'and I like it on the hill. It's very peaceful and she can't get at me there.'

'I'll walk up to the road with you then,' said Kay. 'I want to catch the bus.'

The steepness of the incline out of the valley effectively limited conversation and it wasn't until they reached the top that either of them had sufficient breath to speak more than a few words.

'You're looking peaky this morning,' said Kay. 'Are you all right?'

'Yes, I'm fine. I had a restless night, that's all.' That's the first of the lies, thought Catherine, but Kay was no fool; she had probably put two and two together and got the right answer. 'I can see the bus coming. If you see any ten-bob notes going for a shilling today you can bring me back a few.'

Kay laughed. 'Not before I've filled my own pockets.'

Beneath Catherine's feet as she walked, the little yellow flowers of tormentil and the violet faces of butterwort looked up at her. Skylarks rose up, their song growing fainter as they winged their way up. Curlew and whimbrel warbled, but the busy oyster-catchers, running about in red stockings did nothing but utter shrill and continuous kleep-kleeps.

When she reached her peat bank, Catherine saw others working. Some raised their hands in greeting, but none came to speak except Billie. He had lost much of his shyness and came leaping from bank to bank, laughing all the while.

'Good to see you, Catherine,' he said.

'And you, Billie. How are you?'

'I'm braaly weel.'

Although Billy spoke with a marked accent, as did most other people, sometimes he used an expression or word she hadn't heard before. 'And what does that mean?' she asked.

'It means, I'm very well.'

'You're going to have to speak, "proper," as you say, if you ever go off the island,' said Catherine.

'Ah, well, I'm been thinkin' about that.' Billie grinned and slowly, with an exaggerated pronunciation said, 'What are you going to do about your sheep?'

'You're a tease.' Catherine made a fist and punched him lightly. 'I've been thinking and the best I can do for now is to read up as much as I can first.'

Billie kicked a clod of peat. 'You'll just be wasting time,' he said.

'No I won't. If you want to help we can go to the shows and the market together and you can help me study in the winter.'

'It'll not be enough, but,' Billie's expression lifted, 'if we do that then you can teach me to speak proper.'

'I can but try. Now go, I've got work to do.'

With the midday sun the day had turned quite warm. When Catherine decided she'd worked long enough, not being in a hurry to go home she sat down to watch a skylark rising and falling, a lone gull hanging in the air and a tuft of white cloud drifting across the sky. She was tired and, putting her hands behind her head, she lay back. There was a charm of larks now and the gull had been joined by another. She watched as the pair drifted slowly on the thermals rising from the land. It was a lazy day, a do-nothing day, and it was all hers. Head cushioned on her hands she relaxed, closed her eyes and listened to the breeze, the little breeze that crept through the heather to whisper in her ear of faraway places, to sing softly and lull her to sleep and to dream.

'Are you all right, lass?' A tall man bent over Catherine. 'Are you all right?' he said, raising his voice.

Waking with a start Catherine took one look at the bearded giant of a man looming over her and screamed.

'OK, OK,' said the man. 'You're not dead then.'

'Dead? Of course I'm not dead,' said Catherine. 'Who are you?'

'I'm Norrie.'

Catherine stood and looked at him while a pair of brown eyes studied her.

Norrie Williams was tall and well built, and the expression on what she could see of his face, behind the beard, was kindly.

Norrie smiled. 'Everybody's gone home,' he said. 'I wasn't going to leave you here in case you weren't well, but you're all right so I'll go.'

'Thank you for being concerned,' said Catherine. 'That was kind of you.'

'Ay,' said Norrie, making no attempt to move. 'You're … ah … Robbie Jameson's …ah …' He faltered and came to a stop.

'Widow,' said Catherine. 'I thought you were leaving.'

'Ay,' Norrie smiled again, his teeth bright against his beard. 'Take care when you're on the hill, lass, don't go alone.'

'If you say so,' said Catherine and watched as he strode away with never a backward glance. She picked up her bags of peat and started for home.

Widow, she had said. What a dreadful word that was. Although she had heard Mina say it she had never thought of herself as such and the thought was foreign to her. How could she be a widow? Widows were old and wrinkled and grey and had lived a lifetime. She was not like that … but a widow she was, nonetheless.

The bags of peat were heavy and made her arms ache; she stopped frequently to put them down and was only too glad when at last she was going down into the valley. Jannie saw her coming and came out of her house, a sock hanging from the needles that flew back and forth in her hands. 'What are you carrying bags of peat for?' she asked.

'Because I wasn't coming home empty-handed,' said Catherine.

'You need a kishie.'

'And what's that when it's at home?'

Jannie pushed the sock into the pocket of her apron. 'Come wi' me,' she said. Catherine put down her bags and followed Jannie to the byre. Hanging on a beam were some straw baskets. Jannie took one down. 'You put the strap across the front of your shoulders and the kishie sits on your back. You have to fetch your own peat home,' said Jannie. 'You should get one of these.'

'But I thought …' Kay had told her Daa would bring it home, but still Jannie was insisting she had to fetch her own peat.

'Likely you would have to get one made,' Jannie went on, 'but you'll not be lucky. Kishies is made in winter.'

'Then why even suggest it,' said Catherine. 'Why not show a little kindness and offer to lend me one of yours? Or is there to be no end to the way you try to put me down? You won't win, Jannie, you won't win.'

FIFTEEN

CATHERINE AND DAA climbed the hill behind the Deepdale houses, at the top they turned and looked back. The valley was laid out below them. Smoke spiralled up from chimneys and Catherine could smell the now familiar aroma of burning peat.

'Now,' said Daa, 'you see the land is marked out in strips, they're called rigs and they belong to the houses. You have one.'

'How will I know which is mine?'

'It's not fenced because we let the sheep come down off the hill in winter for the better grazing. You can't grow flowers, they'll eat them.'

The land had lost its rough uncared-for look. Daa had ploughed and with Jannie and the aunts' help had sown potatoes. Catherine had joined the others to hoe between the rows of growing crops. Oats were springing up, adding their own sweet green. Catherine knew now that she would have a share of all the crops. How closely knit these families were, how dependent on each other.

It was Sunday morning and there was rain in the offing. As they walked Daa pointed out various landmarks: a huge lump of white quartz was called the Nort Stane, a hill loch beyond it, Eela Water. They crossed the main road. A rough wooden gate was set in a low wall on top of which was a fence.

'That's the hill dyke, not all the same, bit dyke bit fence.' Daa opened the gate; they walked through and climbed again. 'The sheep go on the hill when we plant the rigs,' said Daa.

Catherine had seen the wiry little hill sheep, first when she and Robbie had walked across the moor to visit Rose and again when she had been working with the peat. Some of them must belong to her, but which ones?

'All sheep look alike to me,' she said. 'How do you tell them apart?'

'They're marked. You'll find yours when they come down to be clipped.'

They were on the moor now and Catherine said, 'I love it up here. Just look at the view. I've never seen anything like it; the sea is endless and always changing and when the sun shines the hills come alive. Can we go higher up?'

Together they plodded on and the rough grass and heather of the moor gave way to bare peaty earth, stony ground and boulders. At last Catherine said, 'That's far enough,' and sat down on a lump of rock. Daa pointed out more landmarks and told her the names of different areas. 'You have to know,' he said.

'What's that house there?' Catherine asked as she pointed at a building on the far side of the peat banks. 'It's a long way from anyone else.'

'Ah,' said Daa, 'when folk were quarrelsome they were hounded out and had to build where they could. It's not been lived in for a long time.'

'I've noticed a lot of ruined houses. What happened to those people?'

'There were the clearances, you'll know about that, and some folk emigrated after the potato famine. That happened here as well as in Ireland, and then TB carried off a lot.'

'Tell me more.'

'Ask Kay, she knows all about it.'

'So it's always been a hard life then?'

'That would be right.'

'Let's go home,' said Catherine.

'Why are your bags of peat still outside your door?' asked Kay.

'I got fed up with the sight of them. Jannie said I ought to have a kishie. She showed me hers, but said they're only made in winter so I'd be out of luck.'

'Uh, that woman,' grunted Kay. 'What will she do next?'

'You're not surprised are you?' said Catherine, as she made a pot of tea. 'Would you pass me those cups, please? She wants to make me go home, doesn't she? I believe she'd do anything to get me off the island.'

'Would you like to go home?'

For a moment Catherine did not reply. Then she smiled. 'Yes, I would, but only for a holiday and that won't happen for a long time. I have plans.'

'Sounds interesting. What are you up to?'

'I've been out with Daa; he took me round the croft and showed me what was mine. Have a bannock. He's going to teach me how to be a crofter.'

Kay laughed. 'A crofter?'

'Yes. I want to carry out Robbie's plans, if I can. I don't know anything about sheep but Daa's going to teach me and I'm going to bone up on—'

'Catherine …'

The cup in Catherine's hand stopped halfway to her mouth. 'What?'

'In your condition do you think that's wise?'

The cup was placed back on its saucer. 'You know? It doesn't show and I only knew myself a few days ago.' She had been right. Kay had definitely put two and two together and got the right answer. 'How do you know?' she asked.

'Put it down to a lifetime of experience,' said Kay. 'Shetland folk aren't slow when it comes to reproducing, but won't it upset your plans?'

Catherine's answer, 'No, why should it?' was said with conviction. 'Women have always worked while they were pregnant. Why shouldn't I?'

'No reason I suppose. Have you talked to the doctor yet?'

'No.'

'Then I suggest you do. Best to be on the safe side, eh?'

'You won't say anything to Jannie, will you? She'd only use it as another lever to make me go home. But I'm home now.' Catherine fought back tears; they were not for now, but to be kept for the dark and lonely hours of the night.

'It will be our secret,' said Kay. 'I won't breathe a word.'

Cleaning Doctor Lumsden's surgery and waiting room did not take a lot of time, but Catherine enjoyed working there. She was not earning a lot but, added to the small widow's pension she was getting, it would do. She had managed to put a little of her nurse's pay in the bank and had added to it money that had been given to her in lieu of wedding presents. There was also the money she and Robbie had put aside for improvements to the house. It all totted up to a tidy sum and would be enough to cushion her when she had to stop work.

It was Monday morning, and mindful of the conversation she had with Kay she decided she really should see Lumsden and tell him she was pregnant. She didn't see him often, but next morning his car was still outside the house. She met him as she went in. 'I want to see you,' she said.

'And I'd like a word with you,' he replied. 'Come with me.'

Catherine followed him into his consulting room. 'What have I done wrong?' she asked, 'Is there something I've forgotten?'

Neil Lumsden laughed. 'No, I'm very satisfied with what you do. No, my dear, I'm really sorry you lost your husband, but I wondered if now might be the time to think about training to become the health visitor.'

Catherine bent her head and looked down as she clasped her hands and laced her fingers. Health visitor: couldn't be better, but not now, oh no, not now. 'Is anything wrong?' asked Lumsden when she didn't answer him.

She looked up. 'I'd love to be your health visitor, but it'll have to wait … I believe I'm pregnant.'

'So that's why you wanted to see me?'

'Yes, I'm afraid so.'

'Right, let's have a look at you then.'

When the consultation was over Lumsden said, yes, Catherine was pregnant and he could give her a date, but babies come into the world when they're ready. 'Just don't let him decide to arrive in the middle of a snow storm,' he said, beaming at her, 'or I may not get to you. Perhaps we should book you into the hospital.'

'I'd rather have it at home.'

'Mm, well, there's time yet. We'll see how you go on. Are you happy?

'Um … Daa was going to teach me how to look after my sheep.'

Lumsden shook his head. 'That's a no, no. Pregnant women and sheep are a bad mix; you should have known that.'

'Yes, I did, but I didn't want to think about it. I'm disappointed, but …'

'No buts. Go home and start knitting bootees and bonnets.'

'I can't knit.'

Lumsden had the grace to laugh. 'Now you really are in trouble,' he said.

SIXTEEN

'YOU'LL NEED A dog to work your sheep,' said Daa. A collie pup was tucked under his arm. He held it out to Catherine. 'I'm gotten you this pup.'

'Oh, it's lovely.' She smoothed the puppy's soft coat. It looked up at her and reached out to lick her. 'Hallo,' she said, then sighed, 'but I've news for you. I'm going to have a child and that means I'm forbidden to work with sheep.'

'You're going to have a bairn?' A broad grin stretched across Daa's face. 'Ah, that's good. The sheep will still be there after you've had it.'

Anxiously Catherine said, 'You'll not tell anyone, will you? I don't want anyone else to know yet, but I do want to learn about the croft.'

'But if du can't work wi' the sheep … are you sure?'

'I'm really quite sure. There must be other things you can tell me.'

'Train your dog to be obedient, then, and keep it always by you. You have to get to know one another. A good dog has to obey orders and to know what you're thinking. If it's a good one it'll likely teach you.'

Catherine smiled at that. 'Don't worry, Daa, I'll look after it.'

'It's come from good stock, enjoy it, I'll show you how to train it later on.'

Far from being a month of sweltering days and hot nights August spread mist and fog over the islands and Catherine spent many hours poring over books she had borrowed from the library. Into a notebook she copied drawings and information she considered vital. Words like scab and scald confused her, then there was something Daa called 'the skitters'.

When the door opened one evening to admit Billie she said, 'You're the very one I want to see. Here, look at this and tell me what it means?' She pushed a book across the table to him, her finger on a word on the open page.

Billie didn't reply and she looked up at him. He wasn't looking at the book but at her. 'Are you all right?' he asked.

'Yes, of course I am, why do you ask?' Surely word hadn't got out?

'You're not working with the sheep.'

'How do you know that?'

'Everybody knows what you're doin'.'

'Do they? What a nosy lot people are? Never mind, Daa said there's not much for me to do out there at the moment so I thought it best to study my books. I'm finding there's an awful lot to learn and it seems like a lot can go wrong. You'd sort of think as long as you fed them sheep could just get on with it.'

It was enough to satisfy Billie so, while Catherine read aloud, they tried to decipher what it all meant.

'There's no' much as goes wrong wi' hill sheep,' said Billie.

'Maybe that's because you're not there to see. Do you know how many lambs you get and how many you lose and how many of the old ones die?'

'No. But you can't be on the hill all the time.'

'Wouldn't it be better if they were closer to home?'

'Likely it would.' Billie thought about that for a moment. 'But it would make an awful lot of work and where would we put them?'

'There must be a way, surely?'

'Na, we have to keep them off the crops. That's why they go to the hill.'

They read and discussed and compared notes and later decided they were wiser than when they'd started. Billie said he'd have to go, but lingered. 'Are you happy, Catherine?' he asked. 'Is it not lonely for you?'

'I've got my work and I keep busy, but I do feel lonely at times,' she said.

'I ken Jannie's not good to you.'

'You could say that.'

Catherine picked up the books they'd been studying and stifled a yawn. It was getting late, but still Billie lingered and made no move to leave.

'I'm thinkin' you don't go very far, just to work and like,' he said.

'That's about it, Billie.'

'Do you not miss your family?'

'Yes, sometimes.' Where was all this leading?

'I ken Jannie thinks you should go home. Would you not like to?'

'Sometimes, but this is my home now.' Billie had wriggled his chair round sideways. He looked as though he wanted to leave but still had something on his mind. 'Is anything bothering you?' asked Catherine.

Billie stood up. 'I ken summer is awful busy, but there'll be dances and things in the winter.' While one hand fiddled with the hem of his jacket he crept imperceptibly towards the door. 'I could take you if you'd come with me.'

He was asking her out. Now she saw what she had failed to see before. Billie at sixteen was filling out and growing into manhood. Soft down covered his chin and top lip. His face flushed pink, he was blushing. She looked away.

'That's very kind of you, thank you for asking me. I'd like that,' she said.

'Ay,' said Billie and bolted out of the door.

'She doesn't do much,' said Mina. 'You would think she would have another job by now.' The three sisters sat in Mina's house, each busy with their knitting. 'She should take up the knitting.'

'She'll not do that,' said Jannie. 'She would likely think it was beneath her.'

'And does she think she's better than us?' asked Mina.

'Robbie told me her folk live in a grand house wi' electric and all. You only have to turn on a tap and you have hot water. That's why she was greetin' when she saw our one.'

'A grand house, you say?'

'Ay, bath and lavatory wi' runnin' water all indoors and carpets on the floor and no shortage of food. Her daa has a grocer's shop.'

'Then why does she stay? Why doesn't she go home to her mam?'

'Likely she's doin' it to spite me,' said Jannie.

'No, no.' Laura looked up from her work. 'She's not like that. She's a bonnie lass and she wouldn't do that.'

'And what would you know?' snapped Mina.

'I like her.'

'Oh, you like her. Is it not time you got us some tea,' said Mina.

'Yea, yea,' said Laura and rose from her chair to do as she was bid.

Mina leaned towards Jannie and said, 'Laura would take her knitting and be in there wi' her, Jannie, if I didna keep her at her work.'

It had been a night of heavy rain and it still fell when morning broke. Small burns that during summer chuckled happily as they tumbled down hillsides had become raging brown torrents. Racing over rocky beds they gouged the gullies they ran through ever deeper. Water poured off the hills into the valleys and filled to overflowing the placid streams that ran through the meadows.

Catherine had cycled to work and pushed her bicycle down into Deepdale. The rain had cut channels in the soft surface of the road, formed miniature streams down which water gurgled. There was no sign of life round the houses; no faces looked out to watch for her and apart from one bedraggled bird the hens had hidden themselves away.

Happy at last to be home Catherine stoked her fire and, because the day was so drear and dark, lit her lamp. She let down the ceiling airer, spread her wet things on it, then pulling on the rope hauled it back up. What a boon it was, her 'pulley' as Robbie had called it; her clothes would be dry in no time.

Taking pen and paper from a drawer she sat down to write a letter.

Dear Mum, she began, *it 's one of those wet, wet days today when it stays dark all day and I have to keep the lamp burning, you wouldn't believe .. .*

'I hope you're not too busy, Catherine,' said Kay as she opened the door and came in. She folded her umbrella and stood it in the corner. 'What a day!'

'Not good, is it?' said Catherine.

'I hope you won't think I'm interfering,' said Kay. 'When you've got your coat on it's OK, but ...' she pursed her lips together and nodded her head.

'You mean it's beginning to show.'

'Yes. I might be able to scrounge a couple of baggy jumpers from my nephew; they'd keep you going for a while and as the weather is beginning to get chilly, you'd need them. That is of course ...'

'If I wouldn't mind something second hand. Thanks, Kay, I don't mind.' Abandoning her letter writing Catherine asked if Kay would stay for a cup of tea.

'No, thanks, I won't stop now. If Norman comes over I'll ask him. I take it Jannie doesn't know yet?

Catherine laughed. 'Don't you think she would have been hammering on my door and telling me to go if she did?'

'Have you got any clothes for the baby yet?'

'I bought these.' Catherine took a small tissue-wrapped parcel from her work box. 'I couldn't resist them,' she said as she unwrapped a pair of tiny bootees, 'and my mum has promised to knit something for me.'

'I could knit for you,' said Kay. 'I've got plenty of time on my hands, but we'll talk about it again. I've got a pot of soup on. I'd better look after it.'

When Kay had gone Catherine went back to her letter.

...how much it rains here. And then there's the wind. It comes from every quarter and there's hardly ever a day without it. But when it does stop it's pure heaven, they call it 'a day between weathers' and it's beau ...

A frantic knocking on her door startled her. It flew open and Jannie, a shawl dripping water wrapped round her head, stood there.

'You have to come – Daa's fallen and I can't get him up,' she cried. Without waiting for Catherine she turned and was gone. Cramming a woolly hat on her head and snatching a coat from a peg behind the door Catherine followed her. Lying on the stone flags outside the Jameson house Daa lay groaning.

When Catherine asked him what had happened he told her he had slipped. Moss had crept between and over the paving stones, safe to walk on while dry, wet it was slippery. But it could not have been that; much more likely he had caught the toe of his boot on an uneven flag-stone. 'Do you think you might have broken anything?' she asked shaking her head to get the rain out of her eyes.

'Get him up, get him up,' cried Jannie, 'if he lies he'll get pneumonia.'

Ignoring her, Catherine said, 'I'll check you over, Daa, just in case.' None of his limbs was lying at a wrong angle, but all the same she ran her hands over them. All seemed to be well.

'Get him up,' shouted Jannie.

'Be patient,' said Catherine. She continued to check that Daa had no broken bones, 'No, it seems you're all right,' she said, and to Jannie, 'Take him under his arms the same way as I do and we'll sit him up.' When he was in a sitting position, 'Get your arm round my shoulder now, Daa,' she said, 'and the other round ...' She hesitated to say Jannie, but Jannie butted in with, 'Round mine.' John Jameson was not a partic-ularly heavy man and they soon got him to his feet, but when he tried to walk he gave an exclamation of pain.

'Is it your ankle?' asked Catherine when he held one foot off the ground. He nodded. 'I'm sure it's not broken, but hang on and hop till we get you indoors.'

Daa hopped and hobbled into the house where they settled him into his chair. Catherine unlaced his boot, pulled out the lace, then spread the leather as wide as she could and gingerly eased the boot off. 'Can you wiggle your toes, Daa?' she said.

The ankle was swelling rapidly, but John Jameson gritted his teeth and slowly moved his toes. Catherine smiled and looked up into his face, 'That's not broken,' she said. 'It's only a sprain.' She looked at Jannie, 'Bathe it with cold water, keep a cold compress on it then bind it up and don't let him walk for a day or two. And get him out of those wet clothes ... yourself too.'

'He cannot sit there all day,' whined Jannie. 'Who's going to milk the cow?'

'The cow will be milked,' said Daa and by the way he said it Catherine knew that he would do it.

'I've never seen such rain,' said Catherine, 'I'm wet too, so I'll have to go.' She was talking to herself for Daa was struggling out of his coat and Jannie had disappeared elsewhere. Oh, well, thanks for nothing, she thought and let herself out. It was still raining; driven by the wind it beat into her; she bent her head and leaning into it went home.

SEVENTEEN

NOT MANY LETTERS came Catherine's way. Her mother wrote from time to time, but Catherine knew what the gist of her letter would be before she opened it. When the postman opened her door it wasn't a letter he brought but a parcel. 'I see your mother's lookin' out for you,' he said. 'I ken the postmark.'

'I guess I know what's in it so I'll save it for later.' Catherine tossed the parcel on the table as though she didn't care. She wouldn't open it while he was there; she knew he would look and then drop in on Jannie to tell.

The parcel held baby clothes, a teething ring and a rattle. She knew she should put them away, but just looking at the delicate pastel colours, touching and feeling the softness of the little things gave her a warm feeling. She had kept hidden all outward signs of her pregnancy so far, but she wouldn't be able to hide her condition much longer; soon everyone would know. She cradled the bump that her stomach had become with her hands. And then she felt it. Holding her breath … she waited. It came again. It was nothing more than the sensation of a bubble bursting, but it was low down in her belly, too low to be her stomach. Her baby was moving and making its presence felt. It was a new life that she and Robbie had created and now she had to bring into the world, nurture and watch grow. Her heart swelled with joy and a happy smile spread across her face.

The sound of footsteps on the stones outside the door destroyed the tender moment, then the latch clicked. Catherine grabbed at the precious items on the table and covered them with her arms. She was too late to hide them all and when the door opened it was Jannie who walked in. Why didn't people knock on the door first like they did back home?

'Daa told me to come and tell you …' Suddenly Jannie stopped, her mouth dropped open and she stood staring at a pair of little bootees that had escaped Catherine's gathering in. A mixture of emotions flitted across her face. 'You're going to have a bairn,' she snapped. 'Why did you not tell me?'

'Because you would have wanted me to go home to my family and I'm not going to do that.'

'But should you not be wi' your mam?'

'No. This is where my baby will be born. It's Robbie's too and your grandchild; would you want it to be born at the other end of the country?'

'But your mam—'

'She has other grandchildren, it's not her first.'

Momentarily deprived of words, Jannie, twisting her hands together stood staring at Catherine. Then she said, 'When?'

'Some time in February.'

'But … how are you going to manage?'

'The same as many others. Women do this all the time.'

'But you cannot go to the sheep wi' a baby.'

Catherine hadn't got as far as deciding what she was going to do when the baby arrived, but a sense of mischief made her say, 'I shall carry it in a sling on my back the same as Red Indian women do.'

Jannie scowled and pulled herself up to her full height. 'You are not fit to have a bairn, talking like that.'

'There's nothing wrong with it,' said Catherine. 'Women all over the world have carried their babies like that; in fact I think it's a good idea.'

Jannie snatched a breath, but before she could launch into a tirade Catherine said, 'Come off it, you don't really think I'd do that, do you? I'll cope with that problem when I get to it.' She stood up, began to refold the baby clothes and put them in a pile. If it had been Kay standing there she would have shown them to her, but Jannie would have to wait. 'By the way, what was it Daa wanted you to tell me? And what happened about the cow?' she asked.

Daa had insisted on hobbling out to milk the cow. He said there was nothing that needed Catherine's attention; it could all wait till he could do it. Jannie seemed reluctant to leave and, seeking a way to get her out, Catherine told her to continue with the cold compresses on Daa's ankle till the swelling had gone. 'I'll come and see him later on,' she said. She went to the door, opened it and held it open. It was the signal for Jannie to leave and one she could not ignore. Well, that wasn't too bad, thought Catherine, knowing that Jannie would tell the aunts then the postman and in a day or two the whole neighbourhood would know.

Mina and Laura lost no time in coming to see her. To all their questions she gave the same answers she had given Jannie. They smiled, even Mina, and said it would be good to have Robbie's bairn in the valley. When they were leaving Laura stepped back, 'Could I make you a shawl, Catherine?' she said.

'Would you?'

'Yes.' Laura smiled and scuttled away.

Billie came to visit, looked shyly at her and asked what she was going to do about the sheep. He had acted with surprise when she told him she had no intention of letting a baby stop her from carrying out her plans. 'It has set me back a bit,' she said, 'and I'm sorry, but I won't be able to go dancing with you this year, but I will next.'

Although it was getting to be more and more of a struggle to push the bicycle up out of the valley Catherine continued to go to the surgery, but at the end of October she told Neil Lumsden she wanted to leave and in mid November she pushed her bicycle into the outhouse and left it there.

'Come outside, quick,' shouted Kay.

Catherine threw down the book she was reading. 'What's wrong?'

'Nothing's wrong, it's the lights, the Merry Dancers.'

The November night was cold and frosty. Catherine shrugged herself into her coat and looked up at a sky filled with colour. Above her a curtain of colour hung suspended, rippling as though blown by a draught. Pastels deepened into vivid primaries then suddenly shot into shafts of red, blue and green that reached from horizon to zenith. Like a kaleidoscope, interchanging bands of colour shifted, changed and transformed. The whole sky except for a small portion to the south was filled with a moving mass of colour.

'Fascinating,' breathed Catherine. 'What a wonderful sight.'

'It's easy to see why they call them Merry Dancers, isn't it? It fairly cuts you down to size though,' said Kay. 'It's not always like this; more often it'll just be a curtain of lights and even they won't last long. The 'aald eens' say a display like we've just seen foretells trouble of some sort. We'll see.'

They stood and watched until the colours began to fade. When Catherine shivered Kay said, 'Inside with you or you'll get a chill.'

'Will you come in?'

'Love to.'

After the frosty air of the outdoors the kitchen was warm. 'You have a good fire going,' said Kay. 'Do you manage to keep it in all night?'

'Mostly,' said Catherine. 'It has gone out a few times, but that was before I got the hang of it. What are you going to have, whisky or tea?'

'I'll have tea. It won't be long till Christmas, basically a non-event here in Shetland, but I still celebrate it. I used to hang a sock for my husband. He'd laugh, but never forgot to get me a present.'

'You said you have a nephew, but do you have any other relations here?'

'No. Norman's parents both died and Callum's other sister went to Australia with her husband and two boys. I've no idea where they are now.'

'So how long have you been on your own?'

'Too long. Fifteen years.'

'Does it ever get any easier?' asked Catherine.

'With time. You have to look ahead. When you get to my age just remembering the pleasure is pain enough. Memories often bring tears.' Kay smiled, but there was sadness in it. 'Enough of that. Would you like to come and have dinner with me on Christmas Day? We could pull a cracker, couldn't we?'

'I'd like that; I wasn't looking forward to it.'

'I understand, but that wasn't why I asked you. It was for a purely practical reason: you see it's very difficult to pull a cracker by yourself'

'Oh, Kay.' Catherine laughed. 'I don't know what I'd do without you.'

'You'd manage,' said Kay, 'but I'm wondering how you will when your baby's born. Do you still want to have it at home? Winter is worse after Christmas. What if the doctor can't get to you?'

'You forget I'm a trained nurse. Childbirth is the most natural thing in the world,' said Catherine, brushing Kay's concern aside. 'Lumsden was very happy with me the last time I saw him and we aren't expecting any trouble.'

'But if we get snowed in ... I don't want to worry you but it is a possibility ... you'll only have me to help and I'm not any sort of a nurse.'

Catherine smiled, leaned forward and patted Kay's hand. 'Don't worry, I'll see the doc again next week and if he thinks I should go into hospital I will. OK?'

'I'm sorry. It isn't as though Jannie's any help and I'm sure your mother would never forgive us if anything went wrong.'

'I believe African women give birth by the side of the road, then wrap the baby up and keep going.' Catherine laughed. 'I doubt if I could do that.'

'I should hope not,' said Kay, 'but if you did wouldn't that give the "aald eens" something to talk about. Mina would probably never speak to you again and warn people not to go to England because folk there were nothing but savages.' They both laughed. 'But joking aside, when you've got everything ready for your confinement you'll have to show me so I'll know where to find it. In the meantime I'm going to teach you to knit.'

'You're joking,' said Catherine.

'No I'm not. You'll need something else to do besides reading books for the next three months. I'll come tomorrow. Now I'm going home to bed.

At the end of November Catherine made a parcel of the Christmas presents she had bought for her family and asked Kay if she would post it for her when she next went to Lerwick. She had pondered long and hard over what she could give Robbie's parents and decided at last on a copy of her wedding photograph. To Kay she said, 'Please don't buy me a present, you're doing quite enough for me as it is.' But for Kay she filled a tin with biscuits she had baked.

Kay showed her how to knit and she made a valiant effort to produce at least one knitted garment for her baby. But she found it difficult. She dropped stitches, and the knitting too, when she nodded off to sleep in the chair, so she stuffed it out of sight behind a cushion. Instead she sewed and made nightgowns stitched by hand with little embroidered motifs on them.

Flurries of snow fell as the December nights grew longer and days darker, but it didn't last and was often gone before daylight came again. The doctor parked his car at the top of the hill and walked down to see Catherine. 'Easier for me to walk in than for you to walk out,' he said. When he had examined her he pronounced her in good form. He'd get the midwife to visit after Christmas and if Catherine was worried about anything at all she was to get someone to call at the surgery and he would come. 'Be good now,' he said. 'Don't overdo the Christmas pudding and I'll see you next year.'

EIGHTEEN

I T WAS MID-MORNING before daylight crept over the horizon on Christmas Day. Catherine looked out of her window at the sea beyond the bay. It was a heaving, rolling mass of menacing steel-grey water. Her house was so close to the beach that she did not need to open her window to hear the roar the waves made as they threw themselves against the cliffs. Driving between the headlands they poured in, rose up to rush at the beach, slap down on the unoffending sand then hiss angrily as they ran across it. There was no boat in the bay now: Daa had sold it. Only the dinghy, muffled in a tarpaulin, lay above high water.

The sun, seemingly apologetic for its low orbit and brief appearance struggled to spread a little cheer, but it was pale, winter-tired, drifted in a low arc over the southern horizon and failed to lift Catherine's spirits. She put on her coat and, unable to fasten the buttons, clutched the edges of it together; it hadn't been designed for a pregnant woman. She picked up the parcel containing the tin of biscuits, stepped outside, closed the door and walked along to Kay's.

'Happy Christmas, Kay,' she said.

'And a happy Christmas to you too,' said Kay. 'Come and sit down.'

Kay's kitchen smelled of meat being roasted, spices and other sweet things.

'I can smell cloves,' said Catherine as she took off her coat.

'That's the pomanders; I've hung a couple on the tree.'

'You've got a tree?'

'Of course I have,' said Kay. She took Catherine's coat and hung it up. 'Can't have Christmas without a tree. I know it's only driftwood but it was growing once and was part of a tree. I found it on the beach.' Kay's 'tree', decorated with tinsel, a few baubles and the clove-stuck oranges, stood in a pot on the dresser.

'It's lovely, but let me give you this.' Catherine gave Kay her present.

'I thought you said no presents?' Kay took the tin, put it on the table and opened it. 'You've been baking. Oh, you shouldn't have.' She laughed. 'Why do we say that? Why don't we just say thank you? But I do thank you, very much.'

'It was the least I could do,' said Catherine. 'You have been the best of friends; I don't think I would have stayed if you hadn't been here.'

'Nonsense, you're a fighter, you'd survive without me.'

'I don't know about that, Jannie takes some—' began Catherine.

'Jannie does not figure in our conversation today. Forget about her. I know you're not supposed to drink, but one small sherry wouldn't hurt, would it?'

'Not at all.'

'My nephew's going to join us for dinner,' said Kay. 'We won't be eating till about three or four o'clock, so would you like a piece of short-bread? Norman's so busy I don't see him very often, and never till he's finished work, hardly at all in summer so it's usually when he's got an evening free in winter. I think I did tell you about him, didn't I?'

'I'm sure you did.'

At Kay's insistence Catherine sat with her feet up while Kay alter-nately sat and talked to her or busied herself with stoking the fire, looking to the meat and putting pans with vegetables ready to start cooking. Time drifted lazily by and Catherine thought how nice it was to be in Kay's house where she was welcome; better than sitting at home and far better than being in the Jameson house.

'I'm going to put the vegetables on to cook now,' said Kay as the hands of the clock crept towards three. 'If Norman isn't here when they're done I'll put his meal on a plate to warm later.'

But he was there, blustering in, stamping his feet and complaining of how cold it was. 'It'll likely snow before long,' he said. 'How are you, Auntie?'

Catherine was aware of a burly bearded figure as the man put a fiddle case on the floor, then wrapped his little aunt in his arms and hugged her.

'I want you to meet Catherine,' said Kay. 'Say hello, Norman.'

Catherine looked up and straight into the bearded face that had frightened her when she'd fallen asleep by the peat bank; it wasn't looking concerned now, but broke into a grin instead.

'You're not going to scream at me now, are you?' said Norrie Williams.

Kay gasped. 'Hey, what's this? Do you two know each other?'

'Not really,' said Norrie.

'No,' said Catherine. 'He frightened me out of my wits when I fell asleep by my peat bank. He thought maybe I was ill so came to see if I was all right.'

'No need to introduce you then. Sit down and talk to her, Norman.'

'You've changed a bit since I saw you last,' said Norrie.

'Oh, you mean this?' said Catherine, patting her stomach.

'Ay. I was at the school wi' Robbie,' said Norrie. 'You'll miss him.' Then, seeing the gathering brightness in Catherine's eyes, he added, 'He'd be proud o' you for stayin'. We all ken how it is wi' ...' He didn't say the name, just inclined his head towards the other end of the valley and she knew he meant Jannie. 'If there's anything you need doin' you can't manage you only have to get in touch wi' me.

'That's very kind of you, but as I've only seen you once in six months how do I do that? It's all right; Billie comes over quite often and gives me a hand.'

'Ay, I'm heard.' Norrie winked.

'What d'you mean by that?'

'Nothin'.'

'I don't know; nothing's secret.'

'Dinner's ready,' said Kay as she put a dish of roast lamb on the table. 'You carve, Norman, while I get the vegetables. Come and sit here, Catherine.'

They ate their dinner by the light of an oil lamp; there was another on the dresser by the window and the two cast a mellow light on the room. The pudding had been made by Kay, and with wartime rationing still in force was none too well endowed with fruit. But it was good and praise was lavished on Kay for the excellence of the meal. Catherine was not allowed to do anything but sit by the fire while Norrie helped his aunt clear the table and wash the dishes.

Comfortable and relaxed, she listened as Kay and Norrie talked and heard again the soft warm lilt of the dialect. But she liked the way they spoke and thought the accent lyrical. She closed her eyes and smiled, remembered Robbie, and, listening to the others, fancied she could hear his voice again. Little by little her head nodded and she dozed.

The music was soft and sweet: rippling notes, long drawn fluting calls and trills. She dreamed of the moor, of the sweet song of the skylarks, the burbling call of the curlews, the wind on a soft day and the endless drift of the sea. She dreamed of Robbie and smiled as she dreamed. The music played on, then stopped and there came a voice, a soft, lilting, Shetland voice. 'Robbie,' she said as she opened her eyes.

'Ay lass, you're awake.' It wasn't Robbie but Norrie, who smiled at her.

'I'm sorry,' she said. 'I shouldn't have gone to sleep, but I couldn't help it.'

'It doesn't matter.' Norrie propped his fiddle on his knee, holding its neck against his shoulder. 'Would you like me to play for you?'

'You … but … haven't you been playing? I thought I heard music.'

'It wasn't me.' Norrie grinned and the lamplight shone on his teeth, white and even in the dark mass of his beard. 'Must have been the trowie men.'

'Get away with you,' said Kay. 'Don't listen to him, Catherine, he's teasing you.'

'I don't mind,' said Catherine, and to Norrie, 'Yes, please play for us.'

So Norrie played reels and jigs and waltzes and they were clapping and tapping their feet in time to the music. The evening sped away until Kay said, 'Look at the time, will you?' and, 'Would you like a drink, Catherine, before you go home?' Catherine said she would and Kay made tea and cut a slice of the cake they had been too full to eat before. When Catherine said it was time for her to go Norrie said he would see her safely to her door.

He took her arm as they walked the path between the houses. 'I must see you safe,' he said. When they reached her door he asked if he could come in and be sure that all was right with things, that the fire hadn't gone out and she had enough peat for the morning. Catherine was tired and not inclined to protest so she let him in. When he was satisfied that all was well she thanked him.

'It was my pleasure,' he said; then, his eyes twinkling, 'but don't go listening when the trowie men play or they might spirit you away.'

She laughed. 'Away with you,' she said. 'Goodnight.'

'Goodnight, Catherine,' he said. He opened the door to leave; then, as he was closing it he stopped, held it open, looked at her as if he wanted to say more, but said nothing and closed the door.

The New Year slipped by without her noticing for Catherine went to her bed early. January began with cold winds, rain and a sprinkling of snow. As the month advanced the weather worsened, frost went deeper, cold winds became bitter and rain turned to sleet. With so few hours of daylight and even those darkened by louring skies Catherine rarely stepped out of doors. She had abandoned her knitting; Kay discovered it behind the cushion and had taken it away to finish. Her sewing all done, the days dragged and even Kay's cheery presence could not always lift the gloom.

January skated into February on icy roads. Anxiously Catherine looked out of her window as soon as it grew light, tried to read the weather and hoped it wouldn't snow. She was finding her condition uncomfortable now. Her legs ached, her back ached, and no sooner did she lie down than she wanted to get up. When she went to bed she prayed that the next day would bring the start of her labour, but day after day went by and still she was on her feet. Kay called every day, but when the middle of the month came and went and there was still no sign of the baby's arrival she said she would bring a camp bed and stay.

Then it began to snow.

'Snow rarely lasts long here,' said Kay in an effort to allay any fear Catherine might have. 'It's usually gone in a day or two, salt air, you see, and something to do with the Gulf Stream running close to Shetland.'

But the frost was deep and the earth cold and snow lay and did not melt. With only a gentle wind to drive them, great feathery flakes, dancing in whorls and loops, fell silently piling one on the other to deepen the layer already covering the earth.

Billie, pushing a pram, appeared soon after the snow started. 'Mam said she'd promised it to you,' he said, 'and told me to bring it over before you get snowed in.'

'Go away with you,' said Kay. 'We're not going to get snowed in.'

Sitting down with a cup of tea Billie said, 'You never know.'

When he had gone Catherine and Kay examined the pram. Kay admired its deep body and chrome wheels, 'Not exactly mint condition,' she said, 'but good and clean and more use than a cot.'

Catherine was more concerned about the weather than the pram and was looking out of the window at the snow and the leaden sky. 'How are we going to get the doctor if the snow gets too deep, Kay?' she said. 'Not that I think we're going to need him, but if we do?'

'We'll have to send Daa to fetch him.'

'Mm. I ought to have agreed to go into hospital.'

'It might have been better,' said Kay, 'but it was your choice. With weather like this you might not have got there and then you would have been in a pickle.'

'You're right; we shall just have to get on with it.'

NINETEEN

WHEN KAY OPENED the door a low wall of snow blocked her way. A flurry of snowflakes floated in round her. 'Oh my goodness, it's drifted,' she said.

Looking over her shoulder Catherine asked, 'Will the track be filled in?'

'I don't know; the wind was north east, if it still is it won't be too bad. We'll have to wait for daylight. Are you worried about the doctor getting here?'

'It had crossed my mind.'

Kay shut the door. 'When it's light I'll put my boots on and have a look.'

Catherine had woken early; staring into the darkness she wondered what had roused her. And then it came, that first indescribable feeling, low, low down. She had lain there waiting for it to come again, knowing that at last it was her time to give birth.

She stood by the table; clenching her teeth she clutched the back of a chair. Kay, watching her, waited till the spasm was over, then said, 'Come on, take my arm and walk, you know you said it helps.' Kay insisted she keep walking, but the contractions were stronger and as each new wave of pain assailed her Catherine held fast to anything in reach till it was over.

'I think it's time we asked Daa to go for the doctor,' she said.

The thin light of day showed that the snow had stopped falling when Kay plunged through the drift outside the door. Catherine sank into her chair by the fire to await her return. A few minutes later Kay was back.

'He's on his way now,' she said. 'Snow's drifted in places but he should get there all right. I think I'll take the shovel and clear it from the door.'

They walked again, round the kitchen to the bedroom and back. Back and forth they went. The hours ticked away, but there was no sign of Daa or the doctor.

'I hope Daa's all right,' said Catherine.

'He will be,' said Kay.

Catherine's contractions were stronger and coming at shorter intervals. To bear the pain she gripped Kay's hand so tightly that it made the older woman grit her teeth and fear for fragile bones. Then Catherine felt warm liquid running down her legs. 'My waters have broken,' she said. 'I'll have to get on the bed; it isn't going to be long now.'

In the last stage of her labour as each spasm gripped her, breathing hard to ride the pain, Catherine contorted her face as she bore down on it, cried out when it became too much. 'Where's the blasted doctor?' she cried when a spasm had passed and Kay was wiping the sweat from her forehead. 'Why didn't I go to the hospital? Oh, Kay, I don't want to do this any more.'

'Hush,' said Kay, 'hold on, you're nearly there.' Plumping the pillows behind Catherine's back, Kay prayed silently for the arrival of the doctor.

'Did you put the water on to boil?' said Catherine as she lay back and waited for the next contraction.

'I did; kettle and pans.'

'And the rest of the stuff is laid out?'

'It is.'

'Lumsden's not going to get here, is he? … aaah,' cried Catherine as another contraction took hold of her. Snatching a handful of sheet in each hand she leaned forward and bent to the effort of putting all her strength into pushing. Her face grew red as she roared through clenched teeth.

Kay held her breath, wrung her hands together and once again prayed for the arrival of Neil Lumsden.

'Will you look to see what's happening, Kay?' said Catherine as she breathed easy again now that the spasm was over.

'I can see the baby's head,' said an excited, but nervous, Kay. 'What should I do?' But there was no need to ask, for Catherine, every muscle straining was pushing again. 'Its head is out now,' cried Kay.

Breathing deep and hard Catherine leaned back. Then, as another urge to push came and while Kay clenched her fists and willed energy into Catherine, she bore down on it and with one last effort pushed her baby into the world.

'It's a boy,' cried Kay as the baby spluttered, opened its mouth and wailed.

Catherine, every muscle relaxing, softening, giving way, closed her eyes and gave a long deep sigh. A boy, she'd given Robbie a son, thank God. 'See to the baby, Kay,' she said and almost without knowing it shed the afterbirth.

'I know you've already told me what to do, but tell me again.'

'Take the cotton wool and wipe his eyes like I showed you; one swab for each eye, then clean his face. Now you have to cut the cord,' said Catherine. 'Can you do that?'

'Yes,' said Kay and swallowed hard at the thought of it. 'Talk me through.'

'Take the string you sterilized, tie the cord in two places about six inches apart, one close to the baby, as tight as you can, very tight, then cut it in the middle.' It was important that Kay should get it right and Catherine forced herself to sit up and watch. 'That's right,' she said. When it was done she held out her arms to receive her son, a warm damp bundle in a soft white swaddling cloth.

'Just look at him, Kay,' she said. 'All that black hair. Isn't he wonderful?' The two women, heads together, looked at the little screwed-up face and tiny hands, then unwrapping the binding, at the rest of him. 'He's perfect,' said Catherine, wrapping him again to hold him close to her. She looked at Kay and saw that the old lady was close to tears. With the arm not holding the baby she gathered her unofficial midwife to her.

'Oh, Kay, thank God you're here. What would I have done without you?' Then as Kay's tears began to fall, 'Shush, don't cry or I'll be crying too.' But despite herself Catherine's own tears came and the two women, heads together snuffled and sniffed as the floodgates opened. At last, with a watery smile as she wiped away her tears, Kay said, 'I'm just so relieved that nothing went wrong. I don't know about you, but I could do with a cup of tea.'

'Couldn't I just,' said Catherine, 'but could clean me up a bit first?'

'I'll do that while the kettle boils.'

Reluctantly Catherine handed her baby to Kay to be settled in the pram while she was made comfortable and given a cup of tea.

The snow had stopped falling, the sky had cleared and become as blue as a cornflower while the sun, at mid-afternoon, stooped low to peep through Catherine's bedroom window. Neil Lumsden, skiing down the hillside, came to a stop by Jannie's door. It flew open and she appeared. 'Where's my patient?' he asked.

'At home,' said Jannie. 'Will I come wi' you?'

'No need,' said the doctor. He dug in his ski poles and pushed off towards Catherine's house. Kay was about to dish up the meal she had cooked when he rattled on the door. He was propping his skis against the side of the house when she opened it. With a cry of joy she said, 'Oh, I'm so glad you're here.'

'My goodness, woman, what's the matter with you? I'm here to see Catherine. Is everything all right? Where is she?'

Wiping her hands on her apron Kay led the way into the bedroom. Catherine was awake. She was leaning over, gazing into the pram. She smiled when she saw who her visitor was. 'You're a bit late,' she said.

'Well I did tell you not to go into labour in the middle of a snow-storm, but you obviously weren't listening. Anyway, I'm here now so let's have a look at you.' He turned to Kay. 'Would you mind?'

'You don't have to ask, Doctor. I'm gone.'

Sitting on the bed after he'd examined Catherine, seen to the baby and weighed it, Dr Lumsden said he was satisfied with everything and beamed at her. 'Why am I not surprised that you managed on your own?'

'But I didn't. I couldn't have managed without Kay.'

'She's a good woman,' said the doctor and chuckled. 'I bet she never did anything like you've just put her through in all the years she taught at school. She was overjoyed to see me; I thought she was going to throw herself in my arms.'

'Poor Kay,' said Catherine. 'Thank God she was here if only for moral support, but it was much more than that. She's a friend in a million.'

'Everybody needs friends.' Lumsden stood up. 'I'd better be off, but take advantage of the fact that you've got someone to look after you. Stay in bed. I'll come and see you again in a day or two.'

In the kitchen Kay was hovering with the teapot in her hand. 'Can I give you a cup of tea, Doctor?' she said.

'Don't you have anything stronger?'

Kay stared at him, then smiled. When she put the whisky bottle on the table her smile was reflected in the beaming face of the doctor.

'Got to wet the baby's head,' he said as Kay poured whisky into two glasses. 'Besides, I have to climb that hill out of here. Bottoms up.'

'Bottoms up,' echoed Kay.

Both glasses were emptied with one gulp. As they were put down Lumsden patted Kay on the shoulder and said, 'Well done, Mrs Burnett, well done.'

'You have visitors, Catherine,' said Kay as she ushered Mina and Laura into the bedroom. Mina stalked in to stand at the bottom of the bed. Laura, carrying a parcel, stood beside her.

'So, you've had a boy, I'm told,' said Mina.

'A boy, a boy,' echoed Laura.

'That's right,' said Catherine, wrapping the shawl Kay had put round her shoulders across her chest. 'He's in the pram.'

The pram was beside the bed. Mina led the way, Laura at her heels, and stopped by the side of it. Leaning stiffly forward she gazed for a long time at the sleeping infant. 'He favours his father then,' she said as she straightened up.

'So he does,' said Laura. Then, as she handed the parcel she was carrying to Catherine, 'I've brought you this.'

'Thank you, Laura.' Catherine opened the loosely wrapped parcel and lifted out a shawl so fine and soft it took her breath away. 'This is absolutely beautiful,' she said as she touched it to her face, 'so fine. You're so clever.'

Laura twittered and said it was nothing. Mina turned up her nose and sniffed disapprovingly, 'What are you going to call him?' she asked as she inclined her head to look into the pram again.

'I haven't decided yet,' said Catherine. But she had for there was only one choice of name for her son.

'Ay … well, you'll think of something. Now we'd better go.' Away she went and Laura, trotting behind her, stopped briefly by the bedroom door to give a little wave, then she was gone too.

'Come and look at this, Kay,' said Catherine when she heard the outer door close behind them. 'Laura has knitted me the most beautiful shawl. It seems too good to wrap round a baby.'

It was late before Jannie came. She was empty handed and walked in ahead of Kay to give Catherine a brief nod before going straight to the pram. There was the suggestion of a smile on her lips as she looked at her grandson. She reached out with both hands as though she would pick him up, then quickly drew back. For long moments she gazed at the child, 'He's like his daa,' she said. 'Robbie had the same black hair.' She looked at Catherine. 'He's awful bonnie.' From her bending position over the pram Jannie straightened up. 'I didna think you would stay to have him, I thought you would go home.'

'No, it was right for him to be born here. Would you like to pick him up?'

'Pick him up?' Jannie hesitated, but then lifted the baby, cradled him and looked at his little face. 'He's just like his daa.'.

The woman does have a heart, thought Catherine, when she saw how Jannie's expression softened, how her lips twitched into a smile when she touched her grandson's face with a fingertip. When she put the baby back in the pram she looked at Catherine. 'I'm braaly glad du stayed,' she said. There seemed nothing more to add and abruptly she turned on her heel and was gone.

Catherine stared after her then, turned to look at her baby. 'You, my son, may be the one to melt your grandmother's heart,' she said and was amused to see the baby's lips spread in the semblance of a smile.

Snuggling down in her bed Catherine pulled the covers up to her chin. Kay was away at her own house, the baby sleeping and the house was quiet. Content and happy to think that at last Jannie was about to accept her Catherine settled down to sleep too.

'Cathie.' The voice came from a long way off. 'Cathie.' There it was again. Was she dreaming? Catherine roused herself from sleep and sat up in bed; no one called her Cathie but her mother and she was 1,000 miles away. She must have imagined it and, not expecting an answer, she said, 'Mum?'

'Oh, there you are.' Catherine's mother, divesting herself of scarf and gloves, came into the bedroom. 'My God, Cathie, what sort of god-forsaken place have you landed yourself in? And what are you doing in bed?' Then, as realization dawned, she gasped, 'The baby's here. Oh, let me look.'

'Why are you here, Mum?' said Catherine.

But Doris Marshall was making little cooing noises. She didn't reply.

Louder this time, Catherine said, 'What are you doing here, Mum?'

Doris looked up. 'What is it, girl or boy?'

'It's a boy.'

'Lovely,' said Doris; then, leaving the baby she sat on the side of the bed. 'I'm here because I thought I ought to be with you and your father said I should.'

'But ...'

'The journey was horrendous; I had to walk from the town. I brought my gum-boots because I thought the farm would be muddy. By the way, where is the farm? I haven't seen anything that looks like one yet.'

'Oh, Mum. Why did you come, *why did you come?*' Catherine lay back on her pillows and covered her eyes with her hands.

'Hmm,' went her mother as she stood up and planted her hands on her hips. 'It seems to me I'm not here before time. Why didn't you tell me you were living in a hovel? You didn't tell me about Robbie till it was too late. Well, now I'm going to find out just what's going on.'

They didn't hear Kay come in. When she said, 'Hello,' mother and daughter turned to look.

'This is my mother, Kay,' said Catherine, 'and Mum, this is Kay, my next door neighbour.' The two women shook hands. Then Kay said, 'I'll make a pot of tea,' and Doris said she'd help.

TWENTY

Daa sat on the bed. 'How are you, lass? None the worse for your ordeal, I hope. And Kay's doin' good by you?'

'No one could do better.'

'Ay, she's a good wife. Now, where's the boy?'

'In the pram,' said Catherine. 'I expect he's sleeping.'

'I'm thinking he's awake,' said his grandfather. 'His eyes are open.'

'Are they? Would you like to pick him up?' Catherine leaned across and turned back the blankets covering her son. 'He's bundled up, quite easy to lift.'

John Jameson slid his big, work-worn hands under the little bundle, lifted the baby and cradled him in his arms. As he did his face softened into a smile. 'He's awful bonnie, looks like his daa.' He turned to look at Catherine. 'Is he good?'

'Hasn't had time to be bad yet. No, he's very good; I'm hoping it's going to stay that way.'

'It will. He's got the right mam.'

With a contented smile on her face Catherine watched her father-in-law's beaming face as he held his grandson. The old man looked long and lovingly into the little face, picked up and examined tiny fingers. At last he spoke.

'You canna mind how little they are, 'he said. 'Do you have a name?'

'Yes. He'll be Robert after Robbie and John after you.'

A smile spread slowly across the old man's face, crinkled the corners of his eyes. He looked at her. 'Thank you, Catherine.' Then he lifted his head and looked off into the distance. 'Robert … John … Jameson … sounds good.' He looked down again at the child in his arms. 'I think I should put him back now.'

When Robert John was tucked up again Daa said he had to go. Giving Catherine's hand a squeeze he said, 'Look after yourself, lass.' He started to walk away but stopped and looked back. 'Have you a visitor? I saw a wife I don't know askin' for you and she was wi' Kay when I came in.'

'That'll be my mother,' said Catherine.

'Ay,' said Daa, nodding his head, 'I thought it might be.'

'Now, Kay,' said Doris when the two women were in the relative privacy of the kitchen, 'tell me what's been going on.'

'I don't think it's for me to say,' said Kay. 'You should ask Catherine.'

'And you think she'd tell me? She doesn't write often and when she does there's never anything much in her letters about Shetland, where she lives, or her in-laws. Was that Robbie's father I met when I asked where Cathie lived?'

'Must have been; he's the only man in the valley.'

'He seemed pleasant enough and Cathie's told me about him, but what about Robbie's mother? There's never a word about her. Don't they get on?'

'Ah.' Kay busied herself with teacups.

'I thought as much,' said Doris. 'She's told me about the funny old aunts and about you and what a good friend you are, but nothing about the old lady. Isn't she kind to her, then?'

'Not exactly.'

'Why not?'

'Some don't take kindly to the English,' said Kay, 'and she didn't know Robbie and Catherine were getting married, let alone when they were coming home. She was very upset and insists she never got the letter Robbie sent.'

'That's ridiculous. I mean, about the English.'

Kay, about to pour out tea, put the teapot down with a thump. 'Oh, come now, Mrs Marshall, you know as well as I do that there are those among us who think themselves superior. The English are notorious for that. They do themselves no good.'

'But my Cathie's not like that.'

'No. I know she's not.'

'Right. I shall have to get to the bottom of this,' said Doris. 'Let's have that cup of tea. That was Robbie's father going in to see my girl, wasn't it?' Kay nodded. 'I'll wait till he's gone.'

Kay poured tea for the two of them.

'It seems to be a desolate place,' said Doris. 'I'm sure I don't know what made Cathie stay after Robbie died, but you're from the south; why do you stay?'

'I've been here a long time so I'm used to it,' Kay said with a smile, 'and it does grow on you.'

'Could have fooled me.'

'Oh, I assure you, there's magic in the islands.'

'And if her mother-in-law is giving her a hard time is it magic that's making my girl stay? Or is there something else I ought to know about?'

'Catherine is a lovely girl; I'm very fond of her,' said Kay, 'and I'm glad she's here, it's time we had some young people in the valley. Not everyone is against her. Have a bannock, Mrs …?'

'Call me Doris,' said Doris.

Daa came through from the bedroom and on his way to the door said, 'Yon's a fine peerie lad, you should be braaly proud.' His accent rich and his speech broad, Daa spoke as he always did. He was gone before anyone could reply.

When the door shut behind him Doris said, 'What on earth did he say?'

'He said the baby was a grand little boy; you should be very proud of him.'

'Do they all speak like that?'

'Most do, but they speak differently when they need you to understand. You must have found that to be able to make your way here.'

Doris thought about this for a moment. 'Yes, I must admit the people in the town were very helpful, even told me where I could leave my suitcase,' she said. 'I think I'll go and see Catherine now.'

Catherine was sitting up suckling her baby. 'What made you risk coming here at this time of year, Mother?' she said when Doris came to sit on the bed.

'I had a feeling things were not as they should be,' said Doris, 'and from what I've been hearing I was right, so you'd better tell me the whole story, I'm not going to go home till you do.'

At that Catherine laughed. 'Have you looked outside? It's snowing again. You'll be lucky if you get home inside a couple of weeks.'

'I don't care how long I'm stuck here; you've got to spill the beans.'

Snow fell silently all night. In the morning it was still filling the air, feather-light it danced and twirled, then settled flake on flake to cover all with a quilt soft and light as eiderdown. Catherine looked out and worried about the sheep, but the hill gates had been opened and they were on land that was closer to home. Kay said they wouldn't starve; Daa would be putting out hay, or whatever else he had, to them.

Slowly, persistently, Doris Marshall wheedled out of Catherine the whole story of what had happened to her. She was aghast at the remoteness, the living conditions and the lack of what she thought of as essentials, and found it hard to understand why Catherine had accepted their absence. She was sympathetic over Robbie's death, but angry when she learned of the tricks Jannie had played.

'If she thinks she's going to treat you like that and get away with it then she's got another think coming.'

'Leave it, Mum, it's all in the past.'

'Leave it? What do you think my name is? I won't have a moment's peace when I get home if I think she's going to go on treating you like that. It's going to be sorted and right now, or I'm a Dutchman.' Doris stormed off to do battle despite Catherine's pleas to forget about it and leave well alone.

'I'm going to give that woman a piece of my mind,' said Doris. Kay stood and watched her push her feet into her boots and put her coat on.

'You mean Jannie, I take it. I wish you luck,' said Kay. There was a smile on her face as Doris went out, slamming the door behind her. Much of the fire that had been in Catherine's mother when she left the house had gone out when she came back. 'Well, I don't know how you understand a word they say,' she said, 'it isn't English they speak, it's a foreign language.

Kay was preparing a meal. 'You didn't get on very well, then?'

'Get on?' Doris took off her coat and hat and hung them up, then took off her boots. 'She's a dragon. I got nowhere at all. He seems nice enough, though.'

'Daa is a gem,' said Kay. 'He'll look out for Catherine. Jannie doesn't get it all her own way.'

Allowed out of bed, Catherine joined her mother and Kay in the kitchen. Kay still came in every day, for Doris forgot about the fire and didn't stoke it, so it frequently had to be coaxed back to life.

'I could do with some fresh air,' said Catherine. She went to the door, then gasped as she opened it. 'Oh, my God! I've never seen snow so deep.'

A dazzling white world met her eye; above it were clear blue skies, out of which shone a sun that was hard and brassy.

'You should be glad you had your baby when you did,' said Kay. 'If you'd left it another day or two Daa would never have got out nor the doctor in.'

'Why, what's been happening?'

'We've had the worst snowfall for years. The roads were all blocked.

To get a lorry through for supplies men had to dig a way through for miles and then do the same again to get it back,' said Kay. 'It's a wonder your mother got through, she must have been determined to see you.'

'My mother is a force to be reckoned with.'

'You can say that again. I told you the aurora we saw last year meant trouble, didn't I? I didn't expect this though. Snowdrifts are bad enough, but add your mother ...'

'Oh, yes,' said Doris, who had been listening. 'I'm trouble, am I?'

'I'm sure Jannie thought you were,' said Catherine. 'How long do you think the snow is going to last, Kay?'

'It's beginning to thaw, we must hope not long.'

'Weren't you afraid you'd run out of food?' asked Doris.

'No, we have milk from the cow, potatoes and carrots in store and flour in the bin. What more do we want? And Catherine's feeding the baby, so,' Kay laughed, 'he'll be all right. You have to know how to keep a store cupboard that'll last through an emergency. Who'd like a cup of tea?'

Although snow had stopped falling the snow that lay did not lessen, but gradually roads were cleared and news came at last that the boat would sail. Doris, who had borrowed her daughter's clothes because her suitcase had been stranded in Lerwick, made plans to be reunited with it and make her way home. This time she would not have to walk, for a lift had been arranged with a local trader. So one day she hugged Catherine, made her promise not to keep any more secrets, kissed the baby and said goodbye.

Then Billie called. 'Mam made you a hufsi,' he said as he dumped a box on the table.

'What on earth's a hufsi?' asked Catherine.

'Take a look.'

'Oh, it's a cake.' Catherine held it to her nose and sniffed. 'It smells good; thank your mother for me, will you?'

'Ay. Where's the boy?'

'So it's the baby you've come to see, not me at all?'

'No,' said Billie, 'I always like to see you, but I would like to see the bairn.' He looked in the pram, pulled the covers back and gazed at the little one.

'Would you like to hold him?' asked Catherine. 'Most people do.'

Billie hesitated. 'I'd maybe drop him; perhaps when he's bigger?'

'Can I ask you a favour? Would you be his godfather?'

'Godfather! I don't know. What does a godfather do?'

'You're supposed to see that he's brought up to be a good, God-fearing citizen, but nobody seems to check on you so ...' Catherine spread her hands, 'I don't know about here, but back home it seems a mere formality.'

'If you think I can, I will,' said Billie.

As Billie left Kay came in. 'Rose sent me a cake,' said Catherine, 'and I asked Billie if he would be little Robbie's godfather.'

'You'll need another godfather, and a godmother too.'

'Will you be godmother? You should be, you were there from the start.'

'I'd love to. Who else are you going to ask?'

'I don't know. I'll have to think about it. Here, hold your godson, I'll make some tea and we'll try that cake.'

Trapped by deep snow Catherine took advantage of the time it gave her to be with her baby. Kay often found her sitting by the fire with him cradled in her arms. When she told Catherine she was making a rod for her own back, Catherine replied that her little boy deserved all the love and cuddling he could get. But as the days lengthened and the sun crept slowly back into the north she began to feel a longing to be out of doors. The desire to begin working with the sheep again filled her waking moments, but until Robbie was big enough and old enough to be left with Kay she would content herself with studying her books.

TWENTY ONE

CATHERINE'S PREGNANCY HAD stolen a lot of her time and she still had much to learn. In the evenings she pored over her books. Leaving Robbie with Kay she went back to her outdoor work and gradually regained her strength and stamina. Never did she wake in the morning and wonder what she was going to do that day. There were hill sheep to see to; rounded up and driven down to collecting pens to be dipped, sheared and for lambs to be marked. Later on lambs would be divided into those to be sold and those kept for breeding. August saw her turning and tossing hay to dry. When the potatoes were ready for lifting she joined Jannie and the aunts to pick them up. October saw her helping to harvest the oats. When winter crept over the horizon, days shortened and nights grew long. Sometimes the Merry Dancers lit the sky and Catherine would look up to watch and wonder.

So the years slid away and with her son, now four years old, winter nights were spent by the fire. With little Robbie tucked into the chair by her side she read to him. He had grown into a sturdy youngster and with the turn of the year, his birthday had come and gone. He spent more time with her now and less with Kay or the aunts.

Spring came in wet and cold and boded ill for the in-lamb ewes. Catherine worried about them and wished she had better outbuildings. There was not enough room in the buildings she had to put them all in to shelter. Added to the hill ewes that were now hers she had a little flock of six pedigree Cheviot ewes. Last year she had put the ram to them in the latter part of October so that they would produce their lambs at the end of March or by the middle of April. On her calendar she had marked the day when she could expect the first lamb. It came and went and day and night after that she donned a jacket and went out to check the ewes. She had learned that sheep often gave birth in the hours before dawn.

The first glimmerings of day were beginning to lighten the sky when she left the house. It had been raining steadily all night and as she trudged along she cursed the foul weather. She found her little flock sheltering in the lee of a wall. In the beam of light thrown by her torch she counted them: one was missing. When she found it she was not surprised to discover that it was giving birth.

The ewe was lying down and Catherine could see she had been labouring for some time; there were scuff marks in the grass where she had pawed the ground till bare earth showed. Catherine drew near then went down on her knees behind the animal. Blinking away the rain that was driving into her face she looked to see what was happening. A swollen head and two little feet protruded; the head should not be lying on the feet; legs should be out first. What did Daa say? Push the head back, then pull the feet out, the rest will follow.

She took a piece of string from her pocket and tied it round the lamb's feet to stop them being lost. Placing three fingers on the unborn lamb's forehead she pushed its head gently back into the womb. Now she took hold of the feet and pulled them forward. Through the nerves of her fingers she felt the joints straighten; pulling again she was rewarded by the sight of the head coming through on top of the legs. She pulled steadily and with a rush the whole body slid out.

There was no birth sac to remove from the lamb's nose, but instead of sneezing and beginning to breathe it lay lifeless on the ground. It was a big ram lamb. 'Come on,' said Catherine as she rubbed its back briskly, 'come on … breathe.' Rubbing vigorously she willed the lamb to suck air into its lungs. But despite her efforts it lay still. What now? Scrambling to her feet she picked it up by its back legs and holding tightly swung it round and round as she's seen Daa do. Then she checked for sign of life, found none, so swung again. It did not respond. It was dead. Catherine laid it on the ground before its mother and watched as the ewe bent down to nuzzle it.

Still the rain beat down; ran in little rivers down Catherine's face and though she knew not every lamb was born to live she hadn't been there to help and this one had died. It was her fault. Sinking to her knees she put out a hand and touched it. It was her first pedigree lamb. And it was dead. Tears now mingled with the rain on her face.

It was Daa's hand that touched her shoulder. 'What are you doing, lass?' he said. 'You'll get your death of cold. Get up.'

'Oh, Daa,' she sobbed, 'the lamb's dead.'

'It's not your fault; you know some ewes have problems. You can't be with them every minute. Come on, get up.' Daa took her hand and helped her to her feet. 'You mustn't get too fond of your animals or you'll break your heart whenever one dies, and sheep don't live that long. You just have to do your best by them.' He patted her on the shoulder. 'Now get away to your bed.'

'Have you finished your breakfast, Robbie?' said Catherine.

'I'm done,' said the little boy.

'Come then, let me put your boots on.' Little Robbie slid off his chair and padded on his stocking-clad feet to his mother. 'You can come with me to see the lambs,' she said as she knelt down to push his feet into a pair of rubber boots.

'Is there a lot o' lambs?'

'No, just the twin Cheviots.'

'Is dat da new eens?'

'You mean, "Are they the new ones".'

'Are they the new ones?' parroted the boy.

Catherine sat back on her heels and looked at him, a sturdy child who spent less time with Kay and more with his grandfather. The aunts waylaid him; Laura scooped him up, Mina knitted for him, Jannie fed him. From all of them he heard the dialect; it was inevitable that he would copy it. What did it matter?

She stood up. 'Coat and hat now, it's none too warm.'

'Is Fly comin' wi' us?' said Robbie as a collie got out of its basket.

'Not now,' said Catherine, and to the dog, 'Go back.'

Separated from the barn and a little way from the house was a small stone-walled shed. A hurdle had been fastened across the doorway in place of a door. Telling Robbie to stay where he was, Catherine put the hurdle aside and went in. A white-faced ewe backed itself into a corner and stamped a foot at her. As it turned its head to look at the lambs by its side its curved Roman nose was only too plain to see. Speaking softly Catherine bent down to pick up one of the lambs. It was a male, bigger of the two and a good weight.

'Look, Robbie,' she said as she held it up to show him, 'isn't he a beauty?'

'Is that the champion?' said the boy, touching the lamb's tightly curled coat.

'I don't know, too soon to tell,' said Catherine. She put the lamb down and caught the other one, knowing it was a female. Both lambs had been born the previous day and though Daa thought it unnecessary she had put them in the shed to let them bond and to protect them from what might have been a cold wet night. It hadn't rained and the day was fine so there was no need to keep them confined.

'Come here, Robbie, help me send them out.' She lifted the little boy to safety and carrying him sent the ewe and lambs out into the park. Away they went, the lambs bouncing along beside their mother, the ewe bleating anxiously as she ran with them. Robbie laughed and clapped his hands while Catherine stood for a moment to watch them.

When the flurry of lambing was over it was time to cast peat. Catherine put a flask of milk and a packet of sandwiches in a bag and, taking Robbie by the hand, set off to climb the hill to the moor. They made slow progress, the hill was steep, the child soon tired so she picked him up and carried him astride her shoulders. The going was easier then and soon they were heading toward the peat banks. She set Robbie down. 'Don't wander off, stay close by me,' she said.

She picked up the tushkar and began to cut. As she cast her peat she constantly raised her eyes to see what her child was doing and called him back when she thought he was straying too far. It had really not been a good idea to bring him; her attention was not on her work but divided between it and him. She drove the blade of the tushkar into the peat and climbed out of the bank.

'Come here, Robbie,' she said, 'let's have a drink and something to eat.' As they sat side by side she poured milk for him and they ate the sandwiches.

'Tell me a story, Mam,' said Robbie.

With her arm round him the little boy leaned close to her and Catherine began with the age-old, 'Once upon a time …'

Climbing the hill and running around while Catherine had been working had tired the boy. When his head drooped and he no longer responded to what she was saying she folded the lunch bag for a pillow and laid him down to sleep. Looking down at him, at his dark hair, at the long dark eyelashes lying on his cheek and could see the resemblance to his father.

The wind whispered through the grass, skylarks sang curlews and whimbrels warbled and the sea rumbled at the foot of the cliffs. Catherine looked around; at the greens and blood-red of moss, yellow tormentil, blues and greys of the sea, black of peat and tan, brown and white of the native sheep. Later the hills would be covered in the pinks, mauves and purple of heather. The same colours that were woven into the Fair Isle-patterned garments that Jannie and her sisters made.

Cutting peat was hard work, but with all the outdoor work she had been doing Catherine was very fit. She had only cut half her bank, there was much more to do, but she would leave Robbie with someone else next time. The sound of someone coming made her look round and she saw Norrie Williams.

'I saw you here and wondered why you weren't working,' he said. 'Now I can see why? How have you been?' He sat down. 'You're lookin' well. I hear you're breedin good sheep.'

'You should come and have a look at them. I haven't seen you for ages.'

'That's because you're always working when I've been over.'

'Well, I do have a lot to do.'

'Hi Catherine,' shouted Billie, striding toward them.

Catherine pointed down at Robbie, then put a finger to her lips and waved a hand to indicate he should be quiet. Billie nodded.

'What are you doing here, Norrie Williams?' asked Billie. 'Do you not have to cut peat?

'Yes, and so have you.'

Catherine looked from one to the other. They were both men, for no longer could Billie be called a boy; at twenty he had filled out and become strong and muscular. The down that had been on his chin at sixteen was now stubble.

'How's your love life, Billie?' said Norrie, lying back and supporting himself on one elbow.

Billie kicked at a turf. 'None o' your business,' he said.

'Ah … so you fancy a lass,' teased Norrie.

'I told you,' protested Billie as a faint flush of red spread up his face.

'Leave him alone, Norrie,' said Catherine.

'No, he has a lass and I want to know who she is.'

'I'm not telling you,' said Billie. He sounded annoyed.

'Ah … she must be awful nice then, if you won't tell us.' Norrie lay on his back and laughed. 'I'm telling you, Catherine, he's only waiting for the dark nights so he can have his way wi' her.'

Blushing now to the roots of his hair Billie spat, 'I'm not going to stay here and listen to you.' Telling Catherine he would see her some other time he turned round and stalked away.

'Norrie!' exclaimed Catherine as she watched a crestfallen Billie making his way across the moor. 'That was very unkind of you; you've upset him.'

Norrie laughed. 'It's you he fancies,' he said. 'Did you not know?'

Forgetting the sleeping child, her voice raised, Catherine said, 'I never heard anything so ridiculous.' At that Robbie began to stir. 'Now look what you've made me do,' she said. She smiled when Robbie opened his eyes and looked at her, gathered the still sleepy child into her arms. 'Say hello to your godfather, Robbie,' she said, then to Norrie, 'I don't know why I asked you to be that. You haven't been to see us more than a couple of times since he was born.'

Norrie sat up. 'I ... didn't want to be talked about, you being ... well ... wi' your Robbie not so long away. I would come along just to see you, if you'd let me,' he said.

Conscious of the man who looked at her, at his handsome face and the look in his eyes, Catherine clutched at the child in her arms, felt her heart begin to pound. She bent her head and put her lips to the dark hair of the little boy's head, let seconds tick by before she looked up at Norrie. 'I think I'd like that,' she said.

TWENTY TWO

I N SPRING CATHERINE searched the moor for newborn lambs. The hill sheep lambed easy and rarely needed assistance, but sometimes she was able to save a lamb from the scavenging birds that would peck out its eyes and kill it. She was thankful there were no foxes who would wreak havoc and kill for the sake of killing, but there were still crows, ravens and black-backed gulls. It saddened her to think that the hill sheep had so little protection. One day she would fence more land so that she could keep the ewes closer to home and make it easier to keep an eye on them

She loved being on the hill, liked to think that every rock and crevice was familiar to her, but knew they weren't. It was a dangerous place to go alone; weather could change rapidly, hot sunshine give way in minutes to a fog that Daa called 'the haar' that crept in off the sea to enfold everything in a cold wet blanket. The hill was wide open, there were no fences to mark boundaries and the sheep that roamed there were not only from the Deepdale crofts. Other crofters ran hill sheep too.

'You don't need to come wi' us to walk the hill,' Daa said to Catherine, when a day had been agreed. 'Come along when we have the sheep penned.'

With an eye on the clock Catherine hurried to finish her housework and put food ready to cook for the evening meal. She filled a flask with coffee made some sandwiches, put Robbie in a pushchair and set off for the communal pen where she hoped the sheep would be already gathered.

When she got there it was full of noisy ewes and lambs distressed at being herded together and, in the melee, fearful of being separated. Crofters and some wives were already in the midst of the animals identifying the lambs that belonged to them. A pram and two more pushchairs were parked in a safe spot beside some vans and a car. Catherine put her pushchair with the others, let Robbie out to play and went to join Daa.

She had learned about the way the lambs were marked by cutting patterns in the ears: lug marks they were called, with strange names like 'a bit afore', 'a shear', 'a rit', 'a fedder'. Squeamish about nothing else, she had to admit that she couldn't bring herself to take the knife to them so she held the animals to let Daa do the cutting. Sweating with the exertion of handling extremely lively sheep, her clothes well oiled with lanolin from their fleece, she was glad when it was time to stop for a drink and a bite to eat. She called Robbie to join them and she and Daa sat by the wall of the pens and opened their lunch bags.

Relaxing for a few minutes before going back to work Catherine closed her eyes and leaned back. A strong pungent odour of sheep filled the air. Some of it came from her clothes. She could feel her lanolin-soaked trousers sticking to her legs. Beside her Daa was getting up. She opened her eyes and was about to do the same when a young woman spoke to her.

'Hullo, aren't you the wife from Deepdale?'

'Yes,' said Catherine, 'that's where I live.'

'I bide just over the hill.' The girl spoke with a broad Scottish accent. 'Do you like it here?' She was wearing trousers and a coat that was none too clean.

'Yes, I do.' What did this person want?

'Takes a bit of getting used to for folk from south, doesn't it? I'm surprised you didn't go back home after you lost your man.'

'I had no intention of doing that,' said Catherine. She stood up, picked up her lunch bag and put it on the seat of the pushchair.

'Yea, but you do need a man about the place, don't you?'

As she straightened up Catherine turned to the stranger and looked her up and down. 'Where are you from?' she asked, 'and what brought you here?'

'Me? Oh, um. I'm from Glasgow.'

'And do you like Shetland? Come here, Robbie,' said Catherine. She took out her handkerchief and wiped a spot of jam from the corner of his mouth. 'Now go and play, darling.' She smiled as she watched him go. 'Now,' she said, as she looked at the young woman, 'I have to go back to work. I don't know who you are, but you've made it quite clear that there's something you want to say, so what is it?'

'I'm Sheila McKechnie,' said the girl. 'You'd better remember that.' Her voice was sharp now. 'You have to know who I am because you wouldn't want to cross me, now would you?'

'Really? And why would that be?'

'I have a boyfriend. You might know him, his auntie lives by you. Norrie's his name.' Sheila lifted her lips in a brief but none too friendly smile. 'I know he's been going over to see her a lot lately and I thought you ought to know he's not available … just in case you had any ideas.'

So that was it. Why, if he already had a girlfriend, had Norrie Williams been calling on her? For some absurd reason Catherine's heart turned over, she had begun to look forward to his visits, begun to have feelings for him, begun to think there was to be some happiness in her future after all. Now this girl was telling her that Norrie was deceiving her. Were all Shetland men strangers to the truth? Turning her back on the girl as she went to join Daa, she said, 'You need have no fears on that score.'

'I'm glad to hear it,' said Sheila.

'Is anything the matter?' asked Daa when they were back at work, seeing that Catherine lacked concentration and had problems holding the sheep.

'No, not at all,' she said, but he could see she had something on her mind.

'Could I leave Robbie with you, Kay, while I go up to stack some peat?'

'Of course you can.' Kay's close companionship with Catherine had taught her how to read the other's moods. She could see that something was troubling the girl, but refrained from asking what it was. She would hear about it in good time. 'You know I'm only too happy to have him.'

Mina and Laura were sitting outside their house. The evening was cool, but it was still warm and pleasant enough to sit in a sheltered spot. They were both knitting. As Catherine passed by they asked how she was getting on with her sheep. 'I'm told you have some good ones,' said Mina.

'Yes, I have, but I hope to have some better ones yet.'

Mina nodded her head; Laura smiled and said nothing.

Jannie sat on a chair just inside her door, she too was knitting. She looked up as Catherine drew level with her. 'Where are you going? Where's the bairn?'

'I'm going to stack peat and I left him with Kay.'

'Not to meet Norrie?'

Not wanting to stop and talk, Catherine had been gradually edging past Jannie, but now she stopped. 'What do you mean by that?'

'I thought he was coming to see you.'

'And what if he was?' Catherine wanted to say it was none of her business, but since Robbie's birth she felt she had to try to build some bridges and being antagonistic wouldn't help.

'Your man is not so long away,' said Jannie.

'It's been four years and not four weeks in case you hadn't noticed,' said Catherine. 'You're not thinking I should spend the rest of my life alone are you?'

'No no.' Jannie bent her head and picked up her work.

'Because,' said Catherine, 'if I did decide to take up with someone else it would be my decision and,' she had to say it, 'nothing to do with you. But I can assure you I have no one in mind.'

'Dinna take on so,' said Jannie. 'I was just askin'.'

'Well, please don't.'

As she plodded up the hill Catherine mulled over what Sheila McKechnie had said. Why had Norrie led her to believe he had feelings for her? If what Sheila said was true why had he made a point of coming to see her and not just his aunt?

When she reached her peat bank she began to stack the dry slabs, build them up so they would be safe against unexpected rain. The monotony of the job, the sounds all round her, the wind and the surge of the sea were soothing and made her forget her troubles. It was still early when she'd finished building the stack and, not wanting to go back to the valley, she walked on across the moor. Undecided whether to climb the hill or go and look in the empty house she decided to climb. At first the vegetation was of rough grass and moss but the higher she went the sparser it became. Partly buried granite boulders stuck out of the ground, the land between them supporting nothing but thin wiry grass.

Someone was calling her name. She looked back and saw Billie. He waved and beckoned to her. She hesitated. She had really wanted to go further up the hill … another time, perhaps? She began to retrace her steps.

'What are you doing here?' she said.

'I was to stack peat. I would have if you hadn't been here. It's a fine day.'

'It is,' said Catherine. 'I love it here when the weather's like this, it's so peaceful.' She sat on the ground, drew up her knees and wrapped her arms round them. 'Don't you think so?'

'I don't have time to think o' that. I have to work.' Billie sat down too, then stretched out to lie flat on his back, hands behind his head. 'There's an awful lot of sky when you look at it this way,' he said. 'And there's a lot of other worlds out there, and I've not see this one yet.' Billie turned on his side and propped himself on one elbow. 'Do you think …? No, it doesn't matter.'

'What's the problem, Billie? Were you thinking about travelling?'

'Ay, but I've put it from my mind, there's folk I wouldn't want to leave.'

'Oh?' she turned to look at him. 'Would that be the lass you're sweet on?'

'Could be.'

'And would I know her, Billie?'

Billie was busy pulling up blades of grass and wouldn't look at her. 'I wouldn't like to leave you, Catherine,' he said raising his head to look at her. 'You're different, not like the Shetland lasses. I'm awful fond o' you and I think you need me …' He hesitated, then added hastily, 'with the sheep and all.'

He hadn't answered her question directly, but in a roundabout way he had. Norrie had winked and said, "I've heard," when she said Billy came over often and Billie had blushed when Norrie teased him; he had refused to confirm that he had a girlfriend. Then Norrie had said, "It's you." She looked away out to sea.

'I would miss you if you went away,' she said. But not as much as you would like me too, she thought.

'You have to be careful who you go with, Catherine,' said Billie. 'There's a lot would like to be with you and not just for your looks.'

'Really? Well, I'm sure I don't know who they are.'

Billie was sitting up now. 'That Norrie Williams is one for a start.'

'No, he isn't, he's got a girlfriend. Somebody called Sheila McKechnie told me she was his girl and warned me off.'

'She would, she's awful limmer that one. You can't trust her.'

'Limmer? What does that mean? I wish you'd speak English, Billie, I know you can,' said Catherine.

He laughed. 'You're in Shetland, you have to learn to speak like us.'

'I'll never be able to do that. Tell me, would you really like to travel?'

She had to steer the conversation away from what she thought he was really thinking about. Though he had grown to man's stature he was still only twenty and she had to block any attempt by him even to begin to declare his feelings; she had to avoid being alone with him.

'I would,' he said. 'I look at the sea and wonder what's beyond. A lot of folk emigrate, you know.'

'But you wouldn't want to do that, would you?' she asked.

'No, I can't, it would break Mam's heart. But I'd like to have a look at another twartree.' He grinned. 'Two or three places.'

'That's easy enough, isn't it? You just pack a bag, buy a ticket and get on the boat. Take enough money to buy you a bed for the night and there you are. And if you like it and want to stay you get a job … come home when you're ready.'

'I couldn't.'

'If you're meant to go off the island the opportunity will come when you least expect it,' said Catherine. 'I suppose you've got some savings, haven't you? From what I've gathered most Shetlanders have got a long stocking.'

'Now you're speaking in riddles.' Billie laughed.

'Well, you know what I mean.' Catherine got up. 'I'd better go; the midges are beginning to bite. I'll see you again. Bye now.'

'Bye, Catherine.'

TWENTY THREE

'I HAVE A bone to pick with you,' said Catherine the next time Norrie walked through her door. Sewing-box in front of her, she sat at the table darning socks.

'Ay, and what's that?'

'Why are you visiting and making me think you might have feelings for me when you already have a girlfriend?'

'Where on earth did you get that idea?'

'Sheila McKechnie,' said Catherine. 'Does the name ring any bells? It should, because she told me in no uncertain terms that you were not available.'

'*That* one? You should not have believed her.'

'Why not? She seemed very sure of herself'

Norrie was sitting opposite Catherine. 'I can assure you she means nothing to me at all,' he said. 'I felt sorry for the lass when she came here first. She didn't know anybody and I took her to the dances a few times. I've told her I'm not for her and to find someone else, but she'll not leave me alone.'

Catherine continued to darn, weaving her needle in and out as she listened. 'Do you expect me to believe you?' she said when Norrie stopped talking.

'I wouldn't lie to you.'

"I do not want to be mixed up in a triangle,' said Catherine. 'That girl was very threatening, so you'd better sort it out.' She stuck the needle into a ball of wool and folded the sock she had been darning together with its partner.

'What good would it do me to deceive you? I would be the loser,' said Norrie, 'and I've no intention of being that.'

'Well, it's up to you then, isn't it?'

'Why won't you believe me?' asked Norrie.

'I would like to, but please just do as I say, will you?' Catherine picked up another sock, pulled it over her hand and looked for the places that needed darning. She bent her head, hoping that Norrie wouldn't see the silly tears that wanted to fill her eyes. Why did being angry make her cry?

'Well,' said Norrie, 'I don't know what I'm going to do short of buying the girl a ticket and putting her on the boat, because I've tried everything else. She can't object to me coming to see my godson and neither can you.'

'No that's true. Not that you come very often.'

'I do have a job to go to and a croft to run.'

Catherine broke off a length of wool, threaded her needle, began to darn again, hesitated, then put it all down. 'Be completely honest with me. Is there anything between you?'

'Nothing at all. If there was I would not be here.'

'I don't want that girl to accost me again, so make her understand.'

'I will.'

She looked at him and wanted to be sure of him, but thought of the confident way Sheila had spoken. A sudden twinge of jealousy made her realize that she felt more for him than she had thought. 'You'll have to prove what you say,' she said. 'You can see Robbie, but don't think you're coming to see me.'

'You're being too hard.'

Catherine folded the socks together and put wool, needle and scissors in the box. 'I have no way of knowing the truth,' she said. Norrie did not reply and for a few moments there was silence between them. 'Aren't you going to leave?' said Catherine.

'Where's the bairn?' asked Norrie. 'Couldn't we take him to the beach?'

'It's nearly his bedtime,' said Catherine.

'I would like to see him.'

Catherine hesitated. 'Well, as you're here now, all right,' she said.

Robbie was lying on the hearth rug playing with his toys when they went to Kay's to fetch him; he looked up at his mother then went on pushing a toy car around. Kay lay back in a chair, her eyes closed; she didn't move when they went in, seemed not to hear them or know they were there. Catherine thought it unusual for her friend to be sitting so still and was concerned; she went swiftly to her side. 'Kay, are you all right?' she asked.

Kay opened her eyes and with a blank stare looked at Catherine, then she smiled. 'Yes, I'm all right,' she said. 'I was miles away and I was dreaming.'

'Is it too much for you having Robbie?' asked Catherine.

'No, no, I love to have him, he's no trouble.'

'Well, if you're sure. Norrie and I were just going to take him down to the beach before he goes to bed.'

'That's a good idea, he'll settle to sleep more readily afterwards.' Kay started to rise from her chair.

'You don't have to get up,' said Catherine.

'I'll be back in to see you,' said Norrie, 'you take it easy, Auntie.'

It had taken Catherine a long time before she could look at the sea without hating it and even longer before she could bring herself to walk beside the bay from which her husband had sailed away never to come back. She had hated it then. But how long can you hold on to hate? To her mind had come the tales told her of the many fishing disasters when when women lost sons as well as husbands and whole families were devastated. Did they hate the sea? Or did they accept that their loss was the price to pay for being married to fishermen? But time does pass. Catherine had accepted her lot and turned her mind to being glad she had been loved and to have her son as proof.

When they reached the beach she took Robbie's shoes and socks off so he could run barefoot and race the waves as they broke and dropped to run across the sand. She took off her own shoes, took Robbie by the hand and went with him into the shallows. When a wave crashed onto the beach and rushed towards them she ran with him and swept him up when they were overtaken. Again and again they walked into the sea then turned to run, laughing, ahead of the foaming water.

Norrie stood to watch them and love for the plucky young woman, who defied dislike and prejudice and who battled against the odds to fulfil her husband's dream, welled up in his heart. One day he might share in the joy and laughter he was witnessing now. But first he had to deal with Sheila.

'Are you not going to join us, Norrie?' said Catherine.

'No, I'm happy watching you.'

'I canna run any more,' said Robbie.

'Will I carry you?' said Norrie, and when the little boy held up his arms he picked him up and hoisted him on to his shoulders.

'It's time for his bed,' said Catherine. 'We'll go home now.' Swinging her shoes by their laces she walked barefoot beside them.

'Do I get a cup of tea or are you just going to throw me out?' said Norrie.

'You do and you can make it while I put Robbie to bed,' said Catherine. Norrie had it ready when she came to tell him the little lad was sound asleep.

Their talk as they sat at the table and drank tea was of sheep and the coming agricultural show. She told him she was looking forward to it as it would be the first time she'd had an animal to enter. When tea cups were empty, Catherine stood up and when Norrie said he was leaving she went with him to the door.

'Don't forget to go in and see Kay,' she said.

Suddenly Norrie's arms were around her and he was holding her very close. Being held by a pair of strong arms was something that had been absent from Catherine's life for a long time; it was something she didn't want to stop, so she didn't resist.

'Don't turn me away, Catherine. I haven't deceived you,' whispered Norrie, his lips in her hair. 'Don't turn me away.' Then he put a kiss on her forehead, let her go and was out of the door and gone.

TWENTY FOUR

CATHERINE'S PROGRESS IN trying to bring Robbie's dream to fruition was not easy. The animals she had thought to be such gentle creatures she found to be anything but. Some were stupid, some nervous, some aggressive, others plain difficult and all subject to a host of ailments. But with Daa's help she soldiered on.

From the previous year's crop of lambs she had chosen two males which she had not had castrated, hoping that one would be worthy of a prize. They had both developed into fine animals, but she favoured one in particular and in order to gentle it had put it on a tether. By tending, feeding it and handling it, it had become easy to manage. It was tethered on the back green behind her house and was the animal she had decided to put in the show. Every day, whatever else she had to do and whatever time of day it was, she slipped it from its tether and, with a lead rope fastened to its collar, took it for a walk. After a while, Noble, for that's what she decided to call him after Kay had said what a noble beast he was, became used to being led about. He took no notice at all when Mina and Laura came out to watch or when Robbie, held fast by Kay, jumped up and down. Daa told her she was a clever girl to make the ram so docile and manageable.

'You don't think I'm wasting my time then?' she said.

'Making a ram easy to handle is never a waste of time,' said Daa. 'They can be pig-headed when they want, and aggressive.'

Billie laughed when Catherine told him what she'd been doing. 'They're powerful beasts and you'd never handle him if he got nasty,' he said. 'How are you going to get him to the show?'

'I don't know yet,' said Catherine. 'I've got to get someone to help me, I can't walk him all the way and I don't want to borrow Daa's pony cart.'

'I can take him,' said Billie. 'I've bought a van and I'd like to help you.'

With her rising excitement at how well the ram was shaping up, at how it might fare in the coming show and now the problem of how to get him there being solved, Catherine forgot her decision to keep Billie at a distance. She threw her arms round his neck and kissed him. 'Oh, Billie, you are a darling,' she cried.

Billie gasped and clutched her to him. 'You too, Catherine …'

With his face so close to hers Catherine saw the shock on it. 'Stop, stop,' she cried. 'Don't say any more. ' Pushing him from her she turned away. 'Um … ah … I'm sorry, Billie, I'm sorry. Thank you for coming over, but I've got to get on now, can't leave Robbie with Kay too long … she hasn't been too well … um.' She talked too fast and suddenly seemed to run out of words.

Billie took hold one of her hands, 'It's all right, Catherine, I've got to go. I'll see you again.' Then he was off, running as he went.

Catherine stamped her foot in annoyance at having forgotten her resolve not to encourage him. What can of worms had she opened now?

Irritation with herself carried on to evening and to little Robbie. Despite his protests she bundled him off to bed much earlier than his usual time.

Catherine rose very early on show day. She slid out of bed, picked up her clothes and crept out of the bedroom. In the kitchen she dressed, then picked up a bag she had put ready the night before. Quietly she lifted the latch, opened the door and went out to begin working on Noble. She lifted his feet to see that they were sound; there was no need, for she had looked at them regularly ever since she had decided to enter him in the show. Next she saw to his fleece, combed and trimmed it until, standing back and looking at him from every angle, his outline was as perfect as she could make it. She could do no more; final primping would have to be done at the show. She patted the top of his hard white head. 'Do your best for me, Noble,' she said. 'Just do your best.' Then she left him to go and wake Robbie and get their breakfast.

Billie arrived before they'd finished eating. 'Have you had anything to eat?' she asked and when he said no she made him sit and take a bowl of porridge. 'You know it's going to be a long day. What on earth were you thinking of?'

'I thought you might be waiting for me.'

Equipped with a small bag of feed, a comb, clippers and a clean jacket for her, she was ready at last. Billie had driven down the track and his van now stood outside Catherine's house.

'I've put some straw in the van to keep him clean,' he said as

Catherine fastened a lead rope to the ram's halter and undid the tether.

'Do you think he might panic?' said Catherine. 'Perhaps we should have put him in before this to see how he reacted.'

'He'll be all right,' said Billie. 'There's a place we can tie him.'

The back doors of the van were open. With Billie on one side and Catherine on the other they lifted Noble's front feet into it. Then, clasping hands behind his rump, with one heave they pushed him in. Billie tied the end of the rope to a ring set in the floor, then shut the doors.

'Did you put your stuff in?' he asked. Catherine said she had. 'Get in then and we'll go.'

'I'm not getting in there until you get to the top of the hill,' said Catherine. 'I ... I ... It's too steep. I'll walk.'

Billie grinned. 'You're chicken,' he said.

'Chicken or not, I'll join you at the top.'

Hoping the ram wouldn't panic Catherine crossed her fingers. Kay looked out and wished her luck, the aunts too. Jannie stood at her door, nodding her head, and said, 'Hope you do well.' Catherine thanked her, but her attention was on Billie's van and the stones that were flying out from under its tyres as he drove up the hill. Gasping for breath as she puffed up the last few yards of track she was relieved to see Billie looking for her. 'No bother at all,' he said when she asked how the ram had behaved. 'You'd think he did it all the time.'

'Let's hope he's as good when we have to get him in his pen,' she said. The sky had clouded over and the day had become dull. 'Is it going to rain?'

'I wouldn't think it,' said Billie.

'Better for the animals if it's not too hot, but I don't want to see rain.'

'Go and find your pen number,' Billie said when they'd driven into the show ground. Pen number allocated, the pen was found and the ram installed.

'I hope you're not as nervous as I am, Noble,' Catherine said as she gave him a last look over. She'd told Billie off for not eating breakfast but had hardly eaten anything herself; now her stomach rumbled and she was afraid she was going to be sick. She stood by the pen and leaned on the top rail.

'Are you all right?' asked Billie.

'No,' moaned Catherine. 'I feel sick.'

'You cannot be sick here.'

'It's all right, it's my nerves; I just *feel* sick, that's all. What am I doing, thinking I can compete with men who've been working with sheep all their lives? They'll look at me and think I'm nothing but an upstart.'

'No, no,' said Billie, putting a hand on her shoulder. 'Folk like you and if you think none of them ken what you're doing then you're wrong. They ken fine.'

Catherine rested her head on her arms. 'I still feel sick,' she said.

'We have to go home now,' said Billie. 'The judges will be comin' round to do their work. We'll come back later.'

At home, unable to settle to anything while she waited for Billy to come back and fetch her, Catherine fussed about. She picked up things and put them down; decided to put something ready for tea, then remembered Kay was going to do it. She was impatient with Robbie so Kay said she would keep him with her and would bring him to the show on the bus. Able to contain herself no longer, she walked up out of the valley to stand at the side of the road and wait for Billie. And there he was at last.

'I am so nervous,' she said as she got in the van.

'You don't need to be, I think you have a fine animal,' said Billie.

The showground was already full of people, with more queuing at the gate to get in. Cattle and sheep were in pens, chickens, ducks and geese in cages. Horses had been allocated a portion of the field to themselves and young riders there were milling around. Over the clamour of animal noises, voices and laughter, was the booming voice of a man with a loudhailer.

'Oh, Billie, I can't wait to see if I've got anything,' said Catherine when the van had been parked and they were making their way to the sheep pens. As they went along the line they looked at the rosettes already on the pens of winners.

'Do we have one?' asked Catherine as they got closer to the pen Noble was in. Billie took Catherine's arm and stopped her, then put a hand over her eyes.

'Yeh, but you're not going to look till we get to it.'

'What colour is it?'

'I'm not telling.'

Blinded by Billie's big hand Catherine stumbled along beside him until he brought her to a halt and took his hand from her eyes.

'We've got one … it's a second … oh!' cried Catherine. She didn't wait to open the gate to the pen but climbed up and over, dropped down into it and put her arms round the ram's neck. 'You lovely thing,' she said.

'You've done well,' said Billie, 'I didn't think you'd do so well as that.'

'Neither did I,' said Catherine, 'but we'll do better next year.'

They looked at the cattle, then at the ponies and workhorses. They peered into pens of chickens, ducks and geese. There were pets too: dogs and cats, goats and all kinds of furry little animals, rabbits and hamsters. In the village hall they marvelled over delicate pieces of lacy knitting, jumpers in Fair Isle, socks, gloves, hats and fine examples of sewing and embroidery too. They strolled along beside trestle-tables and drooled over fancy cakes, jam and pickles.

'I don't know how people find time to do all this,' said Catherine.

'Well, but they do,' said Billie.

And then they found Kay and Robbie. Robbie had only been interested in the ponies and now he asked his mother if he could have one.

'Please, Mam?' he said.

'Well, I don't know,' said Catherine. 'Maybe next year.'

Robbie was not happy with that and as the afternoon wore on he dragged his feet and grizzled, so Kay begged a lift and took him home.

'You'll let me take you to the dance tonight, won't you?' said Billie. 'You did promise once, remember?'

'So I did,' said Catherine.

The festive air of show day carried on into the evening and the dance, which was always held in the Broonieswick village hall after the show. Billie said Catherine should be there and as it had been such a long time since she had been dancing she had agreed. And now she needed something to wear. Her dresses, the ones she had packed and brought with her all those years ago, were lying unworn, folded and creased in the bottom of a drawer. Anxiously she wondered if they would still fit, but, to her delight when she tried them on they did.

If she hurried there was time for a quick bath. She made up the fire and while water was heating put the flat iron on to heat too. The excitement of the day was still with her and when she got out of her bath and towelled herself dry she became aware of how well her body was toned. It was a body that needed love, but she had no husband now and her thoughts turned to Norrie. One day ...

The clock struck the hour. She had to hurry or she would not be ready in time and Billie would come rattling down the track. She stood and ironed the dress she had chosen and left it to cool while she combed her hair, powdered her face and put on a dab of lipstick. Dressed and carrying her dancing shoes she walked up to the road. Billie was there waiting for her.

TWENTY FIVE

I N THE CLOAKROOM Catherine hung up her coat and changed her shoes. She looked in a mirror, decided she looked all right and went to join Billie. They sat out the first two dances. Catherine said she didn't know how to do them, but when a waltz was announced she stepped on to the floor with him.

'I see the McKechnie lass here,' said Billie.

'Where?' gasped Catherine. 'Oh. It looks as though she's with a lad.'

'Ay, I'd say she is.'

'Hello, I'm told you did well today.' It was Norrie.

'Yes,' she said. 'Why weren't you there?'

'Had to go to work, couldn't get time off. You're looking awful pretty.'

Conscious that Norrie had only ever seen her in her working clothes, Catherine blushed. 'Thank you,' she said. 'Have you sorted out that problem?'

'I've had words,' said Norrie. 'It's done with. Can I see you now?'

'As long as you're sure, I don't see why not.'

When the music started again he slid an arm round her waist and despite her saying she couldn't do the Shetland dances they were on the floor and he was saying of course she could. He led her through the steps. When she stumbled he held her, and being wrapped in a pair of strong arms filled her with longing. When the dance was over he smiled and held her longer than was really necessary.

Billie scowled when Norrie took her up for dance after dance. Catherine told him she was sorry, said she wouldn't dance with Norrie again. At the interval she left the dance floor and went up the stairs to the cloakroom. At the wash basin she was splashing cold water on her face when she heard someone come in.

'I told you to stay away from him,' snarled Sheila McKechnie. 'But I saw you in there. Couldn't keep your hands off him, could you?'

Catherine mopped her face. 'We were only dancing,' she said.

'Oh yes,' sneered Sheila, 'you were only dancing. It was more than that from what I saw. I'm telling you, you'd better watch your back.'

'I already told him I wasn't going to see him if he was with you, but he told me only minutes ago that you and he were finished.'

'Oh, he did, did he? Well, that's what he might think. I'm not going to warn you again. Have you got that?'

'And I'm telling you,' said Catherine, 'you can take a running jump. I don't want what belongs to somebody else, but if he's free he's fair game.'

Sheila jumped at Catherine and grabbed a handful of her hair. She gripped it tight and, while Catherine clutched and scratched in an attempt to make the girl let go, made her run in circles. Sheila was strong. 'This is nothing to what I'll do to you if I see you dancing with him again,' she said. 'You keep your hands off him.' Viciously she twisted her hands in Catherine's hair: twisted with such spite that Catherine wished her nails were long and sharp. She raked them down Sheila's arms anyway.

'Little hellcat,' screeched Sheila as Catherine's nails drew blood.

Catherine kicked out and was gratified with the thud as she made contact with Sheila's leg and heard the grunt of pain from her opponent.

'Stop it, stop it at once,' shouted the older of the two women who rushed in. 'Whatever are you doing?'

'None of your business,' shouted Sheila. 'Keep your nose out. I'm just putting her in the picture, OK?' Gathering force she swung Catherine round and round, then let go so quickly that Catherine staggered across the floor and crashed into the wall, her head snapping up to hit the wall with a loud crack. Winded from the collision, she sank to the floor. For a moment all went black. When she opened her eyes everything around her was fuzzy.

Sheila glared at the two women, then turned to Catherine and shook her fist at her. 'You haven't heard the last of me. I shall be around,' she said. Then, with a shrug of her shoulders she casually walked away.

'Are you all right?' fussed the women as they helped Catherine to her feet. 'Can we get you anything, fetch anyone?'

'What a nasty girl that one is.'

'She had no right to treat you like that. What was it all about?'

Shocked at the attack and feeling very dizzy, Catherine looked round her in a daze. 'Oh, nothing really,' she said, 'just a disagreement.' She was glad the women had come in, for if they hadn't she would have been at Sheila's mercy.

'Looked like more than that, to me.'

'You should report her to the police.'

Putting up a hand to run her fingers through her hair, Catherine winced when she touched the tender spot on her head where Sheila had almost pulled hair out by its roots. 'It's all right, I'll live,' she said. But she felt bruised and shaken, angry that she'd been caught off guard. Then, giving her head a shake, she said, 'I don't feel like dancing any more. I think I'll go home.' She took her coat from the peg and put it on, didn't bother to change her shoes and ran down the stairs to look for Billie. He was outside drinking beer out of a bottle.

'What's the matter?' he said when he saw her.

'Don't ask questions,' she said. 'Just take me home, please.'

'Home, you want to go home? There'll be lots more fun yet.'

'I think I've had enough fun for tonight.'

Though he questioned her as he drove she told him to shut up. He didn't stop to let her out at the top of the track but drove straight down. Catherine, thinking she'd had enough punishment for one night, clutched the handle of the door and shut her eyes.

Her door was never locked. She went straight in. At the table she felt for matches, found them and lit the lamp. She had been angry that Sheila had dared to attack her and anger had stayed with her all the way home, but now, having kept it at bay shock overcame her and she was trembling.

'Are you going to tell me what happened?' asked Billie.

'There's nothing to tell.'

'No? Then why did you want to leave the dance?'

'Leave me alone, Billie. I can't do the Shetland dances and I didn't want to stay. Thank you for taking me, but you can go home now.'

'I can see you're upset,' said Billie. 'Why, you're trembling. It was nothing to do with not being able to do the dances, was it? Tell me the truth.'

He stood over her and it was obvious he wouldn't give up until she'd told him. 'Oh, all right,' she said. 'Sheila McKechnie attacked me. I don't know what she would have done if someone hadn't come in and stopped her.'

'Attacked you? What for?' said Billie.

'She thinks I'm going out with Norrie and she says he's hers and she was just giving me a warning. She didn't have to be so violent,' said Catherine. Her eyes were filling with tears. 'Get the whisky, Billie, I need a dram.' Then she was crying and Billy was on his knees, looking up into her face.

'Don't weep, Catherine, I don't like to see that. I'll look after you; you don't have to worry about her or Norrie.' He smiled at her and with tears coursing down her cheeks she stared at him. 'I've loved you for a long time, Catherine,' he said, his voice gentle. 'Marry me, Catherine. I'll look after you and little Robbie.'

'Oh Billie, don't,' she cried.

The smile on Billie's face slid away. 'You need someone to care for you. I can do that. You don't have to struggle alone.'

'Stop it, stop it,' sobbed Catherine.

'Why? I want to look after you. Don't you love me? I thought you did … you kissed me and I thought you did. '

'No, you can't love me, Billie.' Catherine shrank back into the chair, away from him. 'I don't love you.' Slowly he let go of her hands. 'I do love you, but not in the way you would want me to.'

'What's going on?' shouted Norrie Williams as he burst in. 'Get up off your knees, Billie Robertson; you're making a damn fool of yourself'

'And what's it got to do with you?' said Catherine. She jumped up, sending Billie rolling on the floor. 'What do you mean by bursting in to my house like that? Have you never been taught to knock?'

'I was told you were set on and I wanted to see if you were all right.' One look at her tear-stained face told him she was not. 'Am I not allowed to do that?'

'Well, now you can see I am, so you can go.' She turned on Billie who was hauling himself to his feet, 'And you can go too, Billie,' she said.

'I can see you're not all right,' said Norrie. 'Who's been making you cry? If it's young Billie I'll skin him.'

'Well, it isn't,' said Catherine.

'It's not me she's in trouble over,' shouted Billie, 'it's you; it was that Scots lass that attacked her; she thinks you belong to her.'

'Well, she's wrong. I've told her enough times,' said Norrie.

Billie had balled his hands into fists, Norrie too; both looked ready to fight.

'Then you'd better tell her again.'

'I'm not going to; she's got no claim on me.' Norrie's nose was perilously close to Billie's.

'Then you'd better tell Catherine,' said Billie through clenched teeth.

'And who do you think you are to be tellin me…?'

'Stop it both of you,' shouted Catherine, 'and get out. I've had more than enough today without listening to you two. Go.'

The fact that Catherine was shouting at them made both men stop their arguing and stare at her.

'*Go go go,*' she screamed. They didn't move, but just stood and stared at her. 'And *don't come back … either of you … ever.*'

TWENTY SIX

WARM AUGUST AND cool September had given way to rain. It had been falling continuously for days on end. October crept in with muddy feet and each day when Catherine drew back her curtains and looked out of the window there was the same leaden sky, the same steadily falling rain drumming on the roof, running in little rivers down the hillside and filling bums to the brim. Her heart ached for Daa who, she knew, worried about his crops of oats and potatoes. If only the rain would stop and the wind would dry things up he could get them harvested.

A louring sky filled with rain-bearing clouds made the already dark nights of a winter closing in seem even darker. Winter was going to be a long one, it seemed, and for the first time since she had stepped off the boat that March morning so long ago Catherine had a desperate urge to get away.

What was there to stay for? After the night of the show, when Billie had declared his love for her and she had sent him away, he had disappeared. It was thought he'd gone away on the boat and Jannie had raved at her.

'You're an ill-favoured lass. Robbie should never have brought you here. It's been nothin' but trouble since he did. Go home … go home.'

'It's not my fault,' cried Catherine. 'I didn't tell him to go. What he does is nothing to do with me. He's a man and old enough to make his own decisions.'

But Jannie would not let up. 'You've been encouraging him; he never was over here so often till you came.'

'I'm not going to stand here and argue with you, Jannie; think what you like.' Catherine went back to her house and slammed shut the door.

Norrie stayed away. Once or twice she had seen him when he visited Kay and she happened to be there. He didn't ask her out again. She missed him. She missed him now as rain wept on the window. Missed him and his nonsense and the way he made her laugh, missed the sound of the fiddle and the lilting strains of a slow waltz he played: a melody that always touched a chord in her heart. Never during her struggle to make good and be accepted had she felt so alone.

'Why did you have to be taken from me, Robbie?' she cried. She was sitting by the fire and, burying her face in her hands she gave way and wept.

'What's the matter, Mam?' said little Robbie, taking Catherine's hands in his and pulling them away from her face. 'Are you all right?'

'Oh, Robbie, it's just a little sadness, but I'll be all right.' She pulled the boy on to her lap and wrapped her arms round him; wiped some of the tears away with her hand and let the others dry on her face. 'I was missing your daddy.'

'Where is my daddy?'

Catherine, whose cheek was resting on the little boy's head, moved him away and leaned back so she could look at him. He was nearly five years old and for the first time he had asked about his father. It was time she told him.

'Cuddle up then and I'll tell you,' she said. She described the man who had walked into her life, whose quiet presence lulled her after stressful days, who had brought her to Shetland and to Deepdale. Told how he had gone out to fish for lobsters and how he had drowned and that, after she had lost him, she knew she was going to have a baby. 'And that baby is you,' she said.

The little boy was silent for a moment or two. 'Do you have a daa?' he asked and when she said, yes, 'Where is he?'

'He lives in England. You have another grandma and grandpa and aunts and an uncle and lots of cousins too.'

It took some time for the little boy to accept this. 'Where's England?'

England, Southampton, home. Was her mother still fussing over meals? Had everybody got enough? Would they like some more? Was her sister still trying to ape the latest fashions? Was her father still smoking his pipe while he read the paper? And were the city-centre shops, where anything your heart desired could be bought and wouldn't have to be ordered and waited for, alive with the hustle and bustle of eager shoppers? Days would still be warm. Suddenly home seemed very attractive.

'I think it's time we had a holiday,' said Catherine. 'How would you like to meet your other relations? Don't answer that; I've decided. We shall go.'

*

Bags packed and tickets in her handbag, Catherine looked at the clock. Twenty minutes yet before Billie's father had promised to pick them up and take them to the boat. There was time to say goodbye to her friend.

Kay was sitting in a chair; her hands were idle, her knitting on her lap.

'We'll be off soon,' said Catherine. 'Just come to say goodbye.'

Kay looked up. 'Never say goodbye, my dear, it's so final. Have a safe journey and give my love to England. I don't suppose I'll ever see it again. And you,' she looked at little Robbie, 'bring me back a stick of rock, will you?'

'You look tired, Kay,' said Catherine. 'Are you all right?'

'As much as I ever will be,' said Kay. 'I'm getting old; in fact I'm old already. Can't complain, I've had a good life and old age comes to us all if we're lucky. Don't worry about me, just come back safe, this valley needs you.'

Catherine kissed the old lady and Kay leaned forward to put a kiss on Robbie's forehead. 'Don't forget my stick of rock; I haven't had one for ages. Have a lovely time and tell me all about it when you come home. Now go, I can hear Bobbie Robertson tooting his horn.'

Billie's father had already put Catherine's luggage in the back of his van, all she had to do was shut the door of her house. She wouldn't lock it for Kay had the key and would look after it while they were away.

'Have you had any news of Billie?' she asked when they were on the road.

'Never a word.'

'Which is not bad,' she said. 'If he'd come to grief you'd have heard.'

'I would hope so,' said Bobbie.

'I'm a bit worried about Kay,' said Catherine, 'she doesn't look well. Do you ever see Norrie Williams in your travels?'

'Ay, now and then.'

'When you do would you ask him if he would look in on her?'

'I'll do that,' said Bobbie, and Catherine knew he would.

The boat trip was passable; Catherine was thankful that it was made at night and that she and Robbie were able to sleep. For her the journey on the train to London seemed endless, the follow-on to Southampton bearable. But used to the bare hills of Shetland, the little boy was fascinated by the countryside they were flying through and drank in the sight of green fields, trees and hedgerows. Catherine felt at home with the banging of train doors, passengers coming and going, the smell of a station, the hiss of steam, the clank of an engine, the guard's whistle and the click-clack of wheels over points.

By the time they reached Southampton she was tired and Robbie exhausted. He'd been asleep, she had wakened him and he clung to her while she looked out to see who had come to meet them. Her father and youngest sister were there. They saw her and waved and her father came aboard to greet her. 'It's been a long time,' he said as he hugged her. Then, looking at Robbie, he said, 'And who's this?'

'Robbie, say hello to your granddad,' said Catherine.

'He's no my granda,' said Robbie, clinging to his mother's skirt.

'Yes, he is. We'd better get off and find our luggage, Dad.'

Their suitcases were on the platform, offloaded from the guard's van by a porter. Janet, Catherine's sister, had identified them and was standing by them. 'My God, how you've changed, our sis?' she cried as she threw her arms round Catherine. 'You're thinner and you've cut your hair and … no … don't tell me that's the coat you wore when you went away.'

'Yes, it is.' Catherine looked down at her coat. 'What's wrong with it?'

'It's out of date. Don't you have papers or magazines where you live?'

'Of course we do, but I don't have much time to sit down and read and nowhere much to go, so I don't need a lot of clothes.'

'Cut it out, you two,' said their father. 'There's a tired little boy here and your mother will be looking out for us and wondering where we've got to.'

'Why didn't she come to meet us?'

'She's cooking a meal, thought you'd be hungry.'

Catherine, in the front seat of her father's car with Robbie on her knee, peered out at the streets as he drove her home. 'The place has changed,' she said when she saw all the building work that had been going on in the city.

'You haven't seen anything yet,' said Janet, 'you won't know where you are. I guarantee you'd get lost if we let you out on your own.'

There were tears in Doris Marshall's eyes as she rushed out of the house and swept her daughter into her arms. 'You're here at last,' she cried. 'I thought you were never going to get away from that dragon you call your mother-in-law.'

'Oh come on, Mum. Don't you think I can stand up for myself?'

'Yes, of course I do,' Doris was riffling in her pocket for a handkerchief, 'but you never know. Come on in, you must be tired after such a long journey.'

Robbie still clung to his mother's skirt. Catherine bent down to pick him up. 'Here's your other grandma, Robbie.' But Robbie put his arms round Catherine's neck and buried his face in her shoulder.

'He must be very tired,' said Doris. 'Give him some supper and put him to bed, then we can catch up on all your news.'

Robbie would eat nothing and when Catherine put him to bed he was asleep almost before his head touched the pillow. Very gently she prised his fingers from the clutch he had on her blouse, waited to make sure she had not disturbed him, then crept back down the stairs.

Her mother patted the seat beside her on the settee, her father put a drink in her hand and her sister leaned over the back of the settee to listen.

'And is that Jannie behaving any better towards you?' asked Doris.

'Yes, what's this I hear?' said Catherine's father. 'Your mother tells me Robbie's mother's been giving you a hard time.'

'It's not that bad,' said Catherine. 'You have to stand up to her and I do.'

'I hear you've no electricity or running water.'

'Ha ha,' laughed Catherine. 'We've got plenty of water; it's just that it's not in a pipe with a tap on the end. But it's coming to us soon – electricity too; they have it in Lerwick now.'

Her mother protested when she told how Noble had won a prize at the show. 'You're a nurse, you shouldn't be doing rough work like that.'

But Catherine said, 'It was a major achievement really, especially,' and she smiled as she thought of it, 'for a woman and an English one at that.' She told them that most wives helped with the work of the croft and if they didn't have other jobs did knitting to earn extra money. 'And I work at the local surgery,' she said. 'It's only a cleaning job. I've been offered the post of health visitor, but it means going to Edinburgh to train and I don't think I could spare the time.'

Catherine's father had been smoking and listening to the ebb and flow of questions and answers, now he knocked the dottle out of his pipe and put the pipe in his pocket. 'And do the others treat you well?' he asked.

'Daa does,' she said.

Her father leaned forward. 'And does that mean the others don't?'

'No, Kay and Laura are fine. Mina's a bit stand-offish and Jannie hasn't got over losing Robbie. She needs to blame somebody and there's only me.'

'But are you happy there? That's what I want to know.'

'Yes.' Catherine smiled at her father. 'I have some good friends,' she thought of Kay, 'and life is never dull with Robbie around.'

'He seems very shy.'

'He probably doesn't understand you, he's surrounded by people at home who speak the dialect and a lot of the time he does too.'

'But you don't. Don't you make him speak English?'

'Why should I? He's a Shetlander.'

When at last there was a lull in the conversation Janet chipped in with, 'When did you last buy any new clothes, our sis?' She had taken Catherine's clothes out of her suitcases and put them away.

'Um, I don't know.'

'You don't know? I don't believe you.'

'Well, apart from underwear and trousers and boots for out of doors I haven't bought anything. I haven't needed to; I don't have a social life, you see.'

'No social life?' Janet grimaced in disbelief. 'You mean to tell me you just stay at home and don't go anywhere?'

'I did go to a dance after the show, but that was a disaster.'

'Why?'

Catherine yawned. 'I'm not going to tell you and I've just noticed what the time is, so I'm going to bed. Hope you don't mind, Mum.'

TWENTY SEVEN

'MAM, MAM, IS du awake?'

Catherine opened her eyes and there was Robbie creeping into bed beside her. 'Hello darling,' she said, cuddling his warm little body close. 'What would you like to do today? We could look at the ships in the harbour or we could find a toy shop and buy you a new toy. How about a kite? Would you like a kite?'

'What's a kite?'

'We'll get one and then you'll see. It'll be fun. Now we'd better get up or the day will be half gone before we see it.'

The bathroom delighted Robbie. He was fascinated to see water spouting from the taps. 'Where's it coming from, Mam?'

'The hot from a hot water cylinder and the cold from a tank in the roof,' she said. Questions came thick and fast then. 'How does it get hot?' and 'Where does it go?' when he pulled the plug and watched the water swirling away in the bottom of the basin.

'I'll tell you after breakfast. Hurry up.'

Catherine's father and her sister had already left for work but her mother was in the kitchen. Breakfast was cereal – cornflakes, and toast. When Doris put a bowl of cornflakes in front of Robbie he looked at it, then looked up at her.

'That's what we give our chicken at home. We dinna have that.'

'Oh, and what do you have then?'

'Porridge mostly,' said Catherine. 'Try it, Robbie. It's nice.'

'What would you like to do today,' asked her mother.

'I told Robbie I was going to get him a kite and teach him how to fly it so I'd like to go to the shops, if that's all right with you.'

'That's fine. Would you like me to come with you?'

'I think you'd better or, like Janet said, I might get lost.'

*

146

Robbie had insisted on wearing a jumper that Mina had made for him. At the bus stop when people walking by looked and smiled at him he tugged at his mother. 'Why do they laugh at me?' he said.

'They're not laughing; they're smiling because you're wearing such a pretty jumper and because you're such a lovely little boy.'

When it came, it was a double-deck bus. The lower deck was full, so they had to climb the stairs to the top and while Catherine and her mother talked the little boy, fascinated by all he was seeing, gazed out of the window.

The city of Southampton had undergone a transformation in the years since Catherine had left; rebuilding was still going on: offices and shops in the city, estates of new houses on the outskirts. In the wake of the devastation left by the German bombs modern buildings were springing up where whole streets had been laid waste. A city was being regenerated.

When they reached the city centre traffic was thick and pavements crowded.

'Where is all these folk come from, Mam?' said Robbie.

'Some live in the city and some have come in from the country,' said Catherine. 'Hold on to me, I don't want to lose you. Let's find a toyshop, Mum.'

If Robbie had been thrilled by everything he'd seen so far the contents of the toyshop left him speechless. When it came to choosing a kite he had no idea what he wanted, so his mother chose it for him. Holding on to it he sat on a chair outside a fitting-room in a department store while Catherine tried on dresses that Doris insisted on buying for her. A family lunch had been planned. 'I don't care what you look like in Shetland,' said Doris, 'but you're going to have something nice to wear when the others come over.' Two dresses, for which Doris gave up some of her clothing coupons, were put in a carrier and handed to Catherine.

'Shall we go to the park now?' said Doris after they had looked in all the departments and Robbie had started to complain. 'I made a couple of sandwiches – only Spam, I'm afraid, but I used some of that butter you brought so they shouldn't be too bad. We can have a sort of picnic.'

There were not many people in the park; children were at school, so no games of football or tag were going on. Late summer sunshine slanted through the trees and cast long shadows on the grass. Pigeons cooed in treetops and sparrows twittered as they hopped about looking for crumbs dropped from lunch bags. From the city came the muted hum of traffic and from time to time the even drone of a plane could be heard high overhead. The air was soft and carried the sweet, nutty smell of autumn leaves. But there was no wind to fly a kite.

'It's so peaceful here, Mum,' said Catherine. 'You don't know how good it is to be able to sit still and do nothing, not to have to watch the clock and think what it was you were supposed to be doing an hour ago; and to be able to sit out of doors and not to be buffeted by the wind.'

'I know it was bad enough when I was there, but surely the wind doesn't blow all the time?'

'There aren't many days without it. We do have good weather; midsummer days are long and stay light round the clock. Sometimes we get one perfect day. They call it "a day between weathers" and that's exactly what it is.'

While Catherine and her mother sat and talked Robbie ran about, looked up in wonder at the trees, picked up acorns and chased squirrels and pigeons.

'There's no ewes,' he said, when Catherine called him to go home, 'all this grass and no ewes.' He was speaking in dialect.

'What on earth is he saying?' laughed Doris.

'He's saying there's no sheep and there's all this grass to feed them on. Grass isn't this lush at home. I'm afraid he's a budding crofter.' With Robbie at her side she patted his bulging pockets. 'What have you got in there?' She put her hand in and drew out a handful of stones.

'They's for my peerie grandma,' said Robbie.

'But Kay doesn't want … oh darling … this is not the rock Kay asked for. A stick of rock is a sweetie. We'll see if we can find some tomorrow.'

Catherine had planned to be away from Deepdale for two weeks, but before even one week had passed she was counting the hours till she could start for home. At first the novelty of shopping in stores with full shelves and in grocers' shops with all kinds of appetizing foods had been a joy. She gazed longingly in shop windows at pretty cotton dresses but knew that if she bought them they would only be folded away out of sight and not worn; what use had she for such things? When it came to shirts and underwear she added several items to her wardrobe.

When the wind blew she took Robbie to the park to fly the kite. She taught him how to run into the wind to get it off the ground and when it did and had climbed high she gave him the end of the line to hold, winding the string round his hand a couple of times so he would not lose it.

'Hold tight,' she said. 'If you pull on it now and then you can make it dance.' When it had been flying a while she said, 'Shall we send it a message?'

'How are you goin' to do that?' said Robbie.

'Like this.' Catherine took a piece of paper from her pocket, dug into her handbag and took out a nail file. She pierced a hole in the paper, took the line from Robbie and slipped the paper over the end of it. The wind soon caught it and Robbie clapped his hands as it fluttered and slid up the line to the kite.

'What did it say?' he asked.

'It said we'll have to go back to Granny's soon.'

They went to the docks to see the ships and on Saturday Catherine's father drove them to the New Forest to look at the ponies. They visited relations and, overcome by a lively hugging and kissing horde of aunts, uncles and cousins, Robbie hid his face in his mother's skirts. Catherine felt she'd talked herself dry, was exhausted by it all and … she'd had enough. 'I don't know what they say,' said Robbie when she was getting him ready for bed and she remembered how she had struggled with the Shetland dialect. Now Robbie was hearing, not a dialect, for much of her own had been forgotten, but a different way of speaking and a different accent. It was no wonder he didn't understand.

'Is it not time for us to go home?' he asked.

They stood waiting for the train.

'Stay longer next time,' said Doris. 'And don't stay away so long.'

'It's not easy, Mum. I'm too busy in the summer and the sea crossing can be pretty rough in winter.'

'You don't need to tell me that. I hope I never have to make a journey like that again. You take care of yourself now, and especially that little boy.'

'Have you got everything?' asked her father. 'Not forgotten your passports, have you?'

'Get away with you, Dad. I still live in Great Britain, you know.'

Her father laughed. 'You could have fooled me. Sounds like they speak a foreign language up there.'

'Like you don't?'

'I'm just joking,' he said. 'I can hear the train, give us a hug.' Peter Marshall took his daughter in his arms and held her tight. 'Look after yourself, my luvvy. You're always in my thoughts. Best of luck with your sheep, but don't work too hard, and write more often.' Then she was in her mother's arms for an emotional embrace and Doris was saying, 'Come back soon. You're so far away and we all miss you.' Though she promised she would, Catherine knew in her heart that it would be a long time before she travelled south again.

With a hiss of steam and a squeal of brakes the train clanked into the station and her father put their luggage on board. Robbie was lifted up to kiss his grandpa and grandma goodbye. Then they were on the train, finding a seat and looking out to wave.

With Peter's arm round her shoulder Doris mopped her eyes, and, when the train began to move they walked beside it until it went too fast and Catherine, looking out, watched and waved till she could see them no more.

It was raining and cold when the boat docked. Telling Robbie to stay close to her Catherine struggled to get their luggage out of the cabin and into the reception area. Waiting there with the other passengers, she looked for familiar faces. The one she did see surprised her. The doctor's wife, Marie Lumsden, was smiling up into the face of a tall blond man. The smile was more than just friendly and the man was not Neil. Catherine turned away and hoped she hadn't been seen.

When the gangway was open she waited for the first rush of passengers to get off before she picked up her cases to follow them, but before she had time to move, Norrie was coming towards her.

'I'll take them,' he said, 'you see to the boy.'

'But … where's Bobbie? He was coming to fetch me.'

'Likely he was, but I told him I wanted to, so I'm here.' He spoke abruptly and there was no smile on his face. Something was wrong. As they drove away out of town she couldn't think why he was so offhand and not his usual self.

'Is anything wrong?' she asked.

'Wrong? What could be wrong?'

'Well, you're quiet and I wonder why.'

'We've had rain ever since you left; it's not good for the sheep. It's held up the work and I've a lot to do. Did you have a good time?'

'We did.' Surely it wasn't just the weather that was making him grumpy. And if he had a lot to do why had he taken the time to come and meet her? There must be something else. 'But I was glad when it was time to come home.'

'You missed us, then?' He glanced at her and a brief smile lit his face.

'I did. Robbie too; he was as glad as I when it was time to leave.

Weren't you, Robbie?' Robbie, curled up on his mother's lap, just nodded his head.

Heavy rain slanted down and Catherine thought of the balmy days spent in the park teaching Robbie how to fly his kite. Would she rather be there than back here where wind and rain were never absent for long? She thought about her house and wondered if Kay had kept the fire going or if it would be out and the house damp.

'Is everything all right at home?' she asked.

'As right as it ever will be.'

'How is Kay? Did Bobbie give you my message and did you go to see her? I didn't think she was too well.'

'What a lot of questions you ask. You'll see.'

He was driving down into the valley, taking it very carefully, for the rain had washed gullies in the track. He drove on until he brought the vehicle to a stop outside her house. He went to her door and opened it, fetched her bags, carried them in and when she went in the house was warm, the kettle singing on the stove.

'Sit down, Catherine,' said Norrie, 'I have something to tell you.'

She had only to look at his face to know the news was not good.

'It's Kay, isn't it?'

'Ay. Auntie died.' Tears started in Catherine's eyes and Norrie took her hands in his. 'She went in peace.'

'She said to me, "never say goodbye, it's so final," and wouldn't let me say it when I left. What am I going to do without her?'

'You have me.'

She looked at him, at this man who had been nothing but kind to her. She had turned him away, but here he was, still offering to look after her.

'Yes, Norrie, I have you,' she said, giving him a watery smile.

'Mam,' Robbie was at her elbow, 'can I have a drink?'

Catherine got up. 'Do we have any milk, Norrie?'

'Ay. I thought you'd want a cup of tea. Will I make it for you?'

'Yes, please.' Catherine poured milk into a cup for Robbie, got out cups for her and Norrie and when the tea was made, sat down.

'Tell me what's going to happen,' she said.

Norrie told her when the funeral would be. Kay was lying in her house and he'd locked the door so Robbie wouldn't walk in on her. She should tell him that Kay had gone away, that's all. He would be seeing to everything, but if there was anything she could do he wouldn't hesitate to ask. He stayed with her a while, asked about her holiday, and she told him how glad she was to come back and that she didn't feel she belonged down south any more, that Shetland was now her home. He left then and she was grateful he had been there; the journey had been long and tiring, but to come home and find she'd lost her friend was too much. Robbie had gone to sleep in the armchair.

She sat down and let her thoughts stretch back over the years. Kay had befriended her, had stayed with her when Robbie was born. She smiled as she remembered how Neil Lumsden had described the relief on Kay's face when he had eventually arrived and how she had downed a whisky in one gulp. Kay had been her best friend. And now Kay had left her.

Tears filled Catherine's eyes, spilled over and ran down her face.

TWENTY EIGHT

Sitting between Norrie and Daa, Catherine looked at Kay's little coffin with Norrie's bouquet of white chrysanthemums. She closed her eyes. "You'll never see me in church again," she had said and here she was a second time. And there were the crows again; black on black, with only an occasional glimpse of a pale shirt front. When the preacher began the eulogy Daa took her hand and tucked her arm under his. She turned to look at him and understanding passed between them without need for words. Oh Daa, she thought, how glad I am you're here.

At Kay's house after the funeral she helped dispense the food and drink that Jannie and the aunts had prepared. Among those who came to pay their respects were many of Kay's former pupils and it was no surprise to hear them sing her praises. How could it be otherwise?

As she had expected, her little boy wanted to know where Kay was and why they were having a party in her house. She had promised to tell him all about it later if he would only go with Daa and look at the sheep for her because she was rather busy.

When everyone had gone and clearing up was finished Catherine pushed the kettle to the middle of the stove and began to put out cups and the teapot. Norrie, who had slumped into a chair, said, 'I'm not wanting tea.'

'Oh yes you are,' said Catherine, 'and something to eat. I watched you seeing to everyone as well as taking too much whisky for yourself.'

'Was I not allowed?'

'You can do what you like,' she said and stopped what she was doing, 'but if you think I'm interfering I'll go home.'

'No no, don't go,' pleaded Norrie. 'Bide a while wi' me.'

'Only if you promise to eat something,' she said. When he agreed she made tea, filled a plate with cold meat and cut bread to go with it. She poured tea for them both, pulled up a chair and sat down. 'Come and eat,' she said.

As he ate she asked him if he didn't have any more family. 'You must have some somewhere,' she said. 'Aren't there any aunts, uncles or cousins?'

'I did have an aunt and uncle, but they went to Australia. Never hear from them. Now both Kay and my parents are dead, I'm alone.'

'What's going to happen to Kay's house?' she asked.

'It's mine now,' said Norrie, 'and the croft. I'm thinking of moving in; it's bigger as where I bide.'

'Oh,' said Catherine and looked away out of the window.

'Would you not like me as your neighbour?'

It would be nice to have someone living in Kay's house; even nicer if it was Norrie. 'I'd rather you came to live here than to have strangers in the valley.'

'You were a stranger once.'

'Yes, didn't I know it? But I'm not now and I'm getting to love the place.'

'I take it, then, that you'll make me welcome? Catherine,' Norrie reached across the table and took her hand, 'Sheila's gone back to Scotland. I was never hers, but will you be mine?'

The door opened and Daa came in with Robbie. Daa was smiling. 'I'm thinkin it'll be a long while before you take this one south again. "There's no ewes," he said, "and muckle big houses and water at comes from nowhere and goes away the same and we rode on a bus wi' an upstairs." '

'I don't think he liked it much.' Catherine laughed. 'Now, Robbie, were the ewes all right?'

'Yeh, they're good.'

'Thank you for looking at them. It's time to go home, so say goodnight.'

Catherine found it strange to walk past Kay's house, to see the door shut and know there was no one at home, no one to look after Robbie when she went to work. She wondered if she ought to give up her job and said as much to Jannie.

'You don't have to do that,' said Jannie. 'I would have him.'

'You would? But you have your work to do,' said Catherine.

'Ay, but it's not all day and he would be wi his grandpa when he's home.'

'That's true,' said Catherine and agreed that Robbie could stay with her.

Mina came out of her house as Catherine was passing by. 'What are you going to do with Robbie when you go to your work?' she asked.

'Well … Jannie's just offered to have him,' said Catherine.

'We would like to look after him for you,' said Mina.

'Oh.' What was she going to do now? Who was she most likely to offend? 'Um … I think you'd better see Jannie and sort it out between you. Just let me know where I have to leave him.'

'We could do that.' Mina nodded went in and shut the door.

Strange woman, thought Catherine; never in a million years would she have said Mina would volunteer to look after a child. Laura, yes, Laura exuded happiness and an air of mischief. Robbie would be bound to have fun with her.

From then on Robbie didn't spend much time with his mother; much of it was spent with the aunts or Jannie and always with his grandfather at weekends. Daa came along to call for him if he was taking the pony cart and going to check on sheep or mend fences. He needed the boy to hold the bucket of nails or the bottle of worm drench, he said, and Robbie would rush to find his boots and be off. Catherine heard him chatting away to Daa as he was swung up into the cart and, happy for him, closed the door and got on with her work.

She often thought of Kay, keenly felt her loss and wondered how the coming Christmas was going to be without her and her driftwood Christmas tree. Another bauble for the branch had been an easy stocking-present to buy.

Norrie moved in to the valley at the beginning of December. One day he wasn't there and the next he was.

'You should have told me you were coming,' said Catherine when she saw him. 'I would have lit your fire to welcome you.'

Norrie laughed. 'Darlin', you light my fire every time I see you.'

Catherine blushed. 'Oh, Norrie,' she chided, 'I shall have to get you a house-warming present now. Is there anything you need?'

The grin on Norrie's face stretched from ear to ear and, realizing how he was going to interpret what she'd said, she blushed. 'I know what you're thinking,' she said.

'Ay, you already know the answer to that, but you owe me an answer to a question I asked a while ago.'

'And what might that have been?'

'You know fine what it was.'

'I'd not object if you came calling again, if that's what you mean?'

'You know it was not that. I asked if you would be mine.'

'I'll have to think about it,' said Catherine.

'But not too long,' said Norrie.

*

Thoughts of Norrie frequently filled Catherine's mind. It was absurd to feel so happy because he teased her, absurd that her heart pounded when he was close, silly that he made her blush. With Christmas so near she wondered if she should invite him to share Christmas dinner with her and Robbie. In the week before Christmas she said, 'Come on, let's see if we can find a piece of driftwood for a Christmas tree like Kay's.' They searched the beach, went every day, but no driftwood came ashore so she said they'd have to do without.

'I wanted a tree,' said Robbie as she was putting him to bed.

'So did I, but we've got paper chains. We'll find something next year.'

That night, as she put the presents she had bought for Robbie into a stocking to hang on the end of his bed, she thought again about Norrie and whether she really ought to ask him to come to dinner. But then the thought of Jannie and the way she had scowled when she thought she was meeting him on the moor made her think again. What would Jannie do if she thought they were together without Kay as chaperone? But, come on: Jannie wasn't her keeper; it was nothing to do with her. She looked at the clock; it wasn't too late to go to Norrie and ask him. She put on her coat, picked up a torch and let herself out. Head down against the wind, she walked in the pool of light in front of her.

'And where do you think you're going?'

Jumping back in fright Catherine raised her torch to see Norrie's burly form. 'I was just coming to see you.'

'And I was coming to see you. Well, which way do you want to go?'

'No need to go anywhere. I was going to ask if you'd like to have your Christmas dinner with me and Robbie,' said Catherine.

'You've left it late.'

'I know. Will you come?'

'I was just going to ask you to have dinner wi' me. Now we shall have to toss for it and I don't have any money.' He was grinning at her.

'And I suppose that means you want to use my money. Well, forget it; you're going to have dinner with us. I can cook, but I'm not sure about you.'

'Ay well. By, you're a bonnie lass. I'll see you in the morning then.'

'Mam, there's somethin' in my sock and I can't see what it is.'

Catherine pulled herself into consciousness, reached for matches and the candle. Robbie had his Christmas stocking with him; he began to empty it on her bed. Wanting to go back to sleep she said 'oh' and 'ah' as each small present was pulled out and examined. At last the sock was empty and Robbie, clutching a woolly toy sheep, snuggled down beside her. She blew out the candle.

At eight Catherine knew, even though it was still dark, that it was time to rise. Hoping Robbie would sleep on she crept out of bed, picked up her clothes and took them to the warmth of the kitchen to dress. She had prepared everything for their dinner the night before. With no animals to see to there was no outside work to do. Daa would walk round the sheep, Noble was off his tether and in a park with the ewes, and she had no chickens of her own to feed. She put porridge on the stove to cook, then laid the table. Robbie, sleepy-eyed and still clutching his woolly sheep came trailing through from the bedroom. She washed and dressed him and they ate breakfast. Table cleared and dishes washed, Robbie lay on the mat in front of the fire, looking at a book.

Catherine went through to the bedroom to wash and change into something more festive than her everyday clothes. It was the one special day of the year and she wanted to look nice. She put on one of the dresses her mother had given her, brushed her hair and put on some makeup. Janet had given her a small bottle of perfume. 'Make the most of yourself, sis,' she had said. Catherine took it out of the drawer where she kept it and dabbed some on her wrists and throat.

'What's that smell?' said Robbie when she went back to the kitchen.

'It's perfume. Your auntie Janet gave it to me,' said Catherine as she put an apron on over her dress, but Robbie's attention had switched back to his book.

The meat, a joint of beef bought from a butcher in Lerwick, was roasting nicely when Norrie arrived. He gave some parcels to Catherine and asked her to clear a space on the press. 'I have something else,' he said. When he came back he kicked the door gently with the toe of his boot.

'I couldn't knock,' he said, when Catherine opened it. 'As you see I have me hands full.' He was carrying Kay's Christmas tree complete with baubles. 'I ken she wouldn't think it was Christmas without it,' he said.

'That's wonderful,' cried Catherine, 'Come and look, Robbie. Norrie's brought Kay's Christmas tree. Isn't that lovely?'

The tree was set up, presents wrapped in brown paper tied with coloured string put beside it. 'Thank you, Norrie,' said Catherine. 'Wait, I think I have just the thing for it.' She went to her bedroom and came back with a small parcel. 'This is going to be hung on the tree,' she said, taking a little glass angel from the paper, 'in memory of Kay. Not that I could ever forget her.'

'You really did care for her, didn't you?'

'She was my friend; I don't know what I'd have done without her. Now let's get on. We'll open the presents after we've eaten. Dinner's not ready yet, so would you like a dram?'

'That would be good,' said Norrie. 'You're looking pretty, and,' he sniffed, 'smellin good too … or would that be the meat?'

'You will be putting your life in jeopardy, Norrie Williams, if you go on like that.' Catherine sounded serious, but as she turned away she was smiling.

After they had eaten the dinner Catherine had cooked for them they opened the presents. From Southampton there were toys for Robbie and silky underwear for Catherine. She gave Norrie a pocket knife while he gave her a fancy glass bowl. Norrie gave Robbie a small boy-sized staff with a carved handle. 'When you start your flock, you're going to need that,' he said. Then he picked up his fiddle, and with an ease born of long practice began to play. Tea time came and went and when Robbie's head began to droop Catherine put him to bed.

Sitting opposite Norrie, Catherine gazed at the fire glowing between the bars. Norrie continued to play softly, and she sighed. This was what Christmas should be like, family coming together for a meal to exchange presents and be together. Norrie was not part of her family, but just now it seemed as though he was or … could very well be.

'Catherine,' said Norrie, putting down his fiddle, 'I can't go on like this, you know I've lost me heart to you. I want you for me wife. Will you marry me?'

'Norrie!'

He stared at her. 'Oh, blast thee English ways, just say yes you will.'

'Norrie … I … I … '

'There you go again.' Norrie was out of his chair and on his knees. 'Don't be so stuffy, lass. I know you like me, why can't you admit it?'

'Of course I like you, quite a lot in fact , but … '

'But what? Are you thinking you're being disloyal to your man?'

'Well …' she turned her head, wanting not to look at him.

'Would you have wanted him to be happy if you had gone?'

'Yes, of course I would.'

'Well then … '

Catherine looked directly at Norrie, looked deep into his eyes, let seconds tick by. 'If I said yes,' she said, 'would you wait for me?'

'Lass, I'd wait for you for ever, only dinna make it that long.'

'All right then,' she said, 'I will marry you.'

Norrie got to his feet and pulled her out of her chair. He wrapped her in his arms and kissed her long and hard.

TWENTY NINE

IT WAS NEW YEAR'S EVE, nearing midnight, and soon Norrie would be coming through her door, her first foot of the year. Catherine put whisky, some glasses and shortbread on the table and sat down to wait. She thought about the year just gone. She had lost Kay, the woman who had told her it would be an uphill battle with Jannie if she stayed, but still encouraged her to do so. Now she had Norrie. Her feelings for him had grown, but was it love? She enjoyed his company and looked forward to being with him, but were they reasons enough to marry him? Was she looking on him as the shield that Kay had been, looking for a father for Robbie and comfort for herself, someone to help carry her load?

The clock on the mantelpiece began to chime the hour. The last note had hardly died away when suddenly the door burst open. But it wasn't Norrie who hugged her and swept her off her feet. It was Billie.

'Billie,' she cried, 'oh Billie, how lovely it is to see you. When did you get home? Where have you been and why didn't you tell us where you'd gone? We've all been so worried about you. Are you all right?'

'You always did ask a lot of questions,' said Billie as he set her down. 'Let me look at you.' He held her off at arm's length. 'You're looking awful bonnie.'

'Tell me what you've been up to,' said Catherine. 'I'm just dying to know.'

'You have the whisky bottle out. Aren't you going to offer me a dram?'

'Yes, of course. I expect Norrie will be here soon.'

'Ay, what's this I hear?' said Billie as Catherine poured whisky into a couple of glasses. 'You and Norrie going together?'

'It's not official,' said Catherine, 'but Norrie asked me to marry him. I said I would, but not yet.'

'You couldn't do better,' said Billy. 'I guess I always knew you'd finish up wi' him.' He laughed. 'I was awful jealous of him once, you know. I loved you, and when you threw us out,' he laughed again, 'you broke my heart and that was why I ran away.'

'You silly twit.'

To the sound of their laughter Norrie came in. 'Aaah,' he sighed and, staggering back against the door, clapped a hand to his chest. 'She promised to be mine and now I find her wi' another. Ah, woe is me.'

'Stop your fooling, Norrie, and come and sit down,' said Catherine. 'I expect you already knew Billie was here.'

'Yeh, I did, but I thought you'd like to be alone wi' him for a minute.'

'That was nice of you. I guess you'll take a dram?'

'Yeh, but I brought this for you, seeing I'm always drinking yours.' Norrie put a bottle on the table. 'It's a malt; better than that stuff you dish out.'

'Norrie Williams!' exclaimed Catherine. 'I don't like malt whisky so you drink yours and I'll keep mine.' She turned to Billie. 'Do you see what I have to put up with? And now he's come to live next door. I don't know if I can stand it.'

'Ah, you will,' said Billie.

They sat by the fire and talked about what had changed since Billie went away. They asked him what he'd been doing, how long he was planning to stay.

'I'm only here for the holiday,' he said, 'I'll be going back south.'

'He's got a girlfriend at last,' said Norrie. 'What's she like, Billie?'

'She's me boss's daughter. She'll come up wi' me next time I'm home.'

'Is it serious?' asked Catherine.

Billie shrugged his shoulders. 'Couldn't say.'

'Your boss must like you if he lets you court his daughter, but you're having fun, eh lad?' said Norrie.

Billie grinned. Then said he had to go, that he had a lot of people to see. Norrie said he would go with him. 'I'll have to see him home safe,' he said, 'for he's not going to be able to turn away the drams he'll be gettin.'

'And I guess neither will you,' said Catherine.

Spring, particularly the month of April when the next school term started, was the beginning of months of hard work. The Cheviots were due to have their lambs in April and when they were done the cross-breds would start. All through the summer Catherine would be kept busy. Not until the last potato had been lifted, the last sheaf of corn brought in and small animals housed would her work load ease. She consoled herself with the fact that it would be the same for many other croft wives.

But it was still winter. Norrie sometimes took her and Robbie to a social evening at the village hall, or, leaving Robbie with the aunts, took her to a dance. Other times she would invite him to have dinner with them and sometimes when he wasn't away playing with a band at a dance he would come along in the evening, bring his fiddle and play for her.

Daa said it was only right she should be looking for someone to spend her life with, and if Norrie was the one she chose he had no trouble with that. Jannie glared at her but said nothing. When she went to collect Robbie from the aunts where he'd spent a morning Mina questioned her closely.

'Is it right that you are going with that man?'

'I think enough time has gone by for me to have another man as a friend.'

'And what do you know about him? I've heard he has another woman.'

'He does not; if he had I wouldn't be with him.'

'But think of your boy; he should have a good man for a father.'

'And Norrie is a good man.'

'Ay, maybe, but do you think it right you should be alone in the house with him?' asked Mina. 'It's not the right thing to do.'

Catherine put her hands on her hips and looked Mina square in the face. 'Oh, Mina,' she said, 'chaperones went out with the Victorians; life has moved on. You can have as many suspicious thoughts as you like, but you can rest assured there is nothing going on for you to worry about.' She shook her head. Mina sniffed and looked down her nose. 'How else do you think we might meet?' said Catherine. 'We can hardly go walking in a gale, can we?'

Laura came bustling in then. 'Do you want any eggs?' she asked. 'The hens is no laying well, but we could let you have a few.'

'I'm right out, so, yes please. I don't have any money on me at the moment, but if you bring some along I'll pay you for them then. Thank you for looking after Robbie for me. I'm very grateful to you. Say thank you to Auntie Mina,' said Catherine as she helped him into his coat.

'It's no bother,' said Mina.

As they ran home through the rain, Catherine said, 'What would you like for your lunch?'

'I'm not hungry,' said Robbie.

'What's Laura been feeding you, then?'

'I'm had bannocks and some tattie soup.'

'Give me your coat,' said Catherine when they were in her kitchen. She let down the pulley; spread their wet coat on the rails and pulled the pulley back up. She pulled the kettle to the centre of the stove. Robbie having been fed, a cup of tea and a sandwich would do for her, but before she could get bread and butter out of the cupboard Laura was there.

'I'm brought the eggs,' she said and put a paper bag with the eggs in on the table. 'Don't take any notice of what Mina says,' she went on. 'It's none of her business what you do. Norrie Williams is a good man, he'll do right by you, don't send him away, if you does you'll be sorry.'

Catherine looked at Laura. 'Why, Laura, whatever brought that on?'

'I have me reasons. Mina can be awful fierce at times and she does like to meddle in other folk's business.'

'What has she done to you?' said Catherine.

'It's a right long time ago now,' said Laura as she sat by the table. 'I was goin' wi' a lad from the town, but Mina put such doubts in me mind I sent him away. He married another. I didn't get a second chance.'

'Oh, I'm so sorry,' said Catherine.

'Don't be.' Laura gave a wicked smile. 'Mina didna get even one.' Then she laughed aloud. 'But there's more ways as one to skin a cat.'

'What do you mean?'

'Never mind, but if Norrie asks you to marry him, you should. You're a hard-working lass. You deserve to be happy. Now I'd better go.' Laura got up and pushed her chair back under the table.

'Here, let me pay you first.'

The winter so far had been open; flurries of snow barely had time to settle and cover the ground before melting. But as January slid away the weather grew colder and February came in colder still. Frost gripped the land with a fist of steel. Sheep had to be fed daily, and as Catherine's flock had increased in number carrying feed to them took longer. It was then more than ever that she missed Kay, but between them the aunts and Jannie helped out and little Robbie was only too happy to spend time with them, making sure the fire was burning well, the kettle filled and on the side of the hob ready for a hot drink when she got back indoors, Catherine kitted herself out with warm clothes and went to work.

As Robbie's birthday drew near she made biscuits and cake, cooked a ham and issued invitations to all the family to come to tea.

'I ken you already have a dog,' said Norrie, 'but have you room for another should I give Robbie a pup for his birthday?'

'I think he'd like that,' said Catherine. 'I'll get it a collar and a bowl and all the things it'll need.'

'Next thing he'll be wantin' will be sheep. You'll have to look to your laurels, Catherine; he'll be beating you at your own game.'

'Good; he'll be following his father. What more could I ask?'

'I'll not come to the tea,' said Norrie. 'Likely it might make bad feeling.'

Still the cold kept up and on the day of Robbie's birthday Catherine was up early to get her outside tasks done. As she went round the inbye sheep she looked up at the hill. It was a bleak, forbidding place in winter and she was glad the hill sheep were brought to pastures lower down. Work done and indoors at last she made herself a hot drink, then went to fetch Robbie.

'Look, Mam,' he said, 'see what Grandma's given me?' His little hands grasped a ginger kitten round its middle. The kitten's legs pawed the air and from time to time it opened its mouth and mewed piteously. 'It's for my birthday.'

'That's lovely. It would be nice to have a cat, but hold it like this.' Catherine showed him how to put one hand under its bottom and clasp it to him. 'There,' she said, 'I'm sure it's more comfortable now. Did you say thank you?'

'Ay,' said Jannie. 'Does he have to go? Can he no bide wi' me a bit?'

'Yes. Why not? You can bring him with you when it's time for tea.'

Jannie was never slow to agree to look after Robbie. Catherine had come to the conclusion that the little boy was a link to her own son. When she went to pick him up she was never invited to stay, never offered a cup of tea, never asked how she was. The aunts, stiff-backed Mina, artful Laura, were different. They too were always happy to have Robbie stay with them. Mina taught him his manners; Laura spoiled him and when Catherine appeared there was always tea and a buttered bannock. Now they were all coming to tea at her house. Catherine looked at her table. Was there enough bread, had she made enough cake and was the ham properly cooked? It was too late now to change anything, so there was nothing left to do but pray that all would go smoothly.

Mina and Laura were first to arrive. Mina gave Robbie yet another jumper and Laura a book about animals. Jannie had already given Robbie the kitten. Daa gave him a card on which he'd written a promise that he and Jannie would get him a bicycle. 'It's so you can ride to school when you go,' said Daa.

'Do I have to go to school?'

'All bairns have to go to school,' said Daa.

'You'll make a lot of new friends,' said Jannie.

'You'll learn to read and write,' said Mina.

But Robbie turned down his mouth. 'I can read now,' he said.

'Come and sit up,' said Catherine. 'Let's have our tea.' She turned to the others. 'Please help yourselves.'

The ham with fresh bread and butter was superb and by the time six plates were filled there was very little left. Mina complimented Catherine on the ham and Laura said how good the little cakes were. Daa nodded and smiled. The birthday cake, bearing five candles, stood on a cake dish in the middle of the table. Catherine put a match to them and as they burned Robbie laughed and clapped his hands.

'Now you have to blow them all out,' said Catherine.

'You have to make a wish, then blow them all out at once,' said Laura. 'But don't tell us what you wish for.'

All eyes were on him. Holding his hand up to his mouth he rolled his eyes and sighed, then a smile spread across his face, 'I wished for …' he began.

'No no, dinna tell us,' chorused the aunts and Jannie.

'It has to be a secret,' said Daa.

'Take a deep breath now,' said Catherine as she put the cake in front of him, 'and blow.' He blew all the candles out and they told him he was a clever boy. The cake was cut and a slice put on everyone's plate.

When the food was gone and the presents opened the party was over. Jannie said she had a piece of work to finish and, telling Daa to come with her, went home. Mina and Laura thanked Catherine for the tea and said they had to go too. Catherine began to clear the table and get ready to wash the dishes.

'Have you enjoyed yourself, Robbie? Do you like your presents?'

'Why does Auntie Mina always give me a jumper?' he asked.

'Because she knits them so well and she knows I can't.'

'Here's Norrie,' said Robbie as a smiling Norrie opened the door.

'And how's the birthday boy?' said Norrie.

'I'm five years old now.'

'Ay, you're a big boy. I see your Mam's peat bucket is empty. Would you come wi' me while I get some? I could do wi' somebody to hold the torch.'

Catherine had stored her peat in an outhouse. Robbie, holding a torch, followed Norrie. 'Shine the torch here, boy,' said Norrie as he began to put peat in a bucket, then he stopped. 'What's that noise? Ah, there's a box here. I think there's somethin' in it. Can you not hear?' Coming from the box was a scratching sound and the whimper of an animal. The reflected light of the torch showed him Robbie's puzzled face. 'Shall we see what it is?'

In a hoarse whisper Robbie said, 'Yeh.'

As the lid of the box was untied and lifted a wet black nose, followed by the face of a small dog, peered out.

'Wonder what that's doin here?' said Norrie.

'Is it lost?' asked Robbie.

'I don't think so, there's a label on its collar. What does it say?' Norrie held the label and with Robbie's head close to his, read, 'Happy birthday to Robbie, from Norrie.' Lifting the puppy from the box he held it out to the little boy. 'That's my present to you. Look after him now.'

Robbie threw his arms round Norrie's neck. 'That's what I wished for when I blew me candles out. Wishes do come true.'

'If they only would,' said Norrie, 'if they only would. Now, let's show your mam.'

THIRTY

CATHERINE HAD INHERITED Kay's sewing-machine and while Robbie was away was busy patching and mending their clothes. Robbie's pup lay curled up with Fly and the kitten was asleep in front of the fire. A pot of broth on the stove simmered gently. Jannie had taken Robbie to Lerwick to buy him his bicycle. Catherine hoped she would keep him wrapped up warm for there was a cold east wind. Sewing finished, she put the machine away, cleared the table and turned her attention to the soup. She lifted the lid, gave it a stir and the smell of it wafted under her nose. It was just the right sort of food for such cold weather.

Then Jannie was there with Robbie and a brand-new bicycle. The little boy's eyes were shining with delight.

'Look, Mam,' he said. 'It's good. You have to learn me how to ride.'

'It's lovely,' she said. 'Did you say thank you to Grandma for it?'

'Yeh, I did.'

'Well, I'm thanking you too, Jannie' said Catherine. 'I'm grateful for all you do for him. It's good to know he's in safe hands.'

'It's no more as we should, he's our kin,' said Jannie.

'Are you going to teach me now, Mam?' asked Robbie.

'No,' said Catherine, 'your dinner's ready. You must have that first.'

With hot soup warming their insides, and wearing coats, hats and gloves, Catherine gave Robbie his first lesson on riding his bicycle. With adjustments done so the saddle was the right height and the pedals within reach, she began.

'Pull up the brakes like this when you want to stop,' she said, putting her hands over his, 'then take your foot off the pedal, lean over and put it down.'

Robbie nodded and she hoped he understood. Holding the back of the saddle to keep him upright Catherine pushed him to get him going. Then, when he was moving she ran beside him as he pedalled on, then lost momentum and fell off.

'You were doing well,' she said.

'Again, Mam,' said Robbie as he climbed back on the bike.

Again and again he fell off, but each time he rode further and with more confidence and with Catherine only giving him a push to start him.

Getting off the bike properly, worked … almost … the first time, but the second time was better. The third time she said, 'All you need now is to practise.' By this time they were outside Jannie's house, for the more Robbie grew in confidence the further he rode. Jannie heard them and came out.

'I'm wantin' to see how he's doin',' she said.

'He's doing very well,' said Catherine. 'I'm surprised how quickly he's picked it up. He's fallen off a few times, but no harm done.'

'Gets more like his father every day,' said Jannie. She began to cough, cleared her throat, then, with a hand cupped over her mouth, coughed again. 'It's the cold air,' she said when she'd got the cough under control.

'Maybe,' said Catherine. 'Thank you again for the bicycle.'

'No bother,' said Jannie, then, coughing again said, 'I'm goin' in.'

'Not like you to have a cough,' said Catherine, 'you'd better take care.'

'It's nothin'. Just the time o' year,' said Jannie.

Now that the Cheviot ewes were heavy in lamb Catherine went out to check on them twice a day, once when she fed them and again for a last look round before nightfall. Last year's lambs, Noble's first offspring, were growing well and she thought she might enter one or two in the next show. Noble would certainly be there. Another year had seen him develop into a fine-looking animal. If Robbie had lived, how proud he would have been.

She waited eagerly for the arrival of the first lamb, and as she ticked each day off the calendar her excitement mounted. This would be the year she should see some reward for her investment and all her hard work.

The cold winds continued, but now rain threatened and Catherine prayed that the weather would improve. Though she still had the small outhouse where she could put new-born lambs and their mothers, because her flock was growing in number she would need bigger better accommodation in the future. Perhaps she could do something with the barn at the back of the house. There was another barn, but it needed quite a lot of fixing up. The roof leaked and the wind whistled through gaps in the wall. She knew sheep should not be coddled, and if penned needed plenty of air, but they did not need water dripping on them.

When it wasn't raining Robbie spent his time out of doors on his bicycle. The puppy Norrie had given him romped after him and Catherine smiled when she heard the little boy's laughter. Mina and Laura looked out and smiled too, and Catherine was pleased that her son was bringing joy and happiness to them.

The rain became incessant; sometimes it fell with monotonous regularity; at other times bouts of bright sunshine were interspersed with unpredictable hard storms. When she got caught in a fierce downpour on her way home from work her shoes, full of the water that dripped from her raincoat, squished with every step she took. As she drew level with the aunts' house their door flew open and Laura called to her.

'Come you in, Catherine,' she said, beckoning urgently.

'I can't,' said Catherine, 'I'm soaked. I must get some dry clothes.'

'All right then, but don't be long.'

Catherine put her wet clothes on the pulley, dried her feet and put on some dry things. Then she picked up an umbrella and ran to see what was troubling Laura. Had Robbie been naughty? 'What's the matter, Laura? Is Robbie all right?' she asked. But Robbie was happily curled up in a chair with a book.

'No, no, it's not Robbie; it's Daa, he's not well.'

'So?' What had that got to do with her?

'He's not doin any work, he coughs all the time and he'll not have the doctor, and Jannie says ask you. We're awful worried. Mina's there now; go you along. Robbie can bide with me.'

Catherine hesitated. 'If Daa's that poorly Jannie should call the doctor. Daa wouldn't be able to do anything about it,' she said.

Laura shook her head. 'No, he won't have him, and he wouldn't let him look at him if he came.'

As soon as she put her foot on the step of the Jameson house the door was thrown open. Mina had been looking for her. She greeted Catherine with, 'I'm glad you're here. Give me the umbrella. You ken Daa's not well?'

'Yes, Laura told me. What's wrong?'

'There's nothing wrong wi' me,' said Daa. He was sitting in the chair by the fire. Nothing could have proclaimed more loudly that he was ill for, apart from Sundays, he was never idle. 'You can go, we're not needin' you. You too, Mina.' He doubled over then, and with hands wrapped across his chest he began to cough, on and on: a rasping cough which, when it was over, had him gasping for breath. Catherine watched as Daa sank down in the armchair. There were two high spots of colour in his cheeks: colour that was not normal.

'How long have you been like this, Daa?' she asked.

'There's nothing wrong, it's just a chesty cold.' A fit of coughing seized him again. When it was through he said, 'Go home, lass.'

'It's not just a cold you have, you're fevered. I'm sure you have a temperature,' said Catherine. 'You should let the doctor look at you.'

Jannie glared at Catherine. 'No doctor's comin' to this house,' she said.

Mina stood beside Catherine, hands folded in front of her. 'You should listen to what the lass says, Jannie. You know she's a nurse.'

'Yea, I ken, but I'm tellin' you we dinna need a doctor.'

Daa put a hand to his chest as it rose and fell, his breath wheezing in and out. 'I don't know what you're doin here, Mina. You can go away.' Daa started to cough again.

There was not much doubt in Catherine's mind as to where Daa was heading if something wasn't done. He should be put to bed and looked after, but he was proving to be as stubborn as Jannie. As Catherine picked up her umbrella Mina took hold of her arm. 'He can't go on like this. Is he going to die?'

'I sincerely hope not. But I think you really ought to call Lumsden,' said Catherine. 'His chest is congested. You should get him to bed and make him stay there. Prop him up and if you have any cough mixture give him some.'

'Could you not do that?' said Mina.

Catherine shook her head. 'Surely you realize Jannie wouldn't let me within a yard of him. What makes you think I could look after him?'

'I'm not a nurse,' said Mina, 'but you are.'

'I can only advise. Get him to bed and let me know how you get on.'

During the weekend, when Catherine was free to do as she pleased, her mind turned often to Daa. Something should be done to relieve the congestion on his chest or it could turn to pneumonia. But it was not her problem; Mina or Laura would have to help Jannie look after him.

Saturday went by and Sunday morning. Thinking that no news or call for help from Mina could only mean Daa was not as ill as she had thought, Catherine set about cooking dinner. She would go along and see how he was later. When the piece of meat for her and Robbie's midday meal was in the oven and could safely be left for a while she put her coat on and went out of the house.

At Jannie's house she knocked on the door and opened it. Mina was sitting in a chair beside the box-bed, the curtains of which were drawn back. Jannie was sitting by the fire, knitting unworked on her lap. Daa was lying propped up in the bed. The sound of his breathing was dry and laboured.

'Am I glad to see you,' said Mina. 'I was going to send Laura for you.'

Heavy eyes, flushed face and the fact that Daa had taken to bed was all Catherine needed to know. 'He's certainly not any better then,' she said.

Jannie went to stand beside the bed. Her hands rolling one over the other, she stood there for several moments looking at Daa. Then she turned to Catherine. 'I don't know what to do,' she said, her voice trailing off into a sob.

'I'm no better,' said Mina. 'You should be here, Catherine, for I don't know what to do either. I'm afraid for him. Can you not help?'

Catherine looked at Mina and Jannie's stricken faces. 'I'll stay and help if you want me to, Mrs Jameson,' she said. Jannie was for once out of her depth; she mutely nodded her head. Catherine turned to Mina. 'Would you look after Robbie for me?'

'You don't have to ask.'

Catherine took off her coat and laid it over the back of a chair. Daa, eyes closed, lay back on his pillow. Catherine looked at him; saw the unhealthy flush on his face, the beads of sweat on his brow, the damp hairline and the way his shirt clung to him. She didn't need a thermometer to know his temperature was high. She turned to look at Jannie; the woman who had gone out of her way to make her life unpleasant had now crumbled in the face of Daa's illness.

'Are you all right?' asked Catherine.

'Is he going to die?' Jannie's eyes sent out a mute appeal for help.

'Not if I can help it,' said Catherine, 'but we have a job to do. Fetch me your pots and pans. We have to raise some steam to moisten the air.'

While Jannie fetched her pots Catherine raked out the ash in the stove, opened the dampers and fuelled the fire with more peat. She lifted the kettle that was sitting on the hob; it was light, nearly empty. She took it to where two buckets of water stood just inside the door, filled it and set it back on the stove. When Jannie gave her the cooking-pans she filled them with water too.

'A bowl and a flannel now,' said Catherine. 'I want to sponge Daa's face, help to cool him.' She found it strange to be giving orders to Jannie, but her nurse's training had come to the fore and she found it exhilarating to be in charge.

'What do you want me to do now?' said Jannie.

'Find me a clean shirt for Daa. And do you happen to have an oil stove?'

'Ay, we do, just a little one.'

'Can I stand a kettle on it?' Jannie nodded. 'That'll do then.'

The click of the latch announced the arrival of Laura. 'I was just come to see if there was anything you wanted,' she said.

'Yes,' said Catherine. 'Would you look in the top drawer of the little chest by my bed and get me my thermometer? Another thing: do you have anything I can make a poultice from? Bread's out of the question.'

'Oatmeal?'

'You're a gem. Could anyone could get me a bottle of Friar's Balsam.'

'I think we have some,' said Laura.

'Now, Jannie, let's get to work,' said Catherine as Laura closed the door behind her. How easy it was now to use her mother-in-law's first name.

While Jannie looked for a clean shirt Catherine dipped up some water in a mug, added a dash of hot water and took it to Daa. 'I thought you might need a drink,' she said. 'It's just water.' With no word of thanks he took the cup from her, drank, then pushed it away.

The Jameson kitchen was quite full of steam now. Catherine topped up the pans as the level of water in them fell. Daa still wheezed, still dragged air in and pushed it out of his lungs. The nurse in Catherine wanted to change his shirt, fill a bowl with warm water and sponge him all over, but he would probably not want her to and Jannie would surely not let her.

She put a bowl of tepid water on a chair by the bed, dipped the flannel in it and wrung it out. 'Let me just freshen you up,' she said. Daa put up both hands as if to warn her off, but Catherine caught them in her free hand and held them while she began to wipe the flannel gently over his face. To her surprise he succumbed, but when she suggested helping him into a clean shirt the offer was met with rising anger. 'You'll feel much better if we do,' said Catherine, but Daa would not be moved.

I've got to get it off him somehow, she thought, and wondered if Jannie would agree to help her. Taking her mother-in-law's religious fervour into account she guessed that neither of them had ever seen the other without their clothes, so why would they allow a stranger like her to do so?

Daa was becoming more and more lethargic, his breathing rough and laboured and he was sweating profusely.

THIRTY ONE

Daa cowered in the corner of the bed. Trembling, eyes staring, face distorted, he plucked at the sheets and cried, 'He's come for me. Get him out.'

'Who's come for you?' asked Catherine.

'Yon trowie man, can you not see him? I'm not bad to the wee folk; I've left them a grain o' corn and bits fae da harvest. Make him go away, get him out.' The outburst left him gasping; with shaking hands he pulled up the sheet to cover his face. Delirium had pitched him into a fantasy world.

'Oh, yes,' said Catherine, 'I see him.' As if to a small child she spoke in a soft comforting voice. 'It's all right, I'll send him away.' Going to the corner of the room she lifted her hand and wagged a finger. 'Now you listen to me,' she said to a non-existent trow. 'The man of the house has done everything he should; there is no need for you to be here. We would be obliged if you would go back to where you came from.' She opened the door and made as though to usher the trowie man out, bade him goodbye and closed it. 'He's gone now, Daa,' she said.

'Get you away from me,' said Daa, when Catherine tried to readjust his pillows. 'What are you doin in my house?' Far from thanking Catherine for what she'd done Daa lifted his hand and gave her a stinging slap across the face. There was no recognition in his eyes when he looked at her and, strangely, no animosity in his manner when later she fetched a drink for him. Eagerly he took and drank, then, after wiping his mouth with the back of his hand, cowered back into the pillows. Quieter now that the imaginary trow had been sent away he lay back with his eyes closed; from time to time he moaned gently, then started up to mutter something and look suspiciously at Catherine.

'Come, let me put this to your face,' said Jannie. She put a cloth she had dipped in cold water gently on Catherine's cheek. 'He should not have done that.'

The coldness of the cloth took away the sting. 'He's not himself,' said

Catherine. 'You know as well as I that he would not have done that if he was.'

'It doesn't matter; you want to make him well.'

'And we will.'

'God willing,' said Jannie.

In order to take his temperature in the intervals when Daa was amenable, Catherine tucked the thermometer under his armpit. The reading crept up despite her efforts to keep the fever down and when she found it nearing 104 degrees she insisted that someone must fetch the doctor. The message was sent via the postman and Billie came to tell them that Lumsden had been called away to a difficult birth. Tears started to Catherine's eyes. She had done all she could.

With Jannie's help and a bit of a struggle they had managed to change Daa's shirt. They had made poultices and put them on his chest. They had patted his back, sponged his face and as much else as they could get at, given him warm drinks and held inhalations of Friar's Balsam under his nose. They had kept the fire burning bright, checked the water in kettle, pots and pans. Now, with everything done that could be done, Jannie had collapsed into Daa's armchair and fallen asleep while Catherine sat to wait for the doctor.

Sitting beside Daa's bed in the hot, steamy, kitchen Catherine suddenly remembered the joint of meat she had put in her own oven to cook, sighed and relaxed as she vaguely recalled Laura telling her she had rescued it. Laura had brought bowls of soup for their dinner, had fed the dogs and looked after Robbie. Billie had come over to help and had kept them supplied with peat and fresh water, had done her outside work, fed the ewes and checked that all was well. Now, perhaps Neil Lumsden would relieve her of her responsibility.

She was tired, dead-beat and had nothing to do but wait. For three days and nights, never letting herself close her eyes for more than a few minutes she had sat up while Jannie dozed in the armchair. Her sleep-starved vigil had left her in a state of exhaustion and soon her head began to nod, her eyes to close and, despite all efforts to stay awake, she drifted into the never, never world of sleep. As she went deeper her body softened and relaxed and she began to lean sideways. Then she was falling. Suddenly awake she grasped for something to hold on to. Still drowsy she shook herself mentally and physically. Oh my goodness, I mustn't do that, she thought, mustn't let myself sleep. Instinctively she looked at her patient. Daa lay back against the pillows, eyes closed.

An uneasy feeling made Catherine hold her breath. The room was quiet, too quiet; there was no noise other than the lazy quirk of the kettle, the slither of ash in the fire and the sound of Jannie's snoring breath. Catherine strained to hear the wheeze and whistle of Daa pulling air into his lungs … there was nothing.

'Oh please, don't let it be …' she whispered. She got up and went to the bedside. Daa lay limp and relaxed, his chest that until now had risen and fallen like the swell of the sea, lay flat. A sudden chill made Catherine shiver. Picking up his limp wrist she felt for a pulse, searched and uttered an audible sigh of relief when she found it. It was not strong, but it was there, beating rhythmically. He was sleeping, breathing peacefully. The crisis was over.

'Oh, thank God,' sighed Catherine. She leaned over him again. Yes, his face had softened and regained some of its normal colour and his breathing was slow and regular. All was well and now she too could relax.

'Jannie.' Catherine put her hand on her mother-in-law's shoulder and shook it gently. 'Jannie, wake up.' Looking down at her, she saw the emotions of shock and surprise, hope, quickly followed by despair that flitted across her face. 'It's all right,' she said. 'The worst is over. Come and look.'

They stood by the bed. Jannie looked closely at Daa and touched his hand.

When she turned to look at Catherine tears were running down her cheeks.

'Thank you. I should have known my Robbie'd make the right choice …' She pulled a handkerchief out of her apron pocket and began to wipe her eyes.

'Tea,' said Catherine.

'What?'

'I could do with a cup of tea, couldn't you?'

'Ay, I'll make it,' said Jannie, and smiled as she put her hankie away.

Catherine sat down. Jannie made tea, then ran to tell Mina and Laura the news. Catherine was ladling sugar into her cup when Neil Lumsden arrived. He had become her friend and she greeted him now with, 'You know something? I don't think I shall bother to call you to Deepdale any more. Your patient has passed the crisis, you're too late … again.'

He grinned at her. 'And I don't think I would bother to come if you did. Is that tea? Pour me a cup, would you, while I have a look at the patient?'

Daa slept peacefully while the doctor checked his pulse, listened to his breathing, took his temperature. 'I won't disturb him any more,' he said. 'I'll look in tomorrow after surgery. You've done a good job.' He sat down to drink his tea. 'When did you last have a night's sleep? Is somebody going to take over?'

'Yes, Mina will be here soon,' said Catherine.

As she saw Lumsden out Laura came in. 'What did he say?' she asked.

'Not much,' said Catherine. 'But Daa's over the worst.'

'He's going to be all right?'

'He should be. Can you and Mina help Jannie now?'

Laura nodded. 'We can, and we'll keep Robbie a peerie while longer.'

'Thank you, Laura. Daa'll be hungry when he wakes,' said Catherine. 'Beat an egg and put some hot milk and a spoonful of sugar with it. I'll see if I can get some Bengers food tomorrow. You'll have to feed him like a baby and help him get his strength back before he can have minced beef and tatties or anything like that.'

Laura took both Catherine's hands in hers. 'You have a good heart. You and the peerie lad have brought sunshine to us. Now you have to think of your future, so when Norrie asks you say yes.'

'I already have, but I told him he had to wait.' To Catherine's surprise Laura threw her arms round her and hugged her.

'Then I wish you all the happiness in the world. Norrie's a good man.'

Happy to hand over care of Daa to Jannie and her sisters Catherine went home, turned the key in the door and went to her bed.

THIRTY TWO

WITH THE LAST day of March came the first of the lambs. After that they came thick and fast. But the ewes lambed easy and when the first flush was over Catherine allowed herself a little more time for sleep. Norrie came to look, patted her on the back and said, 'I never thought you'd do so well, not having anything to do wi' sheep before. Daa taught you well.' Then he was away to tend his own flocks.

When the Cheviots had all dropped their lambs there was a brief respite before Robbie was to start school. He had filled out, was growing fast and needed new clothes. Catherine took him to Lerwick to buy them.

'What's it like going to school, Mam?' he asked.

'You'll love it. You'll learn to read and write and there'll be other boys and girls to play with.' They were walking along Commercial Street.

With an air of indignation he said, 'I can read now.'

'Yes, but you'll learn to write too.'

'Is that all?'

'What do you mean – is that all?' Catherine stopped and looked at him.

'Laura was teaching me to read and she got me a pencil and I was learning to write. I'm no needin' to go to school.'

'All children have to go to school. Reading and writing are not the only subjects you'll be taught. There's a great big world out there, you'll learn about countries and people and a lot of things. It's a goldmine.'

'What's a goldmine?'

'Well, there you go, Robbie. That's something you'll have to find out. Come on, I've got to buy you some new shoes.'

When Robbie saw the child's seat fastened to his mother's bicycle he said there was no way that he would sit up there when he had a bicycle of his own.

'Lot's of children get carried to school,' said Catherine. 'Not only you.'

'I'm not goin' to sit on that.' Robbie locked eyes with her. Catherine stared back at him, willing him to give way. When he didn't she foresaw trouble looming in the future. 'Oh well, have it your own way,' she said, 'but don't blame me if you get tired and find it too much.'

The aunts and Jannie came out to see him on his way. Laura gave him a buttered bannock. Mina patted him on the head and Jannie wished him luck. Then they stood and waved him on his way.

Proud to be on the road at last, Robbie pedalled along in front of his mother. Though he still sometimes took a tumble he rode his bike well. It was just a short journey to the school, a little more than a mile but, thought Catherine, it was the first step on his journey away from her. Soon he would become involved in a world of his own, one in which he would have his own friends. There would be things he would not tell her, things she would not know about.

At the door to the school they were met by the head teacher, a warm buxom woman who smiled at Robbie and said she was pleased to see him; wouldn't he come and join the others? She took him by the hand, and with a smile dismissed Catherine. The door closed. Catherine, a knot in her stomach and an absurd feeling that she was going to cry, got on her bicycle and went home.

Never had the day seemed so long. Never, when she'd left Robbie with the aunts or Jannie, had she given him a second thought. But now he was continually in her mind. She marked the day in sections. At ten he would be out to play, at twelve he would eat the bannock Laura had given him, drink the milk and eat the sandwich she made.. At some time after two he would be out in the school yard again and at three she would be waiting for him.

When at last the waiting was over and she was on her way to meet him she pedalled fast, praying that the children wouldn't be let out early or that she would be late. Two other anxious mothers were at the school gate; she wondered if her anxiety was as patently obvious as theirs.

'Is your lad started school today?' asked one.

'Yes,' said Catherine.

'Mine too. Wonder how they're getting on?'

Catherine gave a nervous chuckle. 'Better than us, I expect.'

Then there they were; half a dozen five-year-olds, coats on anyhow, socks wrinkled and hair-ribbons missing. Robbie was last. Everything about him, the set expression on his face and the determined way in which he walked told her he had not enjoyed the day. Wondering what had gone wrong, she went to meet him.

'Hello,' she said. 'Have you had a nice time?'

He gave her a withering glance. 'I told you I didna need to go to school,' he said.

'Oh.' Suppressing a smile Catherine watched as he marched purposefully to where he'd left his bicycle. Talk of school was better left until they were home.

Robbie led the way as they cycled back to Deepdale. Catherine saw how he leaned into his task; his little legs pumping up and down. The poker-straight line of his back told her more than she could ever have seen in his face. She began to laugh. How could she have spent the day worrying about him? If family traits were inherited then he had more than his fair share. No one was going to persuade him to do something he didn't want to, but she would have to make him realize that school was compulsory and he had to attend.

At home she told him to change out of his school clothes; then she took him with her to see the sheep, let him visit the aunts, and didn't broach the subject of school until after they had had their tea.

'Now,' she said, 'tell me what happened. What didn't you like?'

'We didn't do anything and I didna like the others.'

'You must have done something, and what do you mean by the others?'

'The other bairns is silly. We was give some bits of paper and crayons and we had to do a picture. We had to sit in our desk and not get up till teacher said. We didn't learn any letters. I thought you said she would teach me how to write.'

The little boy was so aggrieved that he glowered at his mother and Catherine found it hard to keep a straight face. 'She will, but I expect she was busy today,' she said. 'She would have had a lot of things to do for the first day of term. Was that all that upset you?'

'There was a boy said I didn't have a daa like everybody else and that I lived wi' a lot of old wives.'

How cruel children could be. 'Of course you have a father,' she said.

'But he's not here,' said Robbie. 'Why is he not here?'

'I told you about your father. Don't you remember?' she said. 'He was a good brave man. He died and will be in heaven with Kay; that's what you must tell that boy. And as for the old wives, they're your great-aunts and your grandma.' She got up and went to sit by him, put her arm round him. 'Now listen. One day you will learn about the war in which lots of men went away to fight. Many didn't come back. You aren't the only one whose daddy isn't here.'

The little boy sat thinking. 'Could we get another?' he said.

'We could think about it,' said Catherine with a smile. She began to clear the table. 'School will be better tomorrow. You will like it, I promise.'

Robbie stared at her. 'Do you mean I have to go again?'

She didn't need telling that he was rubbing shoulders with dialect-speaking children for Robbie's accent had changed.

'I'm afraid so. All children have to go to school, every day except Saturday and Sunday.' Disbelief, disappointment and anger crossed Robbie's face. 'Believe me,' she said, 'you should not judge school by this first day. You'll not only learn to read and write but lots of other exciting things too.'

'I have to go *every day* … all the time?'

'Yes, but you will have holidays in the summer and at Christmas and Easter and there will be days off at half-term too.'

Robbie fixed his gaze on the table while he thought about what she said, then he slid off his chair. 'I'm going to see Daa,' he said, and she knew he would have a long conversation about the merits of school with his grandfather.

Norrie laughed when she told him of Robbie's reaction to his first day. 'What did you expect,' he said, 'when he has you for his mother?' She was washing the tea things in a bowl of water on the table and turning up the cups on a tray. 'I thought he'd like it,' she said, 'but he didn't like the other children and said he'd rather stay at home with Daa. He seemed to think he could learn more from him than he could at school.' She dried her hands and picked up a teacloth.

'He could learn a lot from the old man, but he'll be all right.'

'I worried about him all day.'

Norrie laughed. 'That was a waste of time, then. Have you thought about what you're going to put in the show this year'?'

'It will have to be Noble, a Cheviot ewe and lambs and I thought a crossbred and lambs and perhaps some ram lambs. I thought it might be good publicity to put some crossbreds in so that folk have a chance to see what they're like,' said Catherine. She had been drying dishes as they talked; when the last one was done she took the bowl of water and tipped it into a slop bucket, dried the tray and put it away. She took a plate of scones from the dresser and put them on the table, then turned to the stove, poured boiling water into the teapot and made tea.

'You've got it all worked out, haven't you?' said Norrie. 'You time your day so you get everything done, but when are you going to find time to wed me?'

'Don't change the subject.'

She poured tea and as she handed a cup to him Norrie took hold of her wrist. 'How long do you think I can wait?' he said.

'Let go of my wrist or I'll spill the tea.'

'You let go the cup.' Norrie put his hand over the top of it and moved it away as Catherine let go and, standing up he pulled her into his arms. 'I ken I said I'd wait for you,' he said, 'but you're tormenting me.'

Why couldn't she let herself go, when to be in his arms was all she wanted? Why not give in to the powerful need for love that rose in her when he kissed her? Why couldn't she tell him she loved him when she knew she did? When at last his lips left hers he said, 'Do you know what you're doing to me? You can't live in the past; Robbie wouldn't want you to.' Catherine was tracing the pattern on his jumper. 'What's wrong?'

'I don't know.' She looked up into his face. 'That's just it. I want to be with you but somehow I can't …' she pushed him away. 'Drink your tea.'

'It'll be cold.' Norrie took Catherine's hands in his. 'I know you're having a struggle, I'll not push you, but when you're ready,' he smiled and leaned forward to kiss the tip of her nose, 'I'll be here. I'll be off now.'

She saw him out, closed the door behind him and burst into tears. She had been so near to giving in, had wanted to, but yet again she'd held back. Why?

THIRTY THREE

CATHERINE TOOK TIME off from the surgery when it was time for the cross-bred ewes to lamb. Now proficient at assisting at a difficult birth Catherine only called Daa out of his bed on rare occasions. There were casualties: weak lambs from old ewes, a few stillborn and a few orphans, but all in all, the crop was good.

Summer, which had been slow to start, suddenly put on a burst of speed. The weather turned warm and grass rapidly became green. New growth also had a not so welcome effect. It caused the diarrhoea that Daa called 'skitters'. He and Catherine herded their flocks and dosed them. Anxiously she watched Noble, hoping she could keep him free of it; she didn't want to see him lose condition. When she wasn't going to and from school with Robbie or working at the surgery she trudged up the hill to work the peat. In between she cooked and cleaned, washed and ironed, dug her garden or helped Daa plant potatoes. There were the hill sheep to look after too. With her dog, Fly, she and Daa and other crofters met to call the stock in for dosing, foot-trimming or shearing.

Catherine marked off the days on her calendar as they crept closer to show day. Canny crofters eyed her warily. What was this English girl doing? She should be at home, raising a family. When she and Daa overheard some of the men talking about her they exchanged glances and grinned at each other. Fully recovered from his illness, Daa acted as though nothing had happened. His attitude towards Catherine returned to what it had been. It seemed he could not remember her nursing him, or was it that the memory embarrassed him?

One day when Mina was away on the bus to Lerwick, Laura called on Catherine to gossip over a cup of tea. She asked when the wedding was to be and when Catherine told her she didn't know said, 'Well, I'll make you a peerie shawl anyway, for it'll likely be in winter and then you can use it for your bairn.' The thought of having children with Norrie brought a flush to Catherine's cheeks and made her plead work to do. Laura smiled, said thank you for her tea and left.

Now that she knew that sheep were not paraded in the show ring in Shetland, Catherine's work with Noble was much easier. She dosed him, kept his feet trimmed, combed his coat to free him of the bits he picked up. On the crossbred ewe she put a collar: the lambs needed no mark, but she trusted herself to be able to pick out the ram lambs when the time came.

In summer her social life was confined to an occasional meal with Norrie, sometimes in her house, sometimes in his. Robbie liked going to Norrie's house, once Kay's, for Norrie had inherited everything in it and it was familiar territory for the boy. He told his elders about the ornaments, took books from the shelf, and when Catherine said he shouldn't he said that Kay had said he could, but to always put them back.

'Now you see why I miss her,' said Catherine. 'She was a very good influence on Robbie as well as being my friend. She was the only one who welcomed me when I came here.'

'But Jannie must have given you a welcome?' said Norrie.

'Now you know better than that, don't you? Of course she didn't, and I'm sure she'd still rather I didn't exist.' And that was where the matter was left.

On show day she rose from her bed in the small hours. She had penned the sheep she was taking to the show the night before. She had to be ready when Norrie called to pick them up, for he hadn't asked but had simply told her that he would. Noble had been groomed to within an inch of his life. She went up to him and gave him a handful of feed, which he nuzzled from her hand. 'It's up to you now,' she said. 'I've done my bit. You look like a winner, let's come home with a cup, eh?'

'So that's how you do it, is it? You talk to them and give them titbits.'

Catherine spun round. 'Billie,' she cried as she ran to throw her arms round him, 'what are you doing here?'

'I'm home for a holiday,' he said as he hugged her.

She leaned back in his arms and looked straight at him. 'Oh, I'm so happy to see you. When did you come home? Nobody told me. Is your girlfriend with you? How long are you going to stay? You'll have to tell me everything .. .

'There you go, questions, questions, questions,' said Billie. 'I was just come to see what you were putting in the show and if you wanted a lift. Sally will be coming with me; you'll be able to meet her then. Who's taking your stuff in?'

'Norrie.'

'You've not married him yet, then?'

'No.'

'Why not?'

'That's none of your business.'

'I'd better go, then, but I'll pick you up later.'

'Thank you. I've a feeling it's going to be a good day, oh, here's Norrie.'

Catherine watched as her sheep were loaded into the back of Norrie's van and Noble put into a trailer that Norrie'd hitched to the back of it.

'Are you coming with me or do you want to go with Billie?' said Norrie.

'Billie's going home so I'll come with you,' said Catherine. She crossed her fingers as Norrie, having his van in bottom gear, coaxed it up out of the valley.

Catherine closed her eyes and prayed they would all get to the top safely.

'I was wondering if we could do something to the track, Norrie. The tradesmen come down this way now, and it's just getting worse and worse.'

'Might get some stone from the quarry,' said Norrie, 'but that's about all.'

'Well, that would be better than nothing.'

They were on the main road and sailing along to the showground. Catherine remembered, or thought she did, what she had to do to book in her entries. She need not have worried for Norrie was with her and it would not be the first time he had entered stock. When her animals were all penned they looked at the competition, or as much of it as was already booked in.

'If nothing better comes in you're going to do well,' said Norrie.

They went home then, Catherine to change her clothes and fetch Robbie from the aunts, and Norrie to pick up and take his own sheep to the show.

THIRTY FOUR

F OR ONCE ROBBIE was being difficult. 'Come on,' said Catherine, 'put your jacket on.' He was old enough to go to the show with her, but he wanted to stay with his grandfather. It was at a time like this that she missed Kay most of all. 'You're going to love it,' she said in an effort to put him in a better mood. 'There'll be lots of things there besides the animals, stuff for kids, books and toys, just like in a shop.'

'Will you buy me something?'

'Perhaps. Listen, I can hear Billie's car.' Billie had driven down into the valley and stopped by her door.

Billie's girlfriend seemed disinclined to talk, so conversation during the short journey was mostly confined to Catherine and Billie. Robbie screwed himself into a corner of the seat and sulked.

The showground was already crowded. It seemed to Catherine that half the population of the islands was there. But where was Norrie? She searched for him, saw him and waved her hand. He returned the wave and started towards her.

From the moment she stepped from her bed that morning her nerves had jangled; now her stomach churned in anticipation of what might be tied to Noble's pen. Was she going to be bitterly disappointed, or would she have cause to celebrate? She grasped Robbie's hand and clasped it tight. 'Mam, du's hurtin',' he cried as she marched along, dragging him by her side. She said she was sorry and loosened her grip.

'Hold on,' said Norrie. 'Don't be in such a hurry. Have you just got here?'

'Yes.' She wanted to ask how her animals had fared, but couldn't.

'So you've not seen what you've got?'

'No, I was on my way there now. Do you know?'

'Yes, I do, but I'm not going to tell you.'

'Why not?' Catherine's heart sank like a stone.

'It's not for me to say.' He wasn't smiling so he wasn't teasing. It must be bad and he was probably thinking she would burst into tears right where she stood if he told her. Suddenly she was angry with him. 'All right then, *don't* tell me,' she said. 'I'll go and look for myself. Come on, Robbie.' She wheeled about and walked away, stamping her feet as well as she could in the soft turf, dragging the little boy with her, so that he had to run to keep up.

'Mam, Mam, don't go so fast, du's pullin',' cried Robbie.

'Oh, shut up,' she said, never slackening her pace.

Billie and his girl had wandered off, but Norrie was right behind her. Knowing she wouldn't look back, he was smiling. 'I'm coming too,' he said.

As she walked along the row of pens Catherine had to dodge little groups of people: crofters and wives who were looking at the prizewinners, probably comparing them with their own stock. There was quite a cluster of folk round the pen that Noble was in, Billie and Sally among them. Billie's face was wreathed in smiles. Catherine gasped and felt her heart leap.

'Come and see this,' said Billie and stood her in front of the pen.

Fastened to the top rail was a red rosette; next to it a card proclaiming that Noble had won first prize in his class. Lost for words Catherine held her breath.

Robbie tugged at her skirt. 'Is he a champion, Mam?'

'Yes, he is,' said Catherine.

'Happy?' asked Billie, and grinned when all she could do was nod. 'Now come here,' he said. He led her along the pens till they reached the one her ewe and lambs were in. That too displayed a first-prize certificate and red rosette.

Standing behind her, Norrie said, 'You couldn't do better.'

'It's all thanks to Billie and Daa,' said Catherine. 'They taught me as much or more than I learned from all the books.' With their help she had done it, in spite of Jannie's opposition, in spite of Jannie's making her already rough road even rougher. She had cleared the first hurdle in her promise to work towards realizing Robbie's dream. When she turned to Norrie her eyes were full of tears.

'Oh lass, you don't have to cry,' he said and swept her into his arms.

'But I'm just so happy,' she sobbed, weeping into his jumper.

'Don't make my jersey wet; you know how wool shrinks,' joked Norrie.

'Yes, I know,' she said, lifting her head. 'What about the lambs?'

'Ah, you didn't do so well there. Just a second.'

'Just a second,' she echoed. 'Should I complain?' In her excitement she had forgotten Robbie. 'Where's my boy?' she said.

'He's with me,' said Billie. 'We're going to look at the ponies.'

'Look after him,' said Catherine.

'Mrs Jameson.' The man who spoke was big; his hair was black and like his beard, grizzled with grey. He carried a staff with a carved handle, a prized shepherd's staff. 'Are your lambs for sale?'

'Yes.' Who was this?

'I'd be interested to ken how much you're wanting for them.'

'Well …' Catherine began, then gasped. Norrie had pinched her bottom.

'The lambs'll be in the sale ring come autumn,' said Norrie. 'Mrs Jameson's not wanting to sell them till then.'

'By, that's a pity, but I ken,' said the man, 'very wise. You should get a good price. I'll be looking. Good day.' He tipped his hat and walked away.

'Who was that?' asked Catherine, 'and how dare you pinch my bum.'

'That's Hamish Inkster; he has a big place on the west side. It's a good job I was here; you might have said the wrong thing. That's why I nipped you.'

'You mean I can't be trusted to know the value of my stock, right?'

'Ay, but put them in the ring and when you see what folk'll pay you'll ken fine. Now we cannot stand here all day.'

It had been a tiring day, but by eight o'clock the sheep were home and Daa and Jannie had been shown the rosettes and certificates. Robbie was with the aunts, where he would stay the night, and it was time to get ready for the dance. Catherine dressed carefully, putting on one of the dresses her mother had given her and a precious pair of nylon stockings which she fastened to her suspender belt. She combed freshly washed hair, put on powder and lipstick, then a spot of perfume behind ears and on wrists. She was ready.

The kitchen was quiet. Catherine sat to wait for Norrie. At last he was there. 'How are you feeling?' he asked.

'I'm still on cloud nine; I can't believe things went so well.'

'You worked hard for it, lass. You deserve your success.'

They were late and dancing was already in full swing when they reached the hall. When Catherine had told Kay she couldn't do the Shetland dances Kay wound up her gramophone and taught her. Now she was happy to join the set of an eightsome reel, prance through the polka, the Gay Gordons and the Boston twostep, but whomever else she danced with, the slow waltz was always for Norrie.

He held her close and whispered. 'Shall we go? I've a surprise for you.'

They left during the interval.

'Where are you taking me?' she asked when they were about to get into Norrie's van.

He looked at her over the top of it. 'We're going to have a picnic.'

'A picnic? Are you mad?' she cried. 'It's the middle of the night.'

'It's a fine night and there's a full moon. What could be more romantic? It is romance you want, is it not?'

'Norrie Williams,' said Catherine as she slid into the passenger seat, 'you're completely crazy. Only you could think of something like this.'

Catherine wondered where they were going, but when he drove up the steep incline to Spencie's Field she knew. At the top of the hill he parked the van, took out a basket and a rug and told her to follow him. He walked a little way until he came to a depression in the hillside. There he put down the basket and rug and put an arm round her. 'What could you want better than this?' he said as he spread his other arm wide indicating with a sweeping gesture the south mainland.

The moon in a clear sky gave a cold light, sparkled on creaming wave tops and lit up the foam where breakers crashed at the foot of the cliffs. To the south the lighthouse at Sumburgh stood out clearly and Fair Isle showed its presence by the intermittent flash from its light. To the west Foula hovered on the horizon and below them lights glowed in house windows.

'It's magic,' said Catherine. 'How did you know where to come?'

Norrie spread the rug, took a bottle of wine, some cups and sandwiches out of the basket. 'I found it when we were herding sheep one time.' He was kneeling, gestured to Catherine to sit. 'Would you do me the honour, my lady?' he said. 'Why, certainly sir,' she replied, curtseying and entering into the spirit of his nonsense.

He poured wine. 'Fine thing I remembered the corkscrew, is it not?' They ate sandwiches made with cold roast pork and little cakes which he swore he'd made himself, but later confessed he'd wheedled from one of the women behind the refreshment table in the dance hall.

Sitting on the rug, a cup of wine in her hand, Catherine gazed across the vast expanse of moon-spangled sea and counted the rhythm of the Fair Isle light. The song of the ocean and the sigh of the wind was a special kind of music. Norrie was a kind man, the impromptu picnic and the peace of their surroundings made a welcome closure to a day when her emotions had been in turmoil.

'There's so much sky up here,' she said. 'I suppose it's because we're surrounded by the sea. I love living here. Kay once said that islands have a magic of their own and that they claim your soul.'

Norrie lay on his back. 'I wouldn't want to live anywhere else.'

'Not like Billie, then. He wanted to go.'

'No he didn't. You made him.'

'I did not.'

'Yes you did; you broke his heart.'

Twisting herself round Catherine threw a screwed-up paper bag at him. 'I did no such thing,' she said. 'He asked me more than once what it was like in the south. I told him, but he still wanted to go.'

'No no.' Norrie shook his head. 'You broke his heart like you're breaking mine. You're a cruel woman.'

Catherine laughed. 'Aw, there, there,' she crooned. She broke off a stalk of dry grass and leaned over to tickle the end of his nose.

Norrie turned to look at her. Suddenly the world slipped away and her insides began to melt. Norrie was looking at her with his heart in his eyes. He reached out and took her hand. She bent her head and kissed him gently, then lay down beside him and curled herself into the crook of his arm. Neither spoke. Lying there Catherine gazed up at the moon swimming in the dark arc of the sky, at the stars, brittle needlepoints of light. 'I never dreamed you would do anything like this, Norrie,' she said at last. 'It's just perfect. You really are a lovely man.'

He smiled. 'Does that mean you're getting fond o' me?'

She knew what her feelings for him were and didn't want to wait any longer to tell him. 'More than that, I love you,' she said, her lips kissing his as she said it.

'Catherine … Catherine …' stammered Norrie. 'Do you know how long I've been waiting to hear you say that? I knew you were to be mine the first time I saw you, but you were only just a widow. I couldn't say anything.'

'And you've waited all this time.'

'I'd made up me mind, nothing was going to make me change it.'

She covered his mouth with her hand as he was about to kiss her again. 'I know now why I kept making you wait. Making Robbie's dream come true was more important and it was because I couldn't think of bringing anyone else into my house … or my bed: that was a very special bed. I hated the box, wanted a proper bed. We ordered it and waited weeks for it to come.' She paused, then in a voice little more than a whisper said, 'Robbie and I only slept in it the once.'

For a minute or two Norrie made no reply. Raising a hand he gently stroked her cheek. 'Well, darlin',' he said at last, 'when you marry me you'll live with me and sleep in my bed.' He paused, then said, 'When's it going to be?'

'Soon. I won't make you wait much longer.'

He held her tight, so tight she thought her ribs might break. 'I shall love you to my dying day,' he said.

'What about now?'

'Now? I didn't bring you here for that.'

'I didn't think you did.'

'But…'

'Shut up and kiss me,' said Catherine.

THIRTY FIVE

'**D**AA, DO YOU know anyone who would make us a signboard?' asked Catherine.

'Why do you want a sign? Everybody kens where we live.'

'Yes, I know, but Robbie said when he'd got a prizewinner he'd have a sign made to advertise the Cheviots. Well, we've done it and we need the sign.'

'What did you want to put on it?'

'Deepdale Cheviots, Jameson & Son.'

'Not … *Mrs* … Jameson?'

'No. Jameson & Son.'

Daa smiled and nodded his head. 'Yeh, I ken somebody.'

Weeks passed. Catherine had cycled to Lerwick to do some shopping and as she approached the head of the valley on her way home, there it was. She got off her bike and stared at it. Above the lettering, **DEEP-DALE CHEVIOTS JAMESON & SON** had been painted a picture of a Cheviot ram.

Catherine stood for a long time looking at it. It was a dream come true, paid for with long days, broken nights, working out of doors in all winds and weathers and at the same time battling mentally with Jannie's hurtful little tricks. Was it worth it and would she do it again? Yes, if need be.

Summer had been good: hot sunny days with never a breath of wind and Daa had cut, turned and carried hay by mid August. The good weather went on well into the beginning of September. "We shall pay for this," said the old folk. But enough rain had fallen for a plentiful supply of grass and the lambs had grown well. Soon it would be time to sell them.

Little Robbie, not so little now, had spent the summer holidays dogging his grandfather. Though he told Laura he enjoyed games and was good at them, he would not admit that he liked school. He often stayed with Jannie and had a meal with his grandparents when he'd been with Daa all day.

While the weather still held good Daa cut the corn, just in time, as it happened for the very day after he had gathered it in the rain started. Once begun, it seemed as though it would never stop. With the equinox came gales. Ferocious winds lashed anything that dared stand in their way; sent rain to rattle on windowpanes, howled down chimneys, goaded the sea to fury and sent sheep and all other animals to seek shelter wherever they could. A tethered animal had nowhere to run, so Catherine took Noble and put him in the outhouse. His tether was getting frayed; she resolved to get him a new one. She kept Robbie at home with her, did some baking, mending and writing letters.

As September drew to a close the rain stopped and the wind changed quarter. All was calm after the storm. The sun shone weakly, as if apologizing for the commotion. The wind now came from the south and dried the land, potato haulm blackened and died and in October Daa said they would lift the potatoes.

This was the last harvest of the year and everyone was required to help. Mina and Laura looped up their skirts so they wouldn't trip themselves up. When they bent over Catherine could see their legs encased in knitted woollen stockings. What didn't they knit? Jannie's skirts were not as long and she needed to do nothing with them. Catherine wore the trousers which had caused such a stir when she first appeared in them. Robbie abandoned the potato field to play with his puppy. All day they worked, from the minute the first row was ploughed out until the light began to fade. The women, backs aching from stooping, went away to their houses to prepare a meal while Daa carted the crop already gathered to the barn. Next day they worked again and by late afternoon all the potatoes were in and covered with a blanket of straw. There was enough till potatoes came again.

Weary from two days' hard work Catherine filled her pots and pans and put them on to heat; a hot bath to ease her aching muscles was what she needed. After she and Robbie had eaten she fetched the wash tub, poured enough water in to bath Robbie and put him in. While he splashed and tried to blow bubbles with the soap she refilled the pots and put them back to heat again.

The little boy loved his bath and it wasn't until the water had cooled that he would let his mother get him out; but at last he was in bed. Catherine locked the door. She didn't want to be taken by surprise. She stepped into the tub and relaxed into the hot water. It felt so good and eased the pain in her back. She thought about Mina and Laura and wondered if they were having a bath; tried to imagine stiff, unbending Mina getting into a tub. Would Laura be sent out of the room? Then she wondered if they ever did bath, for she'd never seen a tub big enough to hold either of them at their house.

In bed at last, her eyes closed as soon as her head touched the pillow, and she sank into sleep. A voice shouting her name, a fist pounding on her door and the terrified cries of Robbie woke her. She leaped out of bed and reached for her torch. 'It's all right, Robbie, I'm here,' she said as, pushing her arms into her dressing-gown she made for the door. 'Who is it?' she cried.

'It's me, Norrie, let me in.'

'Why aren't you in bed?'

But Norrie was pushing past her. 'Hide me,' he said.

'You're drunk,' said Catherine as she caught a whiff of whisky.

'No, I'm not,' protested Norrie; though it was evident that he was, for he was none too steady on his feet. 'Hide me,' he said again.

'You must be in trouble. Tell me what it is before I do,' said Catherine.

'I'm done nothing.' Norrie's words were slurred. 'Police are after me.'

'They won't be after you for nothing. What have you done?'

'There's no time. You have to believe me. Please help me.'

If the police came to her door whatever was she going to say? Should she do as he asked? And if she did, where on earth could she put him? While he stood holding on to the back of a chair for support she looked at him. This was a Norrie she hadn't seen before. But it was the first time, so she had to give him the benefit of the doubt. There was only one place for him.

'Come with me,' she said and led the way to her bedroom. 'Get undressed and into bed. I'll deal with you later.'

Norrie was in no mood to argue, for there was no kindness in her voice. Catherine watched as he dropped his clothes, climbed into bed and within seconds was sound asleep. She looked at him and wondered what he'd been up to. It must be to do with alcohol; she couldn't imagine him being involved in any sort of crime.

'Mam.' It was Robbie.

'It's all right, darling. Norrie lost his key and can't get into his house. Go back to sleep now.'

In the living room she lit the lamp, stirred the fire and put the kettle on to boil. She was not going back to bed. Not because Norrie was in it, but because it was almost five o'clock and nearly time to get up anyway.

She heard the sound of boots on the stones outside before the knock on the door. She waited a while and let whoever it was knock again before she went to open it. Two policemen stood there. 'We're looking for Norrie Williams,' said one. 'We know he lives in the valley, but we can't get any answer at his house. We saw your light and wondered if you'd seen him? You're up and about early.'

'Yes, I got up to make a drink and, as you see,' Catherine indicated her dressing-gown, 'I shall be going back to bed. Norrie? I see him every day.'

'Sorry, ma'am,' said the officer. 'I meant tonight.'

'Tonight? He's asleep. What do you want him for?'

'Asleep?'

'Yes, and sleep is what you do when you go to bed, isn't it?'

'But … we followed him here from Lerwick.'

'No, oh no,' said Catherine. 'Must be someone else. Oh dear, have they given you the slip? I don't know how you tell them apart, all those whiskers; they all look the same to me. Are you sure it's Norrie you want? I'll go and wake him if it is.' Please, oh please don't let them say yes, prayed Catherine, her fingers crossed. Both men looked at her. She stared back at them. It was obvious they were trying to decide whether to believe her or not. 'I know it's not the done thing to sleep together,' she said, 'but we are going to be married shortly. I'd appreciate it if you'd keep this to yourselves.'

The older policeman smiled while the younger smirked. 'Na, it's all right. Sorry to have bothered you.' They both tipped their caps and said good night.

'That's all right, officer. I hope you find the one you want.' She smiled at them as she closed the door. Then she slid the bolts home, leaned against it and breathed a sigh of relief. 'Now for the truth,' she muttered as she picked up the candlestick and went along to the bedroom.

Norrie lay on his back, his mouth was open and he was making little snoring noises. Such a shame to wake him, but she was going to. She put a hand on his shoulder and shook it. Norrie snorted and turned on his side. She shook him again, harder this time.

'What, what,' said Norrie, starting up from sleep.

'Wake up, I need answers and they'd better be good.'

He grinned. 'I must be dreaming. Is that really you standing there?'

'Who else? I've told lies and sent away the men who were looking for you. I want to know what you've been up to.'

Norrie struggled to sit up. 'Do you really?'

194

'Yes. I might have put myself into a very bad position trying to help you. If you had to go to court I could be in great trouble. Now tell me the truth.'

'I would never lie to you,' said Norrie. 'Me and some of the boys was along at Gibbie's. You know who I mean?' Catherine nodded. 'He'd gotten a barrel brought up on one of the boats, so we was in for a good night, but Magnie and Tammy Halcrow got to blows. Gibbie threw them out and then the police was there. I wasna goin' to stay, but they must have seen me.'

'It's one thing to get a bottle of whisky to drink in your own home, but you know Shetland's dry, so to go drinking illicit liquor in a public house in the middle of the town is asking for trouble,' said Catherine. 'You knew the risk you were taking. I would have thought you'd know better.'

'Aw, come on, what else is there to do?' said Norrie. Catherine turned her head away and didn't answer. 'What did you tell them, lass?' he said at last.

'I let them think you'd spent the night in my bed and that they'd been mistaken and that it was someone else they wanted. I think they believed me. I hope they did.'

With a sigh of relief Norrie pulled her to him and would have laid her down beside him, but Catherine pushed him away. 'Get up, Norrie Williams.' She spoke sharply. 'Get dressed and go home before anyone else sees you. You know Jannie would have me hung, drawn and quartered if she found out you were here. I would never be able to convince her you hadn't stayed the night.'

In the kitchen the kettle was boiling. Catherine made a pot of tea. She poured out a cupful and when Norrie came through from the bedroom relented and poured some for him too.

'Now go,' she said when he'd drunk it.

THIRTY SIX

Now that ROBBIE was at school it was not unusual for him to come home with the sniffles, but this time the cold he caught had developed until his nose was blocked, his eyes were watery, and he was definitely unwell. But Catherine had to work and also go to Lerwick to shop.

'You're late this morning.' Laura had come to collect Robbie.

'He's not very well,' said Catherine. 'I think I should stay home.'

'No no, he'll be all right with us. Go to work; we're happy to have him.'

It was only a cold, after all; nothing serious. He would be warm, well fed and cared for, so Catherine cycled off to the surgery. It was late before she was able to get away, but at last she was on the road to Lerwick. In the town, with a shopping list in her hand, she hurried to make her purchases. She was on her way to where she had left her bicycle when someone called her name.

'Catherine, wait.' Rose came panting up to her. 'My, you are in a hurry. How are you? We haven't seen you in ages.'

'Sorry, Rose, I'll come over soon.'

'It's awful cold. Shall we go for a cup of tea? Maybe you should have something to eat too.'

A cup of tea and a bun would be nice and what difference would another thirty minutes make. Catherine hardly ever met anyone she knew when she went into the town and, anxious to get home, had never stopped for refreshment. Being in the café with Rose was a rare treat and time sped by as they caught up with all that had been going on. When Catherine told Rose about her holiday with her family, a memory of whom she had seen on the boat surfaced.

'I saw Marie Lumsden on the boat,' she said. 'She was with a man.'

'But not Neil,' said Rose.

'That's right. They looked awful close.'

'Not for me to say, but Neil Lumsden deserves better.'

'I thought she was supposed to suffer with her health.'

'It's a convenience, I think,' said Rose. 'I don't want to offend you, but she's English and she's one that doesn't fit in, if you know what I mean. I think she'd like to go back south, but I don't think Neil wants to. Still, that's his problem. Now, when are you and Norrie going to get wed?"

'Soon, but I haven't told Jannie yet so don't say a word.' Catherine looked at the watch on her wrist. 'Is that the time? I'd better get going.' She picked up her bags.

'I'm going too,' said Rose.

As she pedalled home Catherine thought about her wedding. It would be quiet, no white dress, no bridesmaids and, with her family so far away, few guests. Jannie and Daa would have to be told before the banns were read. She thought again about Norrie's escapade in Lerwick. She had been afraid the police would come again. But nothing had happened and life had gone on as before. She had always known that Norrie drank, as Kay did and as did she on occasion, even though Shetland was dry and alcohol hard to get. Kay had bought whisky for her, but where Kay got it she didn't know and had never asked. She smiled, as she always did, when she saw the sign at the top of the hill. She stopped at Mina's house, looked in, and was pleased to see that Robbie was a little better.

'I'll leave him with you till I get my jobs done,' she said.

Despite the refreshment she'd had in the café she wanted a cup of tea before she did anything else. Always on the side of the stove, the kettle soon boiled. She made tea and buttered a slice of fruit bread; it would keep her going until she could cook a proper meal. Refreshed, she changed into her working clothes and put on her outdoor coat, a wonderful garment full of pockets in which were lengths of string, a torch, a pocket knife and other bits and bobs.

She would move Noble first. As she went round the house she called, 'Ked, ked, ked,' to let him know she was coming. When she turned the corner and looked for him her heart stood still. He wasn't there. Had someone stolen him? His tether was lying on the ground. It was broken. She had known it was frayed and that she should have done something about it. But he couldn't be far away; perhaps he was in the outhouse where she had put him when the weather was so bad. She went to look, but he wasn't there. With pounding heart she ran and hammered on Mina's door, opened it and burst in.

'Have you seen Noble?' she cried. 'He's broken his tether and I can't find him.' Both the aunts shook their heads; they had been busy and hadn't looked out. At Jannie's house, where usually she would have knocked and waited, she opened the door and went in. 'Oh, Jannie, there you are,' she cried.

'What's the matter wi' you?' said Jannie.

'I can't find Noble. His tether's broken. Have you seen him?'

'Ay, I did,' said Jannie, 'a while ago. He was headin' for the hill.'

Already moving towards the door Catherine said, 'How long ago was that?'

'Maybe an hour.'

'An hour! Oh God, he could travel a long way in an hour. I shall have to go and find him.' Catherine pulled her hat down over her ears and set off at a run. 'Don't go up the hill, it's going to snow,' shouted Jannie. Standing by her door she shouted again. 'He'll come to no harm. Leave him be … come back.'

But Catherine was already too far away to hear.

At first she climbed quickly, but realizing that she probably had a long way to go she slowed down. When she reached the moor she stopped and turning slowly round looked to see if he was there. There was no sign of him; he must have gone higher up. Turning to face the hill she shielded her eyes and scanned the hillside. Were those sheep that she could see, or just some white quartz rocks? It was hard to tell, for it was a dull day and outlines tended to blur in the distance.

Keeping to the sheep trails she went on to begin the ascent of Stoney Hill. The gradient was steep and soon she was breathing hard. Was she going the right way? Daa had told her to study the way of the wind if she was looking for sheep and she would find them on the lee side. Looking ahead she saw an ominous dark cloud piling up behind the hill. And it was freezing. Her hands were cold even though she wore gloves; she stuffed them up the sleeves of her coat.

She saw him then and called his name. He turned to look at her. A grin of happiness spread across her face, and giving a sigh of relief she climbed again. She had found him. 'Bad boy, bad boy,' she scolded as she drew near. He didn't move. Neither did he come towards her or go away. When she reached him she saw why. The toggle on the part of the tether still attached to him had got caught and stuck in the fissure between two boulders. She remembered the first time she tethered him; protesting at being tied he pulled the rope from her hand and when he ran the toggle had jumped in the air with each bump in the ground. So that was it. It was a good thing the hill had captured him or she might not have found him and he could have died.

As she pulled the toggle out of its prison the first flakes of snow began to fall. She looked up and saw that the sky had grown dark and daylight was fading. What time was it? She felt for the watch on her wrist. It wasn't there – she'd taken it off while she washed her hands when she got home. No point looking for a watch: it would be dark soon, never mind the snow. She had to hurry.

But she couldn't hurry. Loose stones underfoot had her slipping and sliding, and visions of falling and perhaps breaking a leg or spraining an ankle made her move cautiously. *Don't go up the hill on your own.* How many times had that been said to her?

Snow fell gently, big flakes innocent and beautiful floated out of the sky to drift down and settle. Innocent but ominous, relentlessly they grew in number, faster they fell and faster and, like a placid man driven to anger, the mood changed. Beauty turned ugly and gentle became fierce as a blizzard overtook Catherine and her animal. Wind gusted to punch her in the back and to send snow whirling about her head, the beautiful flakes became hard and icy. They stung her face. Everything became wrapped in a blanket of white and her sense of direction deserted her; she could not see and only knew that she had to go down the hill -but which way? Frightened, dragging Noble behind her, she sobbed as she struggled on. It's only a storm, she told herself, it'll soon be over and I'll be able to see. But would she? Wouldn't night have fallen? Wouldn't it be dark? The gravity of her situation was something she dared not think about.

Don't go up the hill on your own.

Once again those words came back to haunt her. In front of her was the moor with its bogs and underground streams and there was no light to show her the safe places to walk. Why hadn't she listened?

What she could see of the ground beneath her feet was as white as the air around her; it was slippery and she'd got the wrong shoes on. She hadn't changed into her boots, hadn't intended to go moun-taineering. As she slipped and slid, her muscles tensed in anticipation of a fall. She held tight to Noble's tether; now that she had found him she wasn't going to let him go. And then it happened.

One foot shot out from under her and then the other. Arms flailing, she tried desperately to regain her balance. Like those of a newborn lamb her legs wouldn't support her and she was falling, sliding, rolling down the hill. She held fast to her anchor: the ram and his tether and, trying to save herself, she grabbed for anything that would be a hand-hold: a rock, a tuft of heather. But she was out of the stony area of the hill, on the bare turf lower down … sliding on a steep slope.

There was nothing she could do to stop her headlong flight, faster and faster she went and then she was in midair … flying. It was a feeling that was quickly shattered when she came to earth with a crash.

And all went dark.

THIRTY SEVEN

'NO, NO, YOU know I don't like those wet kisses.' Catherine put up her hand to push Norrie's face away. But it couldn't be Norrie, for whoever was blowing in her face had bad breath, and he didn't. She opened her eyes. From out of the gloom a long white face peered at her. An indistinct white mass loomed behind it and it was coming closer. She pressed herself hard against whatever it was she was lying on and opened her mouth to scream. Then she heard that familiar throaty rumble and knew that the apparition was none other than Noble. But she was lying down looking up into his face, which was odd. Then she remembered slithering down the hill, being flung headlong into the air, then crashing down.

Feeling around her she discovered that she was lying under a bank. It was a scrape made by sheep, eroded by cloven hoofs, a shelter against the scouring winds. Leaving the snow-covered ground and landing here had been what had given her the sensation of flying. She must have hit her head, which had knocked her out, and she wondered how long she had lain there. She was cold and wet.

Still clutched tightly in her hand was the end of Noble's tether. 'I'm not going to let you go again,' she said. 'You've got to stay with me.' She sat up; it was time to move. Praying that she hadn't broken any bones or sprained anything she gingerly stretched her legs and rotated her ankles. She did the same with her arms, then felt her ribs; good; all was in working order, no damage done. She struggled to her feet. There was still a long way to go.

Then the snow came again. White and blinding it scrambled her senses, stealing any idea she had of direction. And with the snow came utter darkness. She had to go down the hill. It didn't really matter in which direction. At the bottom there would be houses and anyone would take her in. But below her the moor lay in wait. She needed light. There should be a torch in her pocket. There was, and hoping there was still life in the battery she switched it on. She uttered a prayer of thanks when it worked.

With Noble plodding behind her she moved on; treading carefully, she walked in the pool of light thrown by the torch. They must be thinking of her at home now and wondering where she was; but no, only Jannie knew where she had gone. Would she tell Norrie? Would he come to look for her? He would, wouldn't he? She stood still to listen, eager to catch the sound of a voice calling her. The gusting wind buffeted her, screamed and howled around her. Then, in a lull, there it was. Not the wind, but a cry. Was someone calling her?

'Norrie, Norrie,' she shouted. 'I'm over here.'

She cupped an ear with a hand, held her breath to listen for a reply.

It came again, a thin bleating cry. It was not Norrie, just some silly old sheep. Keyed up with expectation Catherine screamed, 'NOOOOO.'

She had to go on, and now that the sheep trails had been covered in snow and obliterated she trod carefully. On she went until the torchlight showed her an area of short-cropped grass that the wind had swept clean of snow. It was a patch where the soil was better and the grass sweeter, which the sheep favoured and ate clean. She swung the torch around, and in front of her she saw a wall: broken down, but a wall. It was not one of the stone built shelters that had been put up as protection for sheep in bad weather; it looked like the wall round a croft yard. And if it was that meant she was close to habitation. She panned the torch round again and there, not a long way off, loomed the outline of a house.

'We've made it, boy,' she cried. Dragging Noble she started to run.

There was no light in the windows. Had the occupants gone to bed? Surely it was not that late. Keeping close to the walls Catherine walked round the house till she came to the door. One look at it and her heart sank to her boots. It was broken; the half that was left hung on rusty hinges. She didn't need to open it; there was enough room for her to go through. This must be the deserted house she had once wanted to explore. Balling her hands into fists she hammered on the rotten wood in anger and frustration. From inside came a scrabbling noise, a sound of movement. It could only be sheep. She folded an arm against the wall and leaning on it gave way and cried, sobbed until the futile tears gave way to the necessity of doing something, anything, to survive. She lifted her head and wiped her eyes on her sleeve. 'You always wanted to look inside,' she said. 'Well, now's your chance.'

It had been snowing steadily since she had found Noble, sometimes soft and gentle, sometimes driven by the wind to pile up in drifts. Now it was falling relentlessly, covering everything and growing deeper minute by minute.

She had two choices now. She could go on down the hill or spend the night in the house. If she went on she risked the batteries in her torch giving out or she might drop and lose it. If either happened she could have an accident and freeze to death. Spending the night in the house was worth looking into.

She squeezed through the gap beside the door and pointed the torch round the room. The glowing eyes of several sheep blinked at her before, surprised and frightened, they scattered away through a doorway into the other end of the house. Hopefully the roof was sound; if she stayed she would at least be dry. She pondered a moment but knew in her heart there was only one choice to make. It was too dark now; no one would be able to find her if they did come to look and it was better for them to worry about her for one night than to grieve for the rest of their lives. That was, provided she made it through the night.

Having made her decision she kicked aside the rubble on the floor and went to the corner of the room next to the hearth. The floor there, thick with dry dung, confirmed her belief that the roof was watertight. It was evident that the hill sheep used the shelter constantly. She sat down and pulled Noble close to her. Her shoes and the bottoms of her trousers were wet and her feet were cold. Although she was under cover and away from the snow hypothermia was her biggest danger; somehow she had to keep herself warm. Noble had lain down beside her. She took off her shoes, pushed her feet into his thick coat and revelled in his warmth.

But there was a long night ahead. Perhaps she could make a fire, there ought to be some dry wood somewhere? To start a fire she needed matches and paper. She searched her pockets. Matches she found, but nothing more in the way of paper than a couple of bills for sheep feed. Would they be enough?

She put her wet shoes and socks on again and shuddered as warm flesh came into contact with cold wet wool. While there was still life in the batteries she shone the torch on the disintegrating remains of a box-bed that divided the 'but and ben' ends of the house. With great delight she began to tear some wood off it. She crumpled the pieces of paper into a ball, put it on the hearth and stacked splinters of wood round it, then she added bigger pieces till they formed a pyramid. Praying that the wood would catch fire, she struck a match.

The paper burst instantly into flame, reached up to lick and scorch the wood, flared up, then died leaving a small heap of red ash. 'Oh please burn,' cried Catherine and threw herself down to lie on the floor. She placed tiny slivers of wood on the ash and began to blow gently until a little yellow flame rose up to lick the wood. She went on blowing softly till the flame grew and crept up to set the wood burning. As she put more small pieces of wood, carefully chosen, against the pyramid, she willed the fire to grow in strength. Gradually she added more until her fire crackled and burned and sent out heat. Sitting back on her heels she spread her hands out in front of it and gloried in the warmth.

The light from the fire illuminated the room, so she was able to turn off the torch. She sat for a while watching the leaping flames, but before they died she got up, stripped as much wood as she could from the old bed and piled it up in front of the fire. She would need a lot of wood to see her through the night, especially in the 'graveyard shift': the early hours when life hangs on a thread and the body is at its lowest ebb, suspended between hope and despair.

Noble had settled himself down by the wall. She kept the end of the tether which was still attached to him close to her so she could grab it in case he should decide to wander off. There was no noise from the animals that had rushed away and Catherine didn't know whether they were still in the house or had escaped through a broken window. Whatever they had done she had no plans to find out.

There was nothing else to do now but wait out the night. Sitting on the pile of boards she had gathered together she once again took off her socks and shoes. Her socks she slipped on to the end of a piece of wood and held them as close as she dared to the fire. She had turned her shoes on their sides and set them too as near as possible to the heat. She stretched out her legs to warm her feet.

As she gazed into the flames she thought of Jannie and Daa. They would probably be having supper, a big bowl of broth. What wouldn't she give for a steaming bowl of broth right now? It was such a long time ago since she had eaten that piece of bread, and her stomach was empty.

They would be missing her now. Jannie would have told Daa and Norrie. Robbie would not miss her; he was with the aunts and wouldn't know she was not at home. She knew they would look after him but hoped Mina would not dose him with any of her old-fashioned reme-dies. Would Jannie be worried? Perhaps, but if she wasn't Daa would be. She had grown very fond of Daa; he had taken her under his wing, believed in her and though he hadn't said so, she knew he did not approve of Jannie's attitude towards her.

And Norrie? Yes; Norrie would be worried, dear, kind, clown of a man that he was. She could imagine him pacing up and down and taking one too many drams as he fretted for her, staying out of his bed and looking out to see if she was coming. He would know that it was useless to look for her in the dark, know he would be putting his own life in danger if he did. He would be waiting for first light of day, the chance to move and come and search for her.

The warmth of the fire made her drowsy. Her eyelids grew heavy, her eyes closed and her head nodded. Fighting off the urge to sleep she shook herself awake. What if she let lack of sleep get the better of her, if she let the fire go out and the cold crept into her bones and she died? The thought of what it would do to those she left behind brought tears to her eyes. She thought of what she would miss. The joy of watching little Robbie grow up, and the things she still had to do, but most of all being with Norrie. What a time to realize how much she loved him. She had been so annoyed with him when he'd come home drunk and she'd lied to the police to protect him. No doubt he would get up to other pranks, but that would be the Norrie she was going to get to know.

Mentally she shook herself and counted her blessings. She was safe and under cover. She was used to night shifts so she wouldn't let the fire die out and she *would* still be there in the morning. She put some more wood on the fire. Her socks and shoes were not dry, but almost, so she put them on and got up to walk about and get her personal central heating system moving. She switched on the torch to look in the box-bed to see if any treasures had been left behind, but there was nothing save a pile of old rags. She shone the torch into every corner, only to find that the place had been emptied of anything that had been worth taking. There was a heap of something to the left of the hearth and under the window, a heap of something that could be anything. She looked more closely at it, stirred it with her foot; was it … could it be peat? It was.

Using the hard, dry slabs she made the biggest fire the hearth could hold. Then, on the floor in front of it, with her arm crooked beneath her head to make a pillow of sorts, she lay down. She had wrapped Noble's tether round her wrist. She slept then, a restless sleep on a hard bed. She dreamed of Robbie, her husband, saw his smiling face and heard him say, "You'll be all right." She raised herself up to feed the fire from time to time, then slept soundly. She woke at last to hear Noble moving. She sat up as he padded softly past her on his way to the door.

'Is it time for home then?' she said. 'Wait till I put my shoes on.'

Dry-shod again, as Noble hopped through the gap by the door Catherine followed him and stepped straight into a snowdrift. She was going home now, so it didn't matter. Standing straight, she looked for sign of dawn. A thin veil of light filled the sky; she looked to see where it was brightest. A narrow sliver on the horizon told her which way to go.

The snow was deep and before she had gone very far her trousers, socks and shoes were wet again and her feet were freezing. But she didn't care; she was alive and soon she would see someone coming to find her. That someone would be Norrie and maybe with Daa not far behind. But she was on the wrong side of the hill and had to go back up and across the moor before she would be in sight of home. She wished she had a staff to help her but she struggled on, stepping and almost falling into drifts until she reached level ground. Water lay in dark pools and sheep that had started moving about long since had left trails for her to follow. Thanks to them the moor was not difficult to traverse. At the top of the track leading down to the road, with Deepdale just beyond, she looked to see if anyone was coming. A figure, no more than a dark shadow against the snow was moving, a man and with him a dog. Was it Norrie? Was it?

And then she was going down. Yes, it was Norrie. She called his name and pulling on Noble's tether began to run, but Noble held her back so she abandoned him, ran, fell, picked herself up and ran again. Slipping and sliding, unable to stop laughing through tears of joy, she crashed into Norrie's open arms and knocked him down. Lying there, holding on to him as though she would never let him go, she smothered him with kisses.

'I thought I was never going to see you again,' she cried. 'Oh, Norrie, Norrie, you'll never know how glad I am to see you.'

'Not half as glad as I am,' said Norrie. 'I've been worried out of my mind. I came to look for you last night, but it was hopeless. I thought you were dead. Oh, lass, don't ever put me through that again.' She clung to him and cried, let the tears she had fought back in the night flow free, tears mingled with her kisses as she kept telling him how much she loved him. And then he said, 'If you hadn't said you'd marry me, I'd have had to make you do it if only for your own safety. You need someone to look after you.'

'And I'll be very happy for you to do that,' said Catherine.

'Ay, but hold off a minute. I ken you had me on the ground once before and had your way with me, but do you not think the rug we have now is too cold?' Though there was a grin on his face she could see the concern for her in his eyes.

'Oh, Norrie,' she cried, 'please take me home.'

THIRTY EIGHT

DAA TOOK CATHERINE into his arms and hugged her. 'Jannie told me I was not to come back without you,' he said. 'I didn't sleep a wink last night for worrying about you. I thought you would freeze to death.'

'I was in the ruined house.' She gave a wan smile. 'I always wanted to look in it; now I have and I never want to see it again.'

With one hand clasped tight by Norrie, holding Noble's tether with the other and he trailing behind her, Catherine walked between Norrie and Daa. She was wet and cold to the knees; on feet that seemed to be made of lead and devoid of feeling she plodded on. She had not realized how cold she was, but now that she was moving her body was coming to life; with life came pain and with every step she took it became more and more intense. She was bruised and shaken and aching from the fall and from lying on a hard floor with only her arm for a pillow.

Daa would not let Norrie take Catherine to her home. 'No,' he said, 'she has to come to us; Jannie wants to help and no doubt she'll be looking out for us.'

When Jannie saw them she clapped her hands. 'Thanks be to God,' she said. The kettle was boiling, porridge already made and a blanket warming on the pulley. She held out her hands to Catherine and looked as though she wanted to embrace her, but then led her to Daa's chair. 'Come sit by the fire,' she said.

After the freezing cold of the night the Jameson kitchen seemed to Catherine almost tropical. Norrie knelt before her and took off her shoes and socks. 'You need to take off your trousers too,' he said.

'She cannot do that wi' you here, Norrie Williams, get away out,' said Jannie. 'And you,' she pointed a finger at Daa, 'give the lass some peace.'

'I'll no' be far away,' said Norrie. 'I'll get you some dry clothes.'

'And I'll see to the ram,' said Daa.

With the men gone out Catherine took off her trousers and Jannie gave her a bowl of hot water to put her feet in. She let down the pulley, gave Catherine a warm towel to dry legs and feet and the blanket to wrap round her, then hung the wet garments over the pulley and hauled it back up. Daa had given Catherine a cup of tea, now Jannie gave her a bowl of porridge laced with cream and sugar.

'I ken that's how you from south like it,' she said.

'Thank you,' said Catherine. Jannie was being kind. It was too much. She had done what everyone warned her not to, had gone up the hill giving no thought to the weather, and it had overtaken her. She was exhausted, her defences were down and she was vulnerable. Only now did she realize how much danger she had been in and how much worry she had given these people. Kind words always tripped her up and to hear Jannie saying them pierced her heart. Hanging her head she wept, the tears tumbling down her face and dripping into the dish of porridge.

'Lass, lass,' said Jannie, tears in her own eyes, 'you don't have to cry. I shouted to tell you not to go but you didn't hear. I should have run after you. I thought I was never goin' to see you again.' Jannie wrung her hands together, seemed not to know what to do and Catherine, looking up at her, could see how stressed she was. 'I ken I've not been good to you,' Jannie went on, 'and I thought about my Robbie and what he would have said.'

Wiping away her own tears Catherine said, 'It's all right, Jannie, it wasn't your fault. I should have known better, but I didn't stop to think. Anyway,' she gave a little smile, 'I'm still here. I didn't die.'

'Ay.' Jannie nodded. She looked relieved. 'Now eat your porridge or it'll be cold,' she said as she too wiped away a tear.

Norrie knocked and asked if it was safe to come in, then lifted the latch and did so. 'I've got some dry stuff from your house,' he said. 'Hope you don't mind.' He was carrying shoes, socks and a pair of trousers for Catherine.

Jannie looked at him disapprovingly, it wasn't right for a man not your husband to go looking through your things. Catherine stretched her feet out towards the fire and wriggled her toes; they had passed the stage when returning warmth brought pain. Daa came in, there was more tea for everyone and he was asking Catherine if she was all right and had she been fed and warmed up.

'I'm fine, just so glad to be home,' she said. 'I'm so sorry I made you worry.' Then she gasped, 'Ah, I forgot about Noble? Where is he?'

Norrie was sitting by her side. 'Daa's put him in the shed; he can stay there till I mend his tether. You didn't think we'd let him go again, did you?'

'I would hope not.'

'What is all this runnin' about?' It was Mina.

'It's a long story,' said Catherine. 'I'll tell you later.'

'The ram broke his tether and ran off and she went after it,' said Jannie. 'She was on the hill all night.'

'Then why are you not dead?' declared Mina.

'She spent it in the old house,' said Jannie. 'Made a fire to keep warm.'

'My dreams came true.' Catherine laughed. 'There was nothing else to burn so I had the greatest joy in pulling a box-bed to pieces and putting it on the fire.'

'And what is that Norrie Williams doin' gittin' hold o' her hand?' said Mina. Norrie was sitting on a stool at Catherine's feet, he smiled at her. 'Do you think we should tell them?' he whispered.

Catherine shook her head, 'Too soon. Let's get it organized first.'

Mina, straining to listen, said, 'You're plannin' somethin'. What is it?'

'Um … Christmas … for Robbie,' said Catherine.

'Are you ready to go home?' asked Norrie.

'Yes.' Catherine stood up. She took the blanket from her shoulders and gave it to Jannie. 'Thank you for looking after me. I'm very grateful.'

'It was no more as I should do,' said Jannie.

As Catherine walked beside Norrie she said, 'Shouldn't you be at work?'

'Ay, but there were more important things to do,' he said, 'like lookin' for some lass as got herself lost.'

'It'll never happen again,' said Catherine.

'No, it won't,' said Norrie. 'That's why you have to marry me.'

While Catherine had been having breakfast, Norrie, as well as fetching dry clothes, had lit her fire. When she opened the door to go in the room was warm.

'You are good to me,' she said. 'I think I shall like being married to you.'

'And when is that going to be?' said Norrie.

'Say a month from today?'

'So it shall be,' said Norrie.

THIRTY NINE

'A RE WE GOING to walk then?' asked Catherine when Norrie called for her.

'I don't have much petrol in the van and it's not far.'

They were going to see the minister at Broonieswick. The November snowfall hadn't stayed but nightfall had brought frost. A shard of moon hung among the stars and grass stood stiff and sparkling in the moonlight.

'What do you think he's going to say to us? Do you think he'll give us a lecture?' said Catherine.

'I wouldn't know,' said Norrie, 'never having been wed before.'

'The preacher that married me and Robbie did go on a bit about being faithful and all that, so I suppose it'll be more of the same.'

But the minister was a kind, benevolent man and welcomed them into his study. 'I have no doubt you are aware of the responsibilities you are about to take on,' he said. 'A marriage should be built on trust; be faithful to one another and strive to be a good example to your children.' He smiled at Catherine. 'It's for you to lead them in the way of God,' he said; then, as he turned to Norrie, 'But I have known you since you were a small boy, Mr Williams, and I think I need have no worries on that score. We all have our weaknesses, of course, and if at any time you have troubles you find too hard to bear, please remember that I am always ready to listen and help if I can. Failing that, God is always on your side.'

'There won't be many people at the service,' said Catherine. 'Do we have to have hymns?'

'Not if you don't want them. Might I ask why there will be so few?'

'My parents live in the south of England and Norrie has no relatives here, so there will only be about ten of us.'

'But would you like the organist to play?'

'That would be nice.'

'Now,' went on the minister, 'let me get my diary.'

Sitting beside Norrie Catherine turned to him and smiled, and so the wedding was arranged.

'Do you want to tell Jannie?' said Norrie when he and Catherine were on their way home.

'Yes, I think she and Daa should be the first to know,' she said. At Jannie's door she knocked, opened it, and holding Norrie's hand went in. 'We've something to tell you,' she said as Jannie looked up from her knitting. 'We've been to see the minister to arrange our wedding.'

Daa got up from his chair and shook Norrie's hand. 'I'm glad to hear that. You would do well to take care of her.'

Jannie put down her work, stood up and took both Catherine's hands in hers. 'I'm pleased for you,' she said. 'I ken Norrie's a good man and it's time you had someone by your side.'

'It'll be a quiet wedding,' said Catherine. 'I don't want a lot of fuss.'

'When is it to be?' asked Jannie.

'Friday after the banns have been called,' said Catherine.

'And will your father and mother be coming?'

'No, it would be an awful journey and I doubt if Dad could get away.'

'And what about you, Norrie?' said Daa. 'You don't have many folk. What about your cousins?'

'I wouldn't know where they are,' said Norrie. 'Nobody ever writes. They could be on the other side of the world or they might be up in Yell.'

'So you see, it can't be anything other than quiet,' said Catherine. 'I suppose we'd better go and tell Mina and Laura now.'

The aunts were surprised when Catherine and Norrie walked in.

'And what are you wantin' from us?' said Mina.

'We've just come to give you our news,' said Catherine. 'Norrie and I are to be married.'

'Well,' said Mina, 'now I ken why Laura's knitting a wedding shawl.'

'You'd surely already guessed,' said Catherine.

'I was thinking that. Marriage was never to be my lot in life so I can't give you any advice,' said Mina as she gave way to one of her rare smiles. 'Instead I'll just wish you all the best for a good life together.'

Laura was agog with excitement. 'I've nearly finished your shawl. Are you going to have a bonny new dress?'

'I haven't thought about that yet,' said Catherine.

'Is your mam and daa going to come?'

'Oh, goodness no, it's much too far. It's to be a quiet wedding.'

A broad smile spread across Laura's face. 'I would'na be too sure of that,' she said.

'Rose, Bobbie, Billie and us aren't going to be a crowd.'

Little Robbie looked at her in silence when she told him and that they would all go and live in what had been Kay's house. It was so long before he spoke that she was afraid he was not going to approve. But then he had smiled and asked, 'Is Norrie going to my daa, then?'

'Would you like that?'

'Yea, I would.'

Now that everyone but Catherine's parents knew she sat down to write them a letter.

Dear Mum and Dad,

I know you'll tell me off if I don't let you know what's going on here. Well, I'm getting married. Norrie asked me and as I could see no good reason to say no, I agreed. That's not quite right, I do love him. Little Robbie is delighted that he's now going to have a Daa the same as the other boys at school.

The wedding is to be on the 17th of December. It's going to be very quiet. I don't want any fuss and it will only be the Deepdale family who will attend as Norrie has no relations here. Don't even <u>think</u> about coming up you know what the boat is like in winter don't you Mum, and I won't expect you.

This is just to let you know that I'm all right and I'm very happy. I'll write a longer letter after Norrie and I are wed to let you know how it all went.

Wish me well, all my love,

Catherine. X X X X X

She folded the piece of paper, put it in an envelope, addressed it, stuck on a stamp, then put the letter on the table. If the postman didn't call she would post it at Broonieswick when she went to collect Robbie from school.

The question now was what to wear. In her bedroom she looked at the dresses her mother had bought her. They were like new. Would either of them do or should she buy a new one? She was sitting on the bed, trying to decide, when someone called her name.

'Where are you, Catherine?' It was Laura.

'I'm in the bedroom. Come through.'

'Yon's awful pretty frocks,' said Laura when she saw what Catherine was holding, 'but you're not thinkin' of wearing one of them, are you?

'I hardly ever wear a dress; it seems such a waste to buy a new one.'

'But you don't need coupons now, so you should.'

Catherine held up the dresses, turned them this way and that, then shrugged her shoulders and said, 'You're right, you know. Quiet wedding or not, it is a special day so it needs a special dress. I shall go to Lerwick tomorrow and see what I can find. Now what can I do for you?'

'I'm brought your shawl.' Laura handed a parcel to Catherine. 'Who are you going to have for your best wife?'

'Best wife? It'll have to be you, of course.'

'I was hopin' you would say that,' said Laura. 'I'd be very proud. Now I have to go.' She had not gone further than the bedroom door when she turned around. 'What is Norrie makin' such a noise for? Sounds like he's pullin' the house apart.'

'What do you mean?' Catherine put down the parcel and followed Laura. As they went out of doors the sound of hammer blows and splintering wood grew louder. 'Whatever is he doing?'

'He'll likely tell you later,' said Laura.

'If he doesn't I shall ask him,' said Catherine.

But Norrie didn't tell her. 'You don't need to know,' he said, 'Go you and buy a dress, do what you have to do and leave me to do mine.'

Shopping for a trousseau, even a small one, was not something to be rushed. Underwear was not hard to find, but when it came to a dress the choice was harder to make. Thanks to Dior's New Look, dress rails had filled with frocks with tight waists and full skirts: not what Catherine wanted. But shop assistants were eager to help when they heard what the new dress was for and Catherine was persuaded to try on one garment after another until at last everyone in the shop smiled and agreed that the one she had chosen could not be bettered. The dress was wrapped and, with the parcels containing her other purchases, put in her basket.

At home work went on as usual and gradually the days drifted by till at last there was none left and the very next was to be her wedding day. Everything that couldn't be left till the last minute had been done. Laura had made cakes, Jannie had cooked a ham and Catherine had ordered and received a wedding cake which was in a box on the table in her kitchen. Her dress was on a hanger, her shoes were placed side by side on the floor and the wedding shawl, wrapped in a muslin cloth, was in the chest of drawers.

There was nothing left to do and everything seemed to have come to a grinding halt; it was the calm before the storm, thought Catherine as she looked out of the window at a grey sky and a restless sea. Through her mind raced all the things that had happened since she first set foot in Deepdale. Was it really nearly seven years? She had reached a turning point now. She loved Norrie and ought to be excited, but the wedding was to be such a quiet affair, nothing like the day she had wed Robbie Jameson. Her mother had taken charge then and for Doris it had to be the whole works. The traditional white dress was borrowed, Janet and one of her friends were bridesmaids and a friend of Robbie's was his best man. Begged and borrowed from friends and relations, rations were stretched to provide a feast for the reception. It had all gone without a hitch.

'Will you read me a story, Mam?'

Little Robbie's voice brought her out of her reverie.

They were beside one another in the armchair, squeezed tight for Robbie was growing fast, when the door opened and Norrie's grinning face appeared. 'Catherine,' he said, 'you have a visitor. I think you'd better sit down … oh, you are.'

'What mischief are you up to now, Norrie?'

He shook his head, 'Nothing,' he said as he pushed the door wide open.

'Did you think we'd let you go to your wedding without us?'

'Mum!' cried an astonished Catherine, 'and Dad too,' as a smiling Peter Marshall looked over his wife's shoulder. She jumped up and ran to embrace her mother. 'Oh, I'm so happy to see you, but … oh … you hated the journey last time. Whatever made you risk it again?'

'We think you've already been through enough on your own,' said Doris, 'and the journey was worth it just to see your face now.'

'It was a hell of a trip,' said Peter. 'I wouldn't like to do it too often. And your mother was right about you living at the back of beyond. I'm surprised, but there must be something special about it for you to stay.'

'Oh there is, Dad. You should see it in summer, it's beautiful then. Uh,' Catherine looked at her father and mother, 'what am I going to do with you, I mean, where are you going to sleep? I don't have enough room.'

'It's all taken care of,' said Norrie.

'I might have known you would have had something to do with this,' said Catherine. 'What other plans have you hatched up?'

'Jannie kens your mother was comin',' said Norrie. 'They're going to sleep at her house.'

Catherine laughed. 'The glorious box-bed, it'll be a totally new experience for you, Mum.'

'What do you mean?'

'I'm not going to tell you. But look, I've forgotten the most important thing. Meet Norrie, if you haven't already; he's the man I'm going to marry. Norrie, this is my mum and dad.'

When Norrie had taken himself off Catherine pulled a chair out from the table. 'Come and sit down,' she said, 'and tell me all your news.'

'I want to see the boy,' said Peter.

Robbie, clutching the book he had wanted his mother to read, was still sitting in the armchair. Catherine gasped. 'I was going to read to him. I'm sorry darling,' she said as she turned round. 'Come and say hello to your grandma and grandpa from England.'

'My, hasn't he grown,' said Doris as Robbie slid out of the chair and came towards her. 'Hello. I have something in my bag for you.'

FORTY

THE MORNING OF Friday the seventeenth of December dawned cold and clear. Catherine woke while it was still dark. She stretched her legs long and her arms wide, then curled herself small. She was warm and cosy and didn't want to get up; in fact she wanted to stay there as long as she could. She had planned her day down to the last detail but now that her mother was here there was little doubt that she would have a hand in it. And what had Norrie been up to? He must have known her parents were coming. Oh well, the day was probably going to be one of surprises. She threw back the bedclothes and got up.

Robbie was still sleeping when she looked in on him. He slept on his back. Holding the candlestick high she gazed down on his face, his cheeks were rosy with health, his hair dark against the pillow. You look more like your father every day, she thought; as long as I've got you he'll still be with me.

She set the kettle to boil and went about laying the table for breakfast. What a boon it would be when electricity – already lighting and warming the houses in Lerwick – came to the valley. Piped water was on its way too. When it reached Deepdale she would no longer have to climb the hill to the well for a bucket of spring water, but would be able to turn on a tap.

Tea made and drunk, she made breakfast and called Robbie to get up. 'You have to have a bath now,' she said when he'd finished eating. 'I'm going to be busy so I want you to go along to Daa and Grandma. But you're not to get dirty; I won't want to bath you again.'

She was busy cutting up bread to make sandwiches when Doris arrived.

'Cathie, love, can I do anything to help?'

'No. Thanks very much. We won't be leaving here till about four o'clock so there's plenty of time. Sit down and tell me how you're getting on with Jannie.'

'Well,' said Doris, 'I can understand most of what she says now. You've been keeping things from me again, haven't you? She told me about you getting caught in a snowstorm and spending the night up on the hill.'

'Oh, that.'

'Yes, oh that. It's a wonder you're still here, she said.'

'But I am,' said Catherine. 'Come and look at my dress.'

'But you're going to walk to the church, aren't you?' said Doris when she looked at the pale-peach dress on the hanger. 'Won't you be cold?'

'Jannie's loaned me her mother's winter shawl. It's better than an overcoat.'

The shawl was lying on the bed. 'Looks more like a blanket,' said Doris. 'I'm glad things are better between you; when I think of you I shall feel happier.'

'How did you get on in the box?'

'I never knew anything like that existed,' exclaimed Doris. 'Your dad couldn't get to sleep for laughing. Just when I thought he'd dropped off he'd chuckle again. I felt like thumping him, he was keeping me awake.'

'I hated it. I made Robbie buy me a proper bed when we moved in here.' Catherine laughed. 'You can sleep in my bed after the wedding if you like.'

They were in the bedroom when Laura came in. 'It's a bonnie dress, is it not,' she said as Doris Marshall was helping her daughter into it.

'It's lovely,' said Doris. 'Now, the shawl is old, the dress is new, so what's borrowed and what's blue?'

'I haven't got anything blue.'

'Neither have I,' said Doris.

'I hope you don't mind,' said Mina as she joined them, 'but I could hear you talking.' She handed a small box to Catherine. 'This is for you.'

A present from Mina! Catherine opened the little box and lifted a turquoise pendant from its nest of white tissue. She held it up for all to see. 'Oh, Mina, it's beautiful. Thank you so much,' she said.

Stiff, upright Mina stood with her hands clasped together in front of her. 'Ay well, it'll look fine on you. You're a good lass, for all that you're English.'

'And now you have your something blue,' said Doris as she fastened the pretty blue pendant's silver chain round Catherine's neck.

'Now for the shawl,' said Laura. She draped the fine cobweb lace over Catherine's head and secured it with some hairpins. 'You don't want the wind to take it away.'

Like a veil the fine white wool sat gently on Catherine's dark hair and clung to her shoulders where it contrasted sharply with the sombre colours of Jannie's heavy shawl. All final adjustments made, Laura stood back to look at her handiwork. She stood smiling at Catherine, then said, 'You are most surely da vire o da isle.'

'And what does that mean?' asked Catherine.

'Doesn't need any explanation,' said Doris, 'you look absolutely beautiful.'

'That's right,' said Laura, 'You are a most beautiful lass.'

Billie, Norrie's best man, pushed Catherine's door open. 'Come on, are you ready? The minister will be waiting.' He looked at Catherine and gave a low whistle. 'Hold on a minute, I'm thinkin' I'll lock Norrie up and run away wi' you myself. You look beautiful, Catherine.'

'Go away with you, Billie. Come on Laura, Mum, it's time to go.'

There were no cars to take them; Norrie had wanted a walking wedding. They and their guests would go to the church on foot. He was waiting outside when Catherine, Billie, Laura and her mother went along to Jannie's.

Any thoughts or plans that she was going to have a quiet wedding disappeared when Catherine stepped in to the Jameson house. It was full of people. Added to Jannie and Daa, the aunts and her father, were others whom she didn't know. There was a man with a fiddle who tucked it under his chin and began to play when he saw her. Robbie, who was sitting on his grandmother's knee, slid to the floor and ran to his mother.

'Why are you dressed like that?' he said.

'We're going to the church. Norrie and I are to be married,' said Catherine. 'You're coming with us. See, Grandma Jannie's got her best hat on and so has Auntie Mina. You can walk with me.'

Fiddler first, playing as he went, they left the house, Norrie with Laura, Billie with Catherine and little Robbie. Catherine's parents next, then came Jannie and Daa while the rest of the company paired off and followed behind. Up the hill they went, the old folk puffing and blowing. At last they were at the top and there waiting for them were more people.

With Rose and Bobbie Robertson were more people and a young man who held a fiddle. The extra folk fell in behind and the little procession set off again. Billie tucked Catherine's arm in his. 'I thought you said you wanted a quiet wedding?' he said. 'You can't have a quiet wedding here. Just listen.'

From behind came the buzz of voices and laughter, the shuffle of feet and the shrieks and cries of children. In front of them the young fiddler, who had joined the other, played and pranced and danced ahead of them. A gusting wind had got up. A hat, which hatpins had been unable to secure, flew through the air to roll along the road, where it defied attempts at laughing children to pin it down.

'Your head will roll if you laugh at me,' said the owner to the boy who had caught and returned it. The merciless wind, not content with stealing the hat, had scrambled the few thin wisps of hair that the hat had covered and stood them up on end.

'You're like an old witch,' laughed the boy and jumped neatly out of the way as the old wife took a swipe at him with her walking-stick.

As they went down the hill into Broonieswick and through the village the procession grew. Folk came out of their houses to join it. Catherine turned to Billie. 'I hope they don't all come home with us,' she said. 'There won't be enough room and certainly not enough food.'

'I dinna think you need to worry about that,' he said.

The windows of the little church were glowing with the light from its oil lamps. The minister was there to meet them. He turned and led them up the aisle.

Catherine had thought she was in control, had her wedding all planned. But when her mother walked in she knew it was out of her hands and when Laura had settled the shawl on her head she had felt she was stepping into a dream. The feeling had grown as the procession had grown larger and people she knew only by sight had smiled at her and fallen into step. Where were they coming from and why? Billie said she needn't worry why they were there or how they were to be fed. Visions of Laura baking batches of cakes saying they were for the church flitted through her mind. So that's what she'd been up to, baking to feed wedding-guests.

The dream went on as she walked up the aisle. An organ played, then the minister was speaking and Billie was grinning at her as he gave Norrie a ring. Norrie put it on her finger, promising to love and cherish her as he did so. She looked up into his face, into his kind brown eyes. Then she too was repeating the words the minister was saying, '... *to love and to cherish, to honour and obey.*'

It was done; she and Norrie were married. With a broad smile on his face the minister said, 'You may now kiss the bride,' but he was too late for Catherine was already being kissed.

'Is there something going on in the hall?' asked Catherine as they walked down the church path and she saw vehicles parked and windows full of light.

'I think they're waiting for us,' said Norrie.

Catherine stopped abruptly. 'You had it all planned, didn't you?'

'Catherine, my love, we all thought we were never going to see you again when you went up the hill and didn't come back. Ken, it takes somethin' like that to tell folk what you're worth and we wanted to show you.' A slow smile spread across his face, then turned into a grin. Dropping into the dialect he said, 'And did du no ken, du canna hae a quiet weddin' in Shetland?'

'Move on, the soup's getting cold,' called a voice.

'Ay, and the tatties'll be ready,' said someone else. Then, as Catherine put her arms round Norrie's neck and kissed him more voices chimed in. 'Time for yon later,' 'I'm dying here for want o' meat,' 'Hey, Norrie, I'm the best man, I should be doin' that.' That was Billie.

'Away wi' you, Billie,' said Norrie. 'Find your own wife.'

In the hall tables were laid for a feast. Dishes of potatoes, platters of roast pork, lamb and beef and jugs of gravy were brought out and set before the guests. Catherine, sitting with Norrie, marvelled at where it had all come from. There were jugs of water and squash; no wine, but when she saw a hand go into an inside pocket and a small bottle being withdrawn she had to smile. Trust a Shetlander to find his own drink. When the feasting was over, tables cleared and put away, the room was swept and the fiddlers began to play.

'Come, we have to start the dance,' said Norrie. Taking Catherine by the hand he led her on to the floor. Hand in hand and in time to a marching tune they went down the centre of the room, then, parting right and left, each took up another partner. At the top of the room they joined together again and this time marched four abreast. Again they parted and took another, circled again till they were eight in number. Now they paired off and formed a set.

The fiddle-players had been joined by a pianist, and a bow drawn across the strings of a fiddle was the signal to start on an eightsome reel. Soon feet were flying and hands clapping. Catherine tripped lightly through the sequence of steps, smiled when they brought her back to Norrie, when they clasped hands and swung, then parted to stand side by side and clap as another couple danced.

'I didn't know you could dance like that,' said Doris to a rosy-cheeked Catherine when the dance was finished.

'I've learned a lot of things, Mum. Dancing's only one of them.'

'Do this with me, love?' asked Peter as a Boston Two-step was announced.

'With pleasure, Dad,' said Catherine.

Happy laughing people filled the floor and with feet stamping in time to the thumping rhythm of the piano and the frantic playing of the fiddlers the walls of the hall throbbed. The minister, devoid of his jacket, shirt-sleeves rolled up and trousers anchored by a pair of red braces, but still wearing his dog collar, danced with enthusiasm. Sitting with Norrie, Catherine watched Neil Lumsden's long legs negotiating the intricate steps of the Lancers. Billie, with a different partner for every dance, was never off the floor.

Mina, who was sitting with Jannie and Laura, came to speak to Norrie. 'Do you not think us old folk could have a dance?' she said.

'Mina,' said a shocked Catherine, 'did I hear you say you want to dance?'

'Ay, you did. The young ones have had their turn and I would like to dance at your wedding. You could ask them to play the Crofters Reel, Norrie.'

Mina, dancing: wonders would never cease. But she had gathered together a set who took their positions on the floor when Norrie spoke to the fiddlers. When the music started other sets were quickly made up. It was a sedate little dance, no frantic swinging of partners and no kicking up heels. It was for dancing in the confined area of a croft house when there was something to celebrate.

At last it was time for supper and trays of bannocks and cups of tea were handed round. The noise now was a hum of conversation, clink of china, hurrying feet as empty trays were carried to the kitchen to be replenished. The minister, who had danced non stop, mopped his brow and asked for coffee. Water, which had been brought in in buckets had run out and only a pot of tea was left. There were hurried whispers in the kitchen.

'What shall we do?'

'We can't tell him there's none.'

'Only one thing to do, pour tea and put two spoonfuls of coffee in, he'll be so thirsty he'll have drunk it before he knows the difference.'

To gasps of, 'do you dare?' the tea/coffee was made and three pairs of eyes peeped round the door to watch as the minister emptied the cup. When the music started he grabbed a partner and was off again. The women in the kitchen laughed at their audacity and having got away with it.

Fiddlers and pianist seemed ready to play all night, but dancers were tiring. It was well into the early hours before the crowd thinned and one by one the guests made their excuses, put their coats on and went home. Little Robbie had long since been put to bed in the back of one of the parked vehicles and was sleeping soundly despite the noise. Norrie had arranged for someone to drive them home for it would be too much to expect the little boy to wake up and walk.

Deepdale slumbered under a sky sprinkled with stars. The moon hung low in the sky to the west. Under its light, grass, stiffened with frost, sparkled with cold points of light. At Jannie's door Catherine thanked her and Daa for all they'd done, said goodnight to them and, with Norrie carrying Robbie, walked on with the aunts and Catherine's parents. 'Robbie can stay wi' us tonight,' said Mina.

'Thank you,' said Catherine, 'but Mum and Dad are going to have my bed so Robbie can sleep in his own. Thanks all the same and thank you, Laura. All that baking of cakes and bannocks wasn't for the church at all, was it?'

'No, but I couldna tell you.'

When they finally stood by Norrie's front door Robbie was handed over to his grandfather. Catherine kissed her mother and hugged her. 'You gave me the best wedding present of them all just by being here,' she said. 'It was the biggest surprise of my life when you walked in. You were very brave to risk the journey.'

'Don't say a word,' said Doris, 'we've got to do it again in a few days' time. Good night, my darling.'

'Goodnight, Mum, goodnight, Dad.'

When they had gone Norrie said, 'I've got you to myself at last.' Catherine, looking up into his face, looked on up at the sky.

'Look,' she said as she raised her arm and pointed. 'The Merry Dancers.'

A curtain of colour hung across the northern sky, rippling, undulating, orange, yellow, red, green, colours fading, then merging.

'I had it laid on especially for you, said Norrie. 'I couldna get any fireworks, you see, so I wondered if this might do.'

Catherine laughed. 'There's always some nonsense with you, Norrie. But please don't ever stop.'

'Never, while I'm with you. But it's time for bed, we have a whole new life to start on tomorrow.'

He opened the door, swept her off her feet, carried her over the threshold then kicked the door shut behind him.